**Also available from Elia Winters
and Carina Press**

Purely Professional

Also available from Elia Winters

Playing Knotty

The Comes in Threes series

*Three-Way Split
Just Past Two
Three for All*

The Slices of Pi series

*Even Odds
Tied Score
Single Player*

D0063828

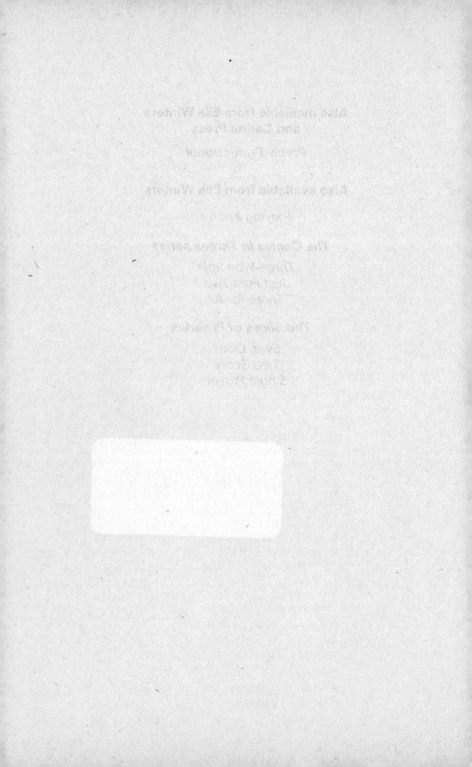

HAIRPIN CURVES

ELIA WINTERS

carina
press

**carina
press®**

Recycling programs
for this product may
not exist in your area.

ISBN-13: 978-1-335-14665-6

Hairpin Curves

Carina Press
22 Adelaide St. West, 40th Floor
Toronto, Ontario M5H 4E3, Canada
www.CarinaPress.com

Printed in U.S.A.

For everyone who spent their quarantine days
wishing desperately for a road trip.

HAIRPIN CURVES

Chapter One

Megan Harris checked the industrial-style clock on the wall, adjusted her glasses, and checked again. How was closing time still an hour away? She could count on two hands the number of tables she'd served since the diner had opened at six. After trying to avoid the clock since her midmorning break, she'd finally caved—and it was barely one. Well, damn. She adjusted her headband, washed her hands, and left the back room to greet the probably-empty diner with a cheerfully insincere smile.

Instead of an empty diner, though, a familiar face looked up from one of the oversized menus, light brown curls pulled up in a pair of retro Princess Leia buns. Scarlett Andrews caught Megan's gaze, her expression turning cautious. Their entire history flashed through Megan's mind all at once: childhood best friends, competitive but loving all through high school, their whole story coming to a swift end when Scarlett bailed on Megan right before college and left her scrambling to find another roommate at the last minute. They hadn't spoken since. Of course, Megan had seen her around now and then, because in a town like Crystal River, you always saw people around. But they hadn't been face-to-face like this. And they certainly hadn't spoken.

Scarlett gave her a closed-mouth smile, no teeth showing, the smile that indicated she was not really happy. "I hoped I might find you here."

Megan leaned against the edge of the booth and folded her arms. She would ignore the little skip in her heart at the idea of Scarlett hoping to see her. That time had passed. "You want breakfast? Or lunch?"

Scarlett licked her lips and opened her mouth to talk, but then hesitated. It was so rare to see Scarlett look hesitant about anything; she had always been a bundle of confidence when Megan knew her well. Funny how a moment's conversation would take her right back to their friendship, back before everything fell apart, back when Scarlett was the person whose approval Megan craved most desperately. "I was hoping to talk to you, actually. You got a minute?"

Megan glanced over toward the open kitchen, where Winston was whistling while scraping the flat-top grill, his cloud of white hair tucked under a hairnet.

"Come on. There's literally no one here." Scarlett gestured around. "Whose table are you gonna wait?"

Megan slid into the booth, her back to Winston. "Tell me if he starts looking grumpy."

Scarlett raised an eyebrow. "Winston never gets grumpy. Even I remember that."

"Yeah, well, it's changed a little since you worked here with me."

Scarlett glanced around. "Hasn't changed *that* much."

Before Megan could respond, Scarlett folded her hands on the table, all business, the menu still lying open in front of her. "So, I assume you checked your email today."

Megan shook her head. "A couple of days ago maybe."

"Don't you have it on your phone?"

"Yeah, but I don't check it much. It's mostly spam and mailing lists."

Scarlett's lip twisted. "You know, you can unsubscribe from those."

Really? They weren't even friends and she was going to give Megan organizational advice? "Thanks. I never thought of that." Megan flushed in annoyance. "Why should I check my email?"

"We got an email from Juliet last night."

"Juliet... Letourneaux?" Megan hadn't heard that name in years. The three of them were best friends as kids, back before Juliet moved away to Quebec halfway through high school. "She emailed both of us?"

"Yeah. She wanted to know if we could get online tonight for a video chat." Scarlett shrugged. "I don't know what she wants. The email was vague."

Megan tried to remember her last communications with Juliet, back in senior year, slowly trailing off over time. "Does she...does she know you and I don't really talk anymore?"

There it was, on the table where they both had to acknowledge it. Megan hated confronting stuff, but some stuff had to be confronted.

"She must not. Otherwise she wouldn't write to both of us on one email." Scarlett looked like she wanted to say more, but didn't. She sat back instead.

"Okay." Megan had no idea why Scarlett was even asking her about this. "So that's it? You wanted to know if I knew what the email was about?"

"I didn't want you to miss the video call. It must be something important." Scarlett's lightly tanned skin turned pinker, a few freckles standing out on her cheeks with the blush.

Megan waited for something else, but Scarlett didn't say much. She just looked across the table at Megan in a way that made Megan feel weird and scrutinized and judged, and she didn't like it. Before Megan could slide out of the booth, though, Scarlett moved like she wanted to put a hand over Megan's. It was a weird, stilted gesture, that ended with Scarlett putting one hand over her other hand instead. "How have you been? Work treating you well?"

"Sure." Megan answered in a knee-jerk positive way, like she always did, but then found herself giving more info without planning to. "Another of the servers quit right after Christmas, so I've been taking his shifts, and Winston and Martha haven't made any moves to replace him. So it's been busy." She'd been meaning to ask them about that, but it never seemed like a good time. Scarlett might say that Winston was incapable of looking grumpy, but lately, Megan had been frequently seeing him poring over papers at his desk with a contemplative frown, or talking quietly to his wife Martha in the back room when Megan was busy waiting tables or covering the grill.

"Right." Scarlett nodded. "Sounds busy."

"I've been busy, but the diner hasn't. It's been dead." Megan looked out the glass front of the diner, out into the parking lot of this strip mall where the Starlite Diner had carved out a tiny niche between Winn-Dixie and the Top Coat Nail Salon. The parking lot was sparsely dotted with cars, and most were over by the Winn-Dixie.

"That's a shame. The Starlite used to be the place to be." Sympathy filled Scarlett's eyes, sympathy that made Megan itchy and uncomfortable. She was never settled under Scarlett's intense gaze. Megan didn't want to talk about this anymore, so she slid out of the booth. "Do you want food?"

Scarlett looked down at her open menu. "Yeah. Sure. thanks. Pancakes and sausage? And a large OJ?"

"Sure." Megan slid out of the booth. "Don't say I never did anything for you."

The words were intended like a joke, a throwback, but she regretted them as soon as they were out of her mouth. They didn't tease like that anymore. They didn't even talk anymore.

Scarlett gave her a ghost of a smile, and Megan left with the same sense of discomfort.

Winston took her order with an undecipherable noise of agreement and set about whipping up some pancakes while Megan drew an orange juice for Scarlett. She wiped down the counters for the millionth time today, wishing there was something else to do. Her time here at the diner was sucking her life dry. She hadn't gone to book group in months, hadn't played any of her favorite video games, hadn't done much of anything but work, sleep, and take care of the house. Christmas was a reprieve, a day off spent with family, but she'd been back into the grind almost immediately after. Adulthood was supposed to be about routines, sure, but this routine wasn't fun at all.

Was Scarlett any better off, though? Megan leaned on the counter and eyed her former friend, who was typing something on her phone. Scarlett hadn't volunteered what she was doing for work, but she was in the diner in the middle of the day on a Tuesday. Socially, Scarlett had the charm and grace Megan could only envy from afar. Scarlett was beautiful, funny, quick-witted, and adventurous. Maybe that was why she had a boyfriend or girlfriend every time Megan turned around in high school, but Megan herself had been a late bloomer. She'd only gotten into the dating scene once she was in college, and that had trailed off after graduating three years ago. There had been a handful of brief flings, mostly out-of-towners she wouldn't have to see again, and a couple of relationships barely long enough to call relationships. Nothing lasting and nothing worth thinking about.

"Order up!" Winston's sing-song call jerked Megan out of her reverie, leaving her with weird guilty, unsettled feelings that rolled in her stomach like a confusing jumble. She slid the plate of pancakes and sausage in front of Scarlett, who put her phone away.

"Thanks." Scarlett flashed her a tight-lipped smile. Megan nodded once, curt, and went into the back room to start washing dishes for pre-close. She didn't want to get into a conversation, especially when she was feeling so unsettled.

Seeing Scarlett again, having Scarlett interact with her like things were normal between them—or at least somewhat normal—had her all aflutter in ways she didn't want to dig too deeply into. First off, she felt like her whole life was standing still sometimes, and having an old friend dip back into it after *years* of no communication made her feel even more like no time had passed. She was a goddamn adult. She was twenty-five years old. She wasn't the hurt eighteen year old who just had her best friend flake off to some fancy private school and never talk to her again. She'd had seven years to get past it. After all these years, she'd thought she *was* over it. But here came Scarlett, smiling and talking about Juliet and expecting everything to be normal. Megan felt itchy all over, a feeling that lingered with her as she loaded the dishwasher.

After Scarlett left, with no other customers coming in after her, Megan was free to start the closing process for real. She'd just finished locking up the safe when the sound of Winston clearing his throat got her attention.

He pulled the hairnet off his head, letting his white wispy hair free. Something in his expression gave Megan pause. He spoke with an uncharacteristic hesitation. "You, uh, got a few minutes?"

Well, this fucking blew. Scarlett put her hands on her hips and stared at the backed-up sink in her kitchen, bubbling disgusting brown water making no signs of retreating down the drain where it *belonged*. The landlord had told her the garbage disposal was working fine, even with the weird noises lately, and she'd believed him. What a dickbag.

"Jacen?" she hollered into the other room. "The sink's backed up."

"What the fuck do you want me to do about it?" Jacen's voice was muffled, like he had a pillow over his head. He probably did; Scarlett's insomniac roommate was prone to catching up from lost nights through naps.

"Fix it?" Scarlett stared back into the sink again. It wasn't moving.

"Did you use the plunger?" Jacen hollered, less muffled. Good; he'd probably taken the pillow off his face.

Scarlett wrinkled her nose at the plunger, now sitting in the other side of the dual sink, dripping brown gross sink-water. "Yes, I used the plunger. It didn't fix it."

Jacen sighed loudly enough for her to hear it from where she was standing. "I may have a penis, but I do not know how to fix a sink."

"What about Zayne?" Jacen's boyfriend had fixed their dishwasher once before.

"He's working, and I am not calling him to come over and unclog our sink. Look it up on YouTube."

Scarlett closed her eyes. Yeah, this was probably her responsibility, and unfair to pawn it off on Jacen or his boyfriend. At least she'd had breakfast. Even if breakfast had involved seeing Megan again, Megan who she'd once been friends with, Megan who she had spent two hours this morning psyching herself up to go see. She probably could have just texted Megan about the whole Juliet thing, but she didn't even know if Megan had the same phone number. Of course, this was Megan; she wasn't really into *change*, was she? Every time Scarlett had seen her around town, she'd looked the same—same unfortunately plain haircut, same unflinching expression, same utilitarian style. She'd seen Megan's old convertible at the Starlite every time she went to get groceries at Winn-Dixie. Still, Megan today with her diner name tag, waiting tables just like she had been forever ago… It was like going back in time.

Too bad she couldn't actually go back in time.

A half hour later, Scarlett was set up on the kitchen floor with a disassembled pipe, a bucket of trash water, and a YouTube video she'd watched a dozen times that seemed to be missing a few key steps. Scarlett leaned back against the stove and took a break, surrounded by under-sink assembly parts. This was not how she'd wanted to spend her day. She still had actual work to do, another data-entry gig she was handling remotely. It wasn't hard, but it took time, and she'd hoped to be done by now. Maybe if she hadn't gone to the Starlite, she could have finished already. She still wasn't sure how to feel about that trip, or about seeing Megan. It had seemed like a good idea at the time, but Scarlett had often done a lot of dumbass things in the name of thinking they were a good idea at the time. Her irritation at the clogged garbage disposal made everything retroactively seem just as irritating.

The thing about seeing Megan again is how her judgment seemed to follow Scarlett home. Megan seemed to stand over Scarlett, arms folded across her chest, frowning slightly, casting aspersions on another one of Scarlett's choices like she always had back in high school. It wasn't mean, per se, but it always implied, *I thought you were better than this*. Even today, she seemed to judge Scarlett's decision to tell her about Juliet's message in person, or maybe judging the very sight of Scarlett in the diner. She'd run from that judgment once, and here it was again, settling into her apartment like another roommate.

Grumbling to herself, Scarlett watched the video again,

zooming in on part of it, and leaned back under the sink again to start her work back up. She could do this.

"How's it coming?"

Jacen's voice drew Scarlett out from under the sink a while later, right when she was putting the last piece into place. She wiped her arm across her forehead. Ugh, she was going to need a whole additional shower after doing this. "I think I've got it." She pushed up to her feet, unsteady after so long on the floor. Her roommate was staring at her, frowning but also looking a little curious.

"You really fixed it? I was kidding about the YouTube thing."

"I fixed it. You look way too nice to have just rolled out of bed." Scarlett looked him up and down. Jacen had the whole "casual chic" look happening, from his skinny jeans to his snug T-shirt, its deep cobalt blue bringing out the rich undertones in his dark brown skin. He had pulled his black dreadlocks back with a blue cloth headband to match, and had finished out the look with a leather jacket.

"Zayne's picking me up in an hour. We're going to the movies. I wanted to look nice." He struck a pose. "This is good, right?"

"Gorgeous. I look like I took a bath in our sink. But look." Scarlett flipped a switch and the garbage disposal roared to life, draining the brown water away in a whirlpool. "Très sexy, non?"

"Magnifique." Jacen chef-kissed his fingers. "What about you? Are you going out with—" he blanched, probably remembering she was single "—anyone?" he finished, somewhat weakly.

"No dates for me." Scarlett started packing up her tools. Ever since she and Gwen had broken up a few weeks ago, she'd struggled to find the motivation to go anywhere. With a freelance job that she could do from home, this was a recipe for not leaving the house much.

"You want to come out with Zayne and me?" Jacen gestured vaguely toward the door. "I'm sure he wouldn't mind."

"No, I don't want to be your third wheel. That—" she gestured to his outfit "—is clearly clothing for a date. I have work to do tonight, anyway. And a video chat."

Jacen frowned again. "You okay? This isn't like you, home on a Friday, video chatting instead of going out. I swear, you're here all the time, now."

"I live here, Jacen." She carried the tools she'd used back to the closet, then stripped out of her shirt on her way to take a shower.

"Well, let me know if you change your mind about coming with us," Jacen hollered down the hall. "I don't like to see you moping."

"I'm not moping!" She left her clothes on her bedroom floor and locked herself in the bathroom, in part just so she wouldn't have to continue that conversation. Sure, yeah, she'd been moping, but that wasn't *Jacen's* problem.

She took her hair down to rinse it, massaging her scalp with her fingertips. With the warm water running over her body, she could close her eyes and relax, if only the tension that had settled into her muscles these last few weeks would go away. It wasn't money; she never had enough of that, but always managed to get by. And she didn't want to think that it was Gwen. They hadn't been good for each other, despite making a healthy attempt at a relationship, and the breakup was the right move. Missing her was normal. But she wasn't actually missing Gwen as much as that physical closeness. Cuddling on the sofa to watch a movie. Spooning together in bed. Kissing, pressing against each other, hands and mouths bringing sweet, mindless pleasure. All that was gone, and her bed was empty.

Scarlett stood beneath the water until it began to run cold, then reluctantly got out and toweled off. Silence in the house meant

Jacen had left. She put on fuzzy pajamas, even though it was the middle of the afternoon, and flopped down on the couch. Her phone stared at her, blank. No one was calling or texting. Gwen came to mind again, and she grimaced. She had better find some way to shake off this funk. In the meantime, though, she had work to do. She pulled her laptop over with a sigh.

"Closing?" Megan had to repeat the word just to make sure she'd heard Winston right. "As in, no more Starlite Diner, forever?"

Winston rested his wrinkled hands on his desk and smiled sadly at Megan across the cluttered surface. His blue eyes turned down at the edges, the smile not reaching them. "We made it through Christmas, and that's as far as the Missus and I were hoping to take things. I'm sure you've seen this day coming."

She hadn't, but she didn't want to tell *him* that. Obviously she hadn't expected the Starlite to stay open forever, but Winston and Martha hadn't given any hints of retiring. Well, other than the travel brochures that had been piling up on the desk... and the shortened business hours after the holiday...and the way Winston had started photographing the place and sighing wistfully after the New Year.

Oh.

Nodding, Winston leaned back in his chair. "We've had a good run, all of us, and you've been darn indispensable these past few years, but we got an offer from the Winn-Dixie that's too good to turn down."

"When?" Her voice cracked, and she tried again. "When are you closing?"

"End of the month."

The end of the month. *That* month. January. Megan's mind tipped on its axis, like her whole center of gravity had shifted, and she wrapped her hands around the arms of the chair. She'd been here for nearly ten years. *Ten years.* The Starlite had been her first job, a part-time dishwashing gig when she was still too young to get a job almost anywhere, slowly increasing in hours and responsibility as she got older. When Scarlett quit to take a job at the grocery store, Megan had continued at the Starlite. After college, without any immediate job prospects in Communications, at least none that didn't require leaving the area, the Starlite had taken her on full-time. She couldn't picture her life without these too-early mornings, brewing coffee before dawn and setting out paper placemats and silverware for the regulars.

Megan loosened her grip on the armrests, taking a breath and trying to regulate her tumult of emotions. "Have you thought about trying to find new owners? Instead of closing it?"

Winston chuckled. "Oh, we talked about it. Wondered if you might want to buy the place."

If she had the money, maybe she would. She leaned forward to say so, then froze, mouth slightly open. This was only supposed to be a temporary job. The fact that a temporary job had grown to a nine-plus-year commitment was not because she loved it.

Winston barely paused, seemingly oblivious that she was about to speak and had stopped. "Martha told me, she said the worst thing we could do is try and saddle you with this place for the rest of your life. Restaurant's on its last legs, Megan. You've seen it. We've all seen it. No, the Winn-Dixie wants the space, and we're giving it to them. For a pretty penny, that is."

Megan's tumble of emotions settled into something like numbness, all feeling draining out of her and leaving an empty stillness behind. She'd been in this cluttered back room so many times, the sights were all familiar, but each object stood out like it was new again. The cork board covered with newspaper clippings from the restaurant's fifty-year history. Framed photos of the T-ball team the diner had sponsored for years, most of those kids grown up and gone off to college by now. Gray filing cabinets crammed into the corners, each drawer filled with decades of vendor invoices and god knows what, since Winston and Martha always resisted digitizing their systems. Stacks of papers on every available surface. There was a whole wall of employee photos from the years, everyone who had ever worked at the Starlite Diner, from busboys to line cooks.

Megan was there, right in the middle of the wall, from back when she was first hired. Her sixteen-year-old face stared back at her. Not much had changed in nearly ten years. Sure, she'd upgraded her glasses, but she still had the same mousy brown hair, practically in the same shoulder-length cut, with the same bland smile. Teenage Megan looked resigned to whatever was ahead of her. Her stomach twisted in discomfort. Was she still the same teenager inside, just in an older body?

And then, next to her, Scarlett's face smiled back. They'd been hired at the same time. Scarlett's hair was a wild light-brown cloud, and she had the same goofy smile as Megan. Back then, Scarlett had seemed so sophisticated, but this photo made her look like just another sixteen-year-old kid.

Megan's gaze drifted over the most recent row of faces in the photographs, the handful of other waitresses and cooks who traded shifts with her. Only a few, now, with the decline in business. "Does anyone else know yet?"

"We thought we'd tell you first." Winston shuffled some papers around, averting his gaze. "You've been with us the longest. I figured you deserved to know first, even if you probably saw the writing on the wall for a while now."

She must've looked stricken, because Winston frowned and shook his head. "Now, don't you worry. We're gonna take care of all of our employees, best we can." He patted his pockets, then got up from the squeaky office chair and began rummaging through the piles. "Let's see. Where is this. It's a big envelope. Ah, here it is," He pulled a manila envelope out from the file and reached inside, peering in as he sorted through the documents. "Here we go. We looked up what was standard, and we threw in a little extra because you've been such a big help, and because we got a good shake from the Winn-Dixie deal." He came around to her side of the desk and handed her a check.

Megan looked down at it, and then looked at it again, disbelieving. "Ten thousand dollars?"

"I know it's not everything, and it's not a salary, but it should at least keep you going for a while." He shifted awkwardly, pushing his glasses up the brim of his nose.

Megan's heart pressed against her ribs. "You didn't have to do this. I can apply for unemployment or something."

"It's the least we can do." He smiled sadly. "You've been part of the Starlite family since you were just a girl. We could barely keep the place open without you."

Megan got to her feet and gave Winston a hug, carefully, the kind of hug you'd give your grandfather if he'd just had surgery. She and Winston had never been on a hugging basis, but this was different. He patted her back awkwardly. "Thank you," she said.

"No leaving before the end of the month, though, all right?" He held her at arm's length and wagged a finger at her. "We're gonna have a lot of stuff to pack up, and a few dozen more breakfasts to cook. Your trip to Vegas will have to wait until February."

Megan laughed, even if she felt more sick than amused. "Sure. February."

Chapter Two

Ten thousand dollars. Megan stared at the check in her hand as she sat in her car in her driveway, not yet willing to move from that spot. What was she going to do with this kind of money? It would pay all her bills for months and months. She had good savings, what with never going anywhere and running up very few expenses. If she was frugal, she could probably make her savings plus this income last…eight, nine months?

But what was she supposed to do without the Starlite? She got tired by 8:00 p.m. She woke up every day at four. Her rhythms were diner rhythms, patterns she'd forced her body into in order to keep this job that she—honestly—didn't really like that much.

Oh, wow, her world spun just thinking that. She said the words out loud. "I didn't really like that job." Guilt, embarrassment, fear, all rushed through her system one after the other. She tried it louder. "I didn't really like that job!"

Her laughter bubbled up, hysterical, the kind of half-wild laughter that would get out of control if she didn't tamp it down. It wasn't happy laughter; it was the fraught, unstrung kind, the kind when a person had reached the end of their rope. She took a few deep breaths to steady herself and got out of the car.

Megan fumbled the key into the lock of her house, jiggling it a few times to get the tumblers to click. She should call the landlord about this one of these days. Still staring at the check, she nearly walked into the doorframe as she went inside. The warmth was a welcome change from outside, where Florida's damp winters made fifty degrees feel like half that. Not that she really knew what twenty-five degrees felt like; it pretty much never got that cold here, and she had never been out of Florida.

Megan stopped in her tracks, right between the living room and kitchen, a jolt running from her head to her feet. She'd never been out of Florida. And here she was, holding ten thousand dollars in her hand, convincing herself to squirrel it away in the bank and stay inside her little box.

Or.

She could do something crazy.

Teenage Megan came to mind, herself at sixteen in that photograph, trying to blend in with the background. That Megan had wanted to have adventures. She'd told herself she was going to do all these things someday, once she'd gotten out of high school, then once she'd gotten out of college, then any day now, always later, after she put a few things in order. There were always reasons to avoid change. Reasons to turn down invitations, to ignore job opportunities, to stay exactly as she was. It was always easier to keep the status quo than to shake up her life. She'd taken the path of least resistance over and over again, and here's where she had landed.

She could take this ten thousand dollars—or not all of it, even just a fraction of it—and *go somewhere*.

Not Vegas, as Winston had joked. Vegas wasn't her style.

Honestly, what was her style? She hadn't lived enough of her life to even develop a style, but she had dreams. She had a whole list of places she wanted to go, a scrapbook full of "someday" visions for her future. With the check burning hot in her pocket, she pulled the scrapbook off the living room bookcase and sat down on the sofa.

"What's that?"

The voice from the kitchen made her jump and slam the scrapbook shut. "Jesus, Matt, I forgot you were home."

Her brother was already poking around in the fridge. "I'm always home."

"Tell me about it." Megan put the scrapbook back on the shelf. She'd look at it later, when Matt wasn't around to make snide comments. "Didn't you have work today?"

Matt chugged his water and leaned against the fridge. If he'd had work today, he'd wasted no time changing back into running pants and an old T-shirt. He didn't look like he'd shaved, either, and his hair was uncombed. "I took today off. I had a headache when I woke up."

Megan wrinkled her nose. Great, another day off for Matt. She approached him in the kitchen. "Speaking of which. You have your share of the rent money?"

"Didn't I Venmo you yet?" He looked at the calendar hanging on the wall, then made a thoughtful noise. "Wasn't that due on the first?"

"Of course it was due on the first, and you told me you'd have it to me once you got paid, so I covered your half." Megan tried to keep her voice calm. If Matt got into a snit, he'd withhold rent for the month just to be spiteful.

"Oh, yeah." He nodded, sipping his water and rubbing his abs absentmindedly with his free hand. "Sure, I can get that to you. Remind me when I've got my phone." Before she could protest, he started out the door, grabbing his phone off the table as he did so. "See ya."

"You've got your phone now," she shouted after him.

"I mean remind me when I'm not busy." He was still on his way out.

"Where are you going?"

"I'm meeting Dan at the gym," he hollered, already leaving.

"I thought you had a headache."

If he answered, the words were lost as he shut the front door behind him.

Megan exhaled through her nose, a hot, angry puff of air. He knew just what to say to piss her off, and always had, ever since they were kids. If he weren't completely incapable of being a responsible adult, he would have his own rental instead of living with her, and she wouldn't have to babysit him all the time for things like paying the bills and cleaning up after himself.

He walked all over her, and she never stood up to him. It never seemed worth the effort. Maybe that should stop.

Megan wiped up the edge of the counter where Matt had spilled some water. Even *Matt* had done his share of traveling, although he'd mooched off the generosity of friends and relatives to do so. But her? She'd been safe. She'd been predictable. She'd stayed home.

And now, she was laid off with ten thousand dollars and very little clue what to do next.

The email from Juliet said only cryptically that she had news for both of them, and asked to video chat around seven that night. Scarlett had already sent back yes, probably assuming that Megan didn't have any other plans. The assumption would have rankled Megan if it wasn't so damn accurate. At 7:05 p.m., a message came through in a newly formed group chat.

Megan stared at the words for an inordinately long time. It just said, Hey! Are you two around?

At this point, it was getting weird not to just announce whatever news she had instead of demanding a video chat, but Juliet had always been a fan of grand gestures. It was part of what made her get along so well with Scarlett when they were kids. Juliet always had the best make-believe games, and Scarlett would be eager to build on her story, and Megan was just happy to be included.

It was also weird to be in a group chat with Scarlett. They'd had that conversation this morning, and then Megan was laid off, and now it was like she was in this twilight zone of worlds being overturned. Once upon a time, things were simpler between them. Scarlett had been the kind of best friend she would go to the moon for. Now? Now was a different story.

Scarlett responded to the chat first, the little circle with her cheerful face popping up on the screen. Sure! What's up? she typed. She was like some kind of poster for an anti-depressant. Surely some of the intervening years should have taken some of that chipperness away.

Megan had to respond, then, because otherwise Juliet was going to think she was the only one in the chat. I'm here too! The exclamation point felt ridiculous. She wasn't an "exclamation point" kind of person, and she never had been. Would they think this looked as fake as she felt?

Hey girls! Oh my god. Let's video chat.

What could she say other than Sure! with another damn exclamation point?

Within moments, all their faces were up on the screen. Nostalgia hit her like a wave of ocean water, the kind you don't see coming that knocks you flat on your ass. Juliet looked amazing, as good as ever, her blonde hair loose and perfect around her shoulders. She was older than when Megan had last seen her, obviously, but she still looked like a model.

Alongside Juliet was Scarlett, whose light brown curls looked cuter in a messy bun than Megan's hair looked when she styled it. Next to their faces, she looked like the friend who was going to tell them not to go to the party because the parents wouldn't be home. The disparity had her pulling self-consciously at her glasses before either of them said anything. Of course, then she couldn't really *see*, so she had to put them on. Now she looked indecisive *and* nerdy. Perfect. Just the way she wanted this weird reunion to go.

"Girls! Oh my god, why haven't we done this before?" Juliet was looking down, staring at their faces rather than the camera, probably.

Because we're not friends anymore! Megan's inner voice said, chipper and too-perky, but Juliet didn't deserve that. *Juliet* hadn't pissed her off, after all. *Juliet* hadn't abandoned her at the most terrifying part of her life to go off to some other prestigious college like Scarlett had.

"What's new?" Scarlett sounded as cheerful as Juliet. Probably her life was amazing now; Megan didn't know.

"First tell me about you! Megan, where are you living? What are you doing?" Juliet rested her chin on her hands.

"Uh. I'm renting a house," she said, trying to sound cheerful. She didn't need to mention that her brother lived with her. "And I'm, you know, I've been working at the Starlite. Trying to pay off that student loan debt. But uh… I'm making some big changes! Career change." She smiled.

"You are?" Scarlett raised an eyebrow, surprise or irritation in her expression. "You didn't mention that this morning."

"Yeah, well, it didn't come up then." Megan's face was so

hot, she must look like a tomato. "It's all still up in the air right now. Very new."

Scarlett was still looking at her like she was trying to understand what was happening when Juliet piped in. "I'm so glad you two are still hanging out! I was worried that you might not be friends anymore and I'd be making everything super awkward by messaging." She smiled brightly, and Megan didn't have the heart to disavow her of her belief. "What about you, Scarlett?" Juliet asked. "What are you up to lately?"

"I'm freelancing, actually." Scarlett sat up a little straighter. "Telecommuting, mostly data analysis for private firms. It's a great setup, because I get to make my own hours, work from home, pretty much living the dream." She grinned with those perfectly white teeth that she hadn't even had to suffer through years of braces to get.

"I'm so glad." Juliet sighed. "The one downside of not being on social media is that I don't get to see what you're all up to. It is *so good* to see your faces."

"Thanks." Scarlett waved her hand in a "get on with it" gesture, and Megan was quite grateful for it. "Now we've got to know. Tell us why you're calling. What's your news?"

"I'm getting married!" Juliet fairly bounced out of her seat. "His name is Gabriel, and we've been keeping things kind of quiet because his family is *very* conservative and wouldn't approve of us living together, but we've decided to make it official. We're getting married on February 19 here in Quebec."

"Congratulations!" Megan and Scarlett said together, their words overlapping. Megan meant all her congratulations, too; Juliet was always so sweet. She deserved somebody really good. But... February 19? Megan looked at the calendar and did some math. "But that's so soon. There's almost no time to plan a wedding."

"Tell me about it." Juliet gave a half-smile. "But his grandmother is not in good health, and we want everyone we love to be able to attend, so we decided to make it really fast. His father has wonderful business connections, and he pulled some strings, so we're at the Château Frontenac for the whole thing." She clasped her hands together. "I know we haven't seen each other in a long time, but we were best friends growing up. It feels so important to me that the two of you attend. Is there any way you can make it?"

"Oh." Megan's heart fluttered. "I...don't know." Quebec? In February? "I've never been on a plane," she said, trying to stall her mind that was already spending the ten thousand dollar check she still had in her pants pocket.

Scarlett looked similarly uneasy. "I...don't know. It's a lot of money for tickets, and I want to say yes, but... I have to think about it, Jules."

Juliet's face fell. "Of course. I understand. I haven't mailed your invitations yet—I don't even have your addresses—but I wanted to talk to you first so you could know how much I wanted you to come. And Quebec will be so gorgeous then. It's Winter Carnival that week, and it's so different from Florida..." Juliet had those big, pleading eyes, like out of a cartoon.

"Maybe it's possible!" Megan found herself saying, with another cursed exclamation point sneaking into her voice. "I mean, I don't know, but I don't want to say *no* right off the bat..."

"Well. Think about it, all right?" Juliet bit her lip. "If you made it, we could totally cover your hotel. But maybe you two could talk more? I'll hang up. Let me know! Please. I'd love to see you. And message me your addresses!"

"Of course. Of course we'll talk." Scarlett was saying it like she wasn't going to hang up on Megan the minute she didn't have the social obligation to talk to her, the way she'd avoided all of Megan's attempts to reach out. She'd later made some attempts of her own that Megan had of course avoided, too, but who was keeping track of that?

"Okay! And let's not be strangers. I miss you both." Juliet gave them beaming smiles and then disconnected, leaving Scarlett as the only face on Megan's screen.

For a minute, Scarlett and Megan just stared at each other.

Scarlett rested her chin on her folded hands. "Career change?"

"Diner's closing, thanks. Telecommuting data analysis?"

"More like data entry."

The silence stretched on some more, and maybe the mercy would be to just hang up and pretend they hadn't talked at all.

"What are we gonna do, Meg?" Scarlett asked.

"About what?"

"About Juliet." Scarlett made a face. "She really wants us to go."

Megan wrinkled her nose. "She also apparently thinks you and I are still best friends."

Scarlett laughed. "Who's gonna tell her?"

"We can't tell her," Megan insisted. "She wants us to go to Canada! I've never even been out of the state."

"Shit, I can't afford to fly to Canada." Scarlett shook her head. "We've gotta say no, right?"

"Right." Megan sighed. "But I don't want to look at that sad face."

"Neither do I. I don't know about you, but I'm gonna take the coward's way out and just RSVP no when the invitation comes." Scarlett leaned back in her chair. "And change my name and go into hiding."

Megan looked at the screen. "I could…" She stopped, the possibility that had come half-formed to her mind suddenly dissolving. "No, it's dumb."

"What?" Scarlett asked.

"I was just thinking aloud. Never mind." Megan shook her

head. "Have a good night. Good luck with whatever you're doing now."

"Yeah, thanks." Scarlett's sarcasm filled her words. She didn't even say goodbye before hanging up.

Megan stared at the screen, at her own face looking at her, and sighed again before closing the window. She had the whole evening to be sad and feel sorry for herself without worrying about what other people thought of her.

Especially Scarlett.

Chapter Three

This was probably dumb. Most of the things Scarlett did were dumb. She wasn't even sure Megan still lived in the same house, but she'd gotten a Christmas card from this address a few years ago when Megan was maybe still trying to keep up appearances, and Megan wasn't the type of person to move. So she sat in the driver's seat of her car in front of a plain-looking beige house, which had a single string of Christmas lights trimming the garage like the saddest scene in a depressing holiday movie, and stared at the light on in the bedroom. It was late. It was late, and she and Megan weren't even *friends* anymore. Sitting in front of her house like a creeper wasn't a good look.

But.

If Megan had an ounce of adventure in her body, Scarlett could wrangle a trip to Canada out of it, and they'd both make Juliet happy. Which was probably the best thing to do in this situation. She'd been thinking about it for days, ever since the video chat. It was late, but she had finally convinced herself to go talk to Megan, and she didn't want to lose her nerve.

So she got out of her shitty car and ran up the front steps to ring the doorbell.

Megan opened the door, her brown hair pulled back in a headband, wearing a matching pajama set because of course she wore matching pajamas, staring up at Scarlett with this expression of bewilderment that hit Scarlett like a punch in the gut.

She used to have a really, really big crush on Megan.

But now, they weren't there anymore, and Scarlett gave her a thumbs-up, like that wasn't the most ridiculous way to greet someone. "Hey!" Scarlett said brightly. "Can we talk?"

"What. The hell." Megan looked past her. "Is this a prank?"

"It's not a prank. But it's cold! Let me in." Scarlett shifted from foot to foot.

Megan stepped aside, and Scarlett stepped into the house. It was the first time she'd ever been in here, and damn, Megan loved beige.

"Your house is nice," Scarlett said, because that is what you said when you were going into somebody's house for the first time. "Nice neutrals."

"I'm not allowed to paint it anything unless I paint over it when I move out." Megan made a face at her. Megan was always pulling these faces, scrunched up and irritated. "What are you doing here? It's late."

"I know it's late. I needed to talk to you."

"The internet is a perfectly reasonable option these days." Megan was wearing bunny slippers, like the kind that had actual bunnies on them, and something about that tweaked a weird little vulnerability in Scarlett's innards that she didn't want to question too deeply.

"Can I sit?" Scarlett went over and sat on the couch anyway without waiting for a response. She looked around the room again. Something seemed off. The art looked like the standard kind of art you'd find at Target, but hell, that wasn't weird. Scarlett got most of her wall hangings at big box stores. It was the stuff on the bookshelves. Megan had always loved romances, so those lined a whole shelf, but she wasn't really a fan of video game tie-in novels, and there were three full shelves of...

"Metal Gear Solid?" Scarlett asked aloud, squinting to read the titles.

Megan flushed. "They're Matt's."

"Matt?" It took Scarlett a moment to remember. "Your brother?"

"He lives here with me." Megan folded her arms.

"Meg, you're not doing the South any favors here by living with your brother."

"Very funny. He lost his job a few years back and needed a place to stay, so I told him he could rent here with me."

"A few years back." Scarlett wasn't friends with Megan anymore, and she should probably keep her nose in her own business, but the curiosity was driving her into the questions she probably had no business asking. "And what's he doing now?"

"He picks up some hours here and there at a few different places." Megan's tone was evasive.

"Where's he tonight? Work?" The answer was probably no.

"He went out with friends. And now he's probably gaming." Megan grimaced.

Of course it wouldn't surprise Scarlett at all if Megan's kid brother was a deadbeat who didn't pay the bills. He'd been a slacker in high school, but hell, lots of people were slackers in high school. Matt was the kind of slacker who liked to mooch off his parents until they stopped him, though. Maybe they'd finally stopped for good and he'd had to move in with Megan.

"What are you doing here, Scarlett?" Megan crossed her arms over her chest. Even standing while Scarlett was sitting, she looked slight. Megan had always been slim, unlike Scarlett's bold curves and wild hair, and her pale skin looked especially pale in the dim light. She didn't seem to ever get much color, even during the hot Florida summers when she and Scarlett used to spend all their time after school swimming and sunbathing outside. Now, the paleness made her look unwell.

"Are you okay?" Scarlett was asking before she thought about it.

Megan waved her hand. "I'm fine. I'm less fine if you don't answer me."

"Okay." Scarlett interlaced her hands, pressing her palms between her knees, and leaned forward on the couch. "Do you actually want to go to Juliet's wedding?"

A softness stole into Megan's eyes. "I can't." Her tone wasn't "I can't," though; her tone was "I wish I could."

"But is it that you don't want to, or don't think you can? Why don't you think you can?"

Megan sighed and spun in a circle. "Do we have to go through this now? It's almost midnight."

"Do you have to get up in the morning?" Scarlett asked.

"Yes," Megan shot back, and then paused. "Well, no." She bit her lower lip. "Winston called and asked me not to come in tomorrow. They're cutting back on hours in the last few weeks the diner's open."

"Great. So you have time to talk."

Megan flopped into the recliner across from Scarlett. "You're impossible. You've always been impossible."

This was the closest they'd come to broaching their past. Scarlett wasn't sure if she wanted to. There were always questions involved, questions she wasn't ready to answer.

"Yes," Megan said when Scarlett didn't respond. "Yeah, sure, I'd love to go. But it's ridiculous. It's a whole different country. I've never been on a plane."

That was the part that had settled in Scarlett's mind, the part she hadn't been able to let go of. "Are you scared to fly?"

"I don't know." Megan sighed. "What do you want me to say?"

"I didn't think it was a particularly difficult question. Lots of people are scared to fly." That didn't seem right to Scarlett, though. For all of Megan's quiet, unobtrusive demeanor, she had never really been *fearful*. She just…didn't expend a lot of effort on things for herself.

"You said it was a lot of money." Megan's tone was accusatory. "Why are you asking me if I'm going to go if you can't afford to go?"

Time for the pitch. "I was thinking maybe we could drive," Scarlett said, and forced the last word out. "Together."

Megan stared at her.

Scarlett stared back.

"Together," Megan repeated. "In the same car." She drew back. "Wait, what car? Not your car, certainly. I saw that thing in the driveway and it's the same one you had in high school. I'm surprised it isn't currently on fire."

Scarlett couldn't even defend herself. "My car's a death trap. We'd take yours."

"So you want me to drive across the entire country with you in *my* car so you can save money on plane tickets?" Megan's eyebrows were so high up they were practically hitting her hairline. "You've got some nerve, Scarlett Andrews."

"Your car's a convertible," Scarlett tried.

Megan gave her a withering look. "It's *winter*."

It really was a terrible plan, wasn't it? But Scarlett had already thought it up, and she was committed. "It doesn't have to be so bad. You and I used to be friends, once." She swallowed, the words suddenly hanging heavier between them than she wanted them to. She forced herself to press on. "Juliet wants to see us both. She was the final member of our trio. We should try to go to her wedding."

Megan wrinkled up her nose. "Gross."

"What?" Scarlett snapped back.

Megan kept the wrinkled-prune expression for another moment. "It's gross that you're getting all emotional about this."

"Unbelievable." Scarlett flopped back on the couch and stretched her arms out over the back of it. "I didn't even want to ask you, you know that? I knew you were going to be an asshole about this, the way you've been a total asshole since we stopped talking."

"Right. Right. I'm the asshole. Obviously. And you're perfect." Megan was getting heated, color rising in her pale cheeks. "How am I supposed to do this road trip? I've never—" She cut herself off abruptly, mouth snapping shut.

"Never what?" Scarlett asked.

Megan shook her head. "Never mind."

"Never *what*?" Scarlett insisted. "Never been to a wedding? Never actually had a valid driver's license?"

"I've never been out of Florida." Megan folded her arms. "There, are you happy?"

"You were serious about that?" Scarlett gaped. "But this state is so bad!"

"This state is *not* bad. I happen to like it here. People come from all over the world to the beaches, and the cost of living is so low, and I have a Disney yearly pass..." Megan ticked off the pluses on her fingers.

Scarlett interrupted her. "It's hotter than Satan's taint, and you can't go thirty feet without hitting a nail salon or a Wal-Mart, and alligators just fucking *show up* in the drainage ditches, and don't even get me started on sinkholes—"

"So move away, then!" Megan said, practically shouting. "Why do you even live here if you hate it so much?"

"Because it's cheap! And because I don't want to shovel snow! And because I grew up here and it's like a damn wart, you can't get rid of it. And…" Her voice fell. "And I like it." Scarlett hated that she actually liked the sunny weather and the beaches and the quirky people.

Megan was nodding like she knew everything, and that was its own annoying bullshit. "I see."

"Ah, yeah, 'I see.' Don't act like you're my therapist." Scarlett waved her hand. "At least I've left the state."

"Don't hold it over me." Megan looked off to one side, something sad coming over her face that made Scarlett feel like kind of an ass for picking on her.

Other obstacles were crashing into place in Scarlett's mind already. "Well, we couldn't drive, then. You probably don't even have a passport, and it would cost a fortune to get one expedited."

"I have a passport." Megan interlaced her fingers in her lap.

"What? Why?" Scarlett couldn't imagine why she'd have gone through the trouble and expense of getting one, if she wasn't going anywhere.

Megan clammed up again, pulling her legs into her chest on the chair. "I don't know why you care."

"I'm curious. For old time's sake."

"I got one back when I first graduated college. I thought—it's dumb." Megan's voice was muffled against her knees. Scarlett wanted to push her, but they didn't have that rapport anymore. But then Megan continued talking. "I thought I was going to travel, and I didn't." She picked her head up and rested her chin on her knees. "Is that good enough?"

She might drive Scarlett mad, and Scarlett might have some unresolved issues with her that she did not want to resolve now, but the curiosity was stronger than the resentment at this point. "Don't you want to use that passport? It seems perfect. We'll drive up to Quebec for the wedding. Go a few days early to see the city, go to that Winter Carnival thing, and then come home. Unless you don't want to leave Florida."

"I want to leave Florida," Megan said defensively. "You think I like never having done anything with my life?"

Scarlett didn't need to tell Megan that she wasn't the only one who hadn't done anything with her life. They would probably have to have that conversation eventually. If they became friends again. "What do you think?" Scarlett asked.

Megan's face went through a number of expressions. "How are we supposed to pay for it?"

"I've got a little money saved up," Scarlett lied.

"But not enough for plane tickets?" Megan asked.

"Okay, so I don't really have any money." Scarlett pulled her legs up onto the couch. "I don't know how we're going to pay for it."

Megan grimaced. She seemed to be considering something for a long time. "Okay. Look. I got a big check from Winston and Martha for severance. I was…thinking of going somewhere with it anyway. I can pay for the hotels and food if you can pay for the gas."

Scarlett did not need to do the math to know she was getting the way better end of the deal, and her conscience wouldn't let her stay quiet about it. "Why would you even have me go if you're going to pay for almost everything?"

"Because I can't do all that driving *myself*," Megan said, like it was obvious. "And I've never done a road trip before. I don't know how to do it."

"You pretty much just drive north," Scarlett said, but then changed her mind. "Never mind. It's okay. I'm just letting you know you're really getting ripped off."

"I think that even if you were paying for half of everything, I'd still be getting ripped off," Megan said, matter-of-factly, "because of the fact that we're going to be stuck in a car together for a week or something."

Scarlett rubbed her chin. "If we drive straight through in shifts, we might be able to do it in less."

Megan raised her eyebrows. "Are you kidding? This is my one road trip, I'm going to make a whole trip out of it. I'm the one paying. We're going to all the places on my list."

"Wait a minute, wait a minute." Scarlett held up a hand. "This suddenly became a carjacking."

"It's not a carjacking when it's my car." Megan gave her a smug smile.

"Ugh. This is the worst." Scarlett rolled her eyes. Megan had her, and she knew it. "Do you at least have good places on the list? I'm not driving out to the fucking Grand Canyon on our trip to Quebec. You're allowed to go two hours off of I-95 in any direction, but no more."

Megan looked defeated, like all the fight went out of her. "I don't even know where I want to go, all right? I was just talking. I don't care."

That was *clearly* a blatant lie, but Scarlett didn't want to examine it or probe into it right now, and Megan was looking all *sad*, which hit some soft place inside Scarlett that should definitely have calloused over by now. She'd pressed her luck enough for one night. "Are you okay if I come by sometime to plan? And maybe message you in the meantime?"

Megan hesitated, then nodded. "Sure. Whatever. Now can you get out and let me sleep?"

Scarlett got up off the couch. "I'd hate to be a bother."

"Yeah, right." Megan ushered her out and closed the door in her face, leaving Scarlett standing in the cold wondering what in the world she was going to do now that Megan had said yes.

Megan stared at the closed door with her heart hammering in her ribs. For all her ability to seem unaffected by emotionally intense conversations, the evening with Scarlett had rattled her. If she hadn't been so exhausted and ready to drop off to sleep, she might have been able to process it better, but right now she just wanted to mull it over after a full night's rest.

But rest wouldn't come, so Megan did what she always did when her mind refused to shut up: she took a bath. She stripped off her pajamas and filled the tub with hot water, hot enough for her skin to barely tolerate, and dumped in some of the Epsom salts bubble bath she'd first bought to soothe her sore legs from standing all day and later just kept around because it was practical. Then, she lit two candles, the generic kind since the official Yankee Candle brand was too expensive for her to justify purchasing, and turned off the bathroom lights.

It was almost midnight. The house was quiet, and would probably stay quiet because Matt would spend the whole night playing video games. She had time to process in the way she liked, and so she sank into the steaming bubbles, hissing as her cold skin contacted the water. She couldn't quite submerge all the way in this bathtub; even though she was slim, her legs were too long, and her knees poked up out of the bubbles like an iceberg. She was able to get her whole torso beneath the water, though, the bubbles brushing her chin, a few bits of foam sticking to her hair. In the dark, only the flickering candlelight to illuminate the room, she ran through what she had just agreed to and what in the world she was going to do next.

She had to be practical, of course. She needed to figure out the exact mileage between Crystal River, Florida, and the Château Frontenac in Quebec. Then she needed to get her car serviced. It was a Toyota, so it was going to last forever, very unlike whatever ridiculous vanity car Scarlett had bought back in high school and then tried to keep limping along nearly a decade later. She was so irresponsible sometimes. Scarlett always blew her money on dumb purchases, when Megan was likely to save and be smart and start a responsible bank account and a Roth IRA. Megan could afford to fly to Quebec if she wanted to. Scarlett could not.

Maybe if she hadn't blown all her money on fancy-ass private college, Scarlett could have afforded it. What was she doing freelancing, anyway? The University of South Florida wasn't *good* enough for Scarlett. A mean little inner voice wondered how she'd even gotten into a private college; it wasn't like her grades were anything special. As soon as she thought it, though, she winced and pulled the words back. She might be jealous, but she wasn't mean. That wasn't like her.

Jealous. She rolled that thought around while she gathered handfuls of bubbly foam and piled them on her knees, only to watch the bubbles slide back down her skin again. Was she really jealous of Scarlett? Certain things, sure. Her amazing body, with those incredible curves that landed everyone Scarlett ever wanted: guys, girls, even people who didn't fit into either of those categories. Scarlett was the first bisexual person Megan had ever known, the first person to be out in their middle school—*middle school*, for crying out loud! She had always known who she was.

And Megan? Megan didn't know shit about herself for most of her life. She hadn't figured out that she wasn't straight until college. She'd been through three relationships before figuring out how to ask for what she wanted in bed, and even then, she was better at doing it herself than getting a partner to do it for her. That was good, because she kind of hated dating. Nobody gave Megan a second glance. Megan was average, and average meant nobody noticed you. Average meant blending in.

Nothing about Scarlett was average, and she was never someone to blend in.

But now, Scarlett was out of money, and she needed Megan's help, and she wanted Megan to drive her to Quebec. And

Megan had...had what? Had volunteered to pay for it, even. God, had she been suckered again? Was Scarlett using her as a way to get to Canada? A little nugget of sickness settled into her stomach. This trip was a terrible idea.

But.

But.

Megan had had twenty-five years to accumulate goals and dreams for herself, and she had a scrapbook filled with the places she wanted to travel to and the goals she wanted to achieve, and she wasn't going to make the first step on her own. She never made the first step on her own; it had always seemed a ridiculous indulgence to put herself first. Even now, even on the other side of their friendship in this morass of weird discomfort between them, Scarlett was pushing her to take the first step.

Megan looked up at the ceiling, where the flames cast long shadows. She was going to have to stay in a car with this woman for a week. Maybe more than a week. What in the hell had she gotten herself into?

Even after her bath, she couldn't settle. She wandered around the house for a while, cleaned some things, and then tried to read a book. That's where Matt found her when he rolled in a little after one, key fumbling in the lock, crashing inside with no attempt to be quiet. "Hey!" He grinned, stumbling a little as he came inside. "You still up?"

"Yeah." Megan closed her book. "Are you drunk?"

"A little." He rubbed his face. "What the fuck do you care?"

"Did you drive?"

"No, I didn't drive. Dan drove me home." Matt yawned. "That reminds me. Can you drive me to his place tomorrow to get my car?"

Megan stared up at him. What a fucking asshole. She sighed. "Sure. You get me the rent yet? I've been asking for days."

"Oh right! Remind me tomorrow. It's one in the goddamn

morning." He went to the fridge and grabbed a Gatorade. "Can you get more Gatorade next time you get groceries?"

"Write it on the list." Megan tried to focus on the book again, but her unease was still unsettling her.

A few envelopes fell onto her lap from above, making her jump. "I got the mail," Matt said. "You actually got something that's not a bill."

Megan held the heavy envelope and knew immediately what it was. She pulled out Juliet's invitation and turned it to catch the light. The navy blue card stock was decorated with golden stars, the fancy golden script proclaiming, *Together with their parents, Mr. Gabriel Bouchard and Miss Juliet Letourneaux request the honor of your presence at their wedding...*

"What's that?" Matt flopped down on the couch next to her, shoving her feet out of the way.

"It's a wedding invitation." She was going to have to tell him at some point. "It's in Quebec."

Matt snorted. "You want me to throw it out?"

Megan pressed it to her chest. "No. I'm going."

Matt stopped, bottle halfway to his mouth, and slowly lowered it again. "You're what?"

"I'm going to the wedding." Megan hated how her voice trembled even when she tried to sound confident. "It's next month."

"You're not going." He laughed and took another sip. "You don't go anywhere. You don't even have a passport."

"Yes, I do." He didn't know her at all.

"Why? Waste of money, if you ask me." He kicked his feet up onto the coffee table. "Look, no offense, Meg, but you're not the traveling kind. Some people are adventurous, and some people aren't. You're not." He patted her shin. "Nothing wrong with that."

"I said I'm going, and I'm going." Megan flared in anger,

all her frustration and confusion suddenly directed at him. "I'm driving up there with Scarlett."

"Scarlett who?"

"Scarlett Andrews."

Matt scrunched up his nose like he was trying to remember her. "Did I ever sleep with that one?"

Revulsion ran through Megan at the mere thought of it. "God, I hope not." Shit, what if he *had*?

"What got into you tonight? That time of the month?" Matt got to his feet, shaking his head. "Ugh. Whatever. I'm going to bed."

He left her there on the couch and wandered into his room at the other end of the house. Megan watched him go, annoyed and for some reason embarrassed. Embarrassed by what? Maybe her past, maybe what she had and hadn't done with her life. She'd been a little uncertain about her decision, but now, she needed to go to prove Matt wrong. She needed to do something to move forward.

She grabbed a pen and the RSVP card. Matt could say what he wanted. She was going to Quebec.

Chapter Four

"Knock knock!"

Megan opened the door at Scarlett's verbal knocking, already bracing herself for the encounter she was about to have. They'd basically tiptoed around each other for the past couple weeks, but Megan had RSVP'd yes to the wedding, and Scarlett did the same, and now they were only a few days away from leaving and the logistics were piling up into a panic-induced extensive list of to-dos. One of those was the actual itinerary, which Scarlett had insisted on reviewing even though Megan was confident she could do it on her own. Okay, that was a lie. Megan wasn't confident she could do any of this on her own. That, after all, was why she was bringing Scarlett into it.

"What are those?" Scarlett asked immediately as soon as Megan led her into the kitchen, stopping short of the table that was currently covered in maps.

"They're maps?" Megan tried not to sound confused but was definitely confused. "What, haven't you seen them before?"

"I've seen maps before, but here in the twenty-first century, most people use the GPS. It's like the future now." Scarlett waggled her fingers like she was showing off a magic trick. "I don't know why you've got ancient technology spread out here like we're taking the covered wagons to Oregon. You worried about dying of dysentery along the way, too?"

Megan rolled her eyes. "Maps are better because you can see the whole route spread out in front of you."

"You could just zoom out on the screen." Scarlett scooted closer anyway and peered across the table full of papers. "Where did you even get all these, a museum? Do they have highways on them, or just horse paths?"

"I got them at AAA, thank you very much. Apparently it's very common. Nobody even looked at me weird." Megan folded her arms. Fuck Scarlett's judgment. She liked maps. "And..." She started to add more, but then stopped, until Scarlett looked up at her with raised eyebrows.

"And what?"

"And...it's kind of classic. You know. The Road Trip." The words were capitalized in her mind. "It feels like it's not right to do it without a paper map." Suddenly saying it out loud, she realized how silly it must sound to Scarlett. "Never mind."

Scarlett's lips curled up, just the hint of a smile. "You don't do anything halfway, do you?"

"Never have." Megan didn't want to admit how intimidating it was to see the whole route spread out in front of her, all those states and even that whole other country sprawling at the far end of the table. She wasn't afraid; she was just new to having adventures. Most of all, she was not going to let Scarlett see her as anything other than perfectly competent. Or at least unbothered about her lack of competence.

"What's your plan?" Scarlett put her hands on her hips and surveyed the maps. "Or *our* plan. I guess I'm in this with you."

Megan had prepared for this. "I expect you to do a lot of the driving, since I'm financing almost everything."

Scarlett shrugged. "Sure. I like driving. It's the least I can do, right? And pay for gas." She put her hands flat on the table and leaned over to see farther. Her curly light brown hair tumbled down over her shoulders. How could she be so effortlessly lovely? Megan always looked like she fell off a barge, and Scarlett was ridiculously attractive. Scarlett probably fell into bed with good looking people everywhere she went. It was supremely unfair.

Scarlett tapped the map. "You don't have anything marked."

"What do you mean?" Megan looked at the map, puzzled. "I highlighted the whole route." She'd traced the entirety of I-95 with her yellow highlighter, up until they changed roads near the border with Canada, and then the rest of the path all the way to the Château Frontenac.

"You highlighted the main road, and that's it. You said you wanted to make a bunch of stops, but you didn't put stars on them or circle them or anything." Scarlett stood the rest of the way up. "You think we'll just take I-95 with no detours?"

Immediately on the defensive, Megan waved an arm across the table with a wild gesture. "You said you wanted to make this as simple as possible!"

"And you said you wanted to do a real road trip. Real road trips have stops." Scarlett was still the picture of nonchalance. "I said we could do two hours in each direction of I-95. There's got to be some places you want to go. Put some detours on there. No need to get all worked up about it."

Megan was still flushed, and suddenly irritated as well. "I don't know why you're *not* worked up about this. I've done all this stuff to get ready. I bought a dress. I got the car tuned up so it would make the trip. I got all of these maps! All you've done is show up and criticize me."

"You bought a dress?" Scarlett tipped her head to the side, a smile flirting with the corners of her mouth. "Can I see it?"

Megan's skin got hot all over. "It's just a dress. You'll see it at the wedding."

"Please?" Transformed, all her previous nitpicking disappeared, Scarlett folded her hands on the table and looked up at Megan with sparkling eyes. "I love dresses. I want to see what you're wearing. I want to make sure you're not wearing the same thing as me."

"I somehow really doubt that." Megan sighed. It was going to be easier to give in than to fight her. "Fine. You want to see it? I'll show it to you."

She led Scarlett into her bedroom.

"Jesus, you always keep your bedroom this clean when nobody's seeing it?" Scarlett folded her arms and looked around.

Megan hadn't thought of her bedroom as particularly clean. It was just a bedroom. But then Scarlett's comment caught up to her. "Hey, who's saying nobody's seeing it?"

"Well, are they?" Scarlett's eyebrow went up in irritating judgment.

Megan turned away toward the closet, her face still red. "None of your business." It was none of her business because no, nobody was seeing it lately. She had been celibate for months now. But Scarlett didn't need to know that.

The dress hung right in the middle of the closet, still in its plastic garment bag. She had not intended on buying something so pretty, so fancy, but this long lilac gown with dark purple lace overlay had spoken to her in a way no little black dress had. Pulling it out of the closet, she prepared for Scarlett's judgey comments. "Here." She put it out on the bed, laying it carefully but trying not to *look* like she was being really careful about it. If Scarlett knew how much she cared about her opinion, still, even after these years, she'd never live it down.

"Oh." Scarlett stepped closer, and her expression was hard to read, so Megan braced herself. Then, finally, she said, "Megan, it's beautiful. It's going to look so pretty on you."

Megan felt even weirder with the compliment than with an insult. "Thanks."

Scarlett touched the fabric. "It's really nice. This must have cost a fortune."

"I got it on after-holiday sale last week. Those are still going on." Megan hadn't wanted to spend money on herself, especially not on something as frivolous as a dress she probably wouldn't wear again, but she hadn't been able to say no to this dress, especially with its reasonable price tag. "What about you? You get a dress yet?"

"I was thinking about maybe wearing...a suit?" Scarlett scrunched up her nose like she was considering. "There's this gray velvet one I saw on sale, and I sometimes think that girls in suits are super hot, but usually that's skinny girls, not, you know." She gestured to herself, all those curves, and flushed. Oh. Was Scarlett embarrassed? How long had it been since Megan had seen Scarlett embarrassed? It brought out a weird desire to comfort her.

"A suit would look great. Maybe with some heels, or boots? And, like, a camisole." Scarlett would look amazing like that, her curves filling out all the parts of the suit, and the feeling was kind of weird. She hadn't thought about *Scarlett* like that since some confusing sleepovers in high school, long before she'd figured out what those feelings meant.

"You think?"

Megan busied herself with pulling the plastic bag back down over her purple dress and hanging it back in the closet. Anything that would prevent or distract her from this weird sensation. "Yeah. Yeah, I think so. It's a good look. You look good in everything you wear."

"Oh, come on." Scarlett huffed out a laugh. "Quit making fun of me."

Megan paused. Maybe Scarlett *didn't* know she was gorgeous. "I'm not making fun of you. You look good in everything. It's one of the things that annoys the hell out of me about you."

There, now they were back to whatever bickering had become normal for them in this brief time of rekindling some kind of friendship. Scarlett rolled her eyes. "Sure. You got any ideas about this road trip, or not?"

"Of course I do." Megan had nothing *but* ideas. She glanced at the scrapbook on her nightstand, the one that she'd been poring over most nights since her conversation with Scarlett.

Maybe she was staring at it for too long, because Scarlett snapped her fingers in front of Megan's face. "Hey! Stop zoning out."

"I wasn't zoning out. I was thinking." Megan snatched the scrapbook up off her nightstand. "I've got a scrapbook here of all the places I want to visit. I didn't put anything on the map because I wasn't sure you'd be up for going to any of them."

"A scrapbook? Let me see." Scarlett held out her hands, which made Megan clutch the scrapbook ever tighter.

"No. I'll go through it."

"Do you have naked pictures of yourself in that scrapbook?" Scarlett waggled her eyebrows, making Megan laugh despite herself.

Two could play at that game. "I keep my naked pictures on my computer like everybody else." She pushed past a gobsmacked Scarlett, taking a bit of satisfaction from that look of shock, and headed back to the kitchen and the maps.

Scarlett trailed after her. "Wait. Seriously. Have you taken naked pictures of yourself?"

"Why, do you want to see them?"

Megan said it as a retort, but Scarlett's eyes went fraction-ally wider, and Megan's face blazed hot all over again. Shit. This was some unspoken territory, and she had no idea how to negotiate it. "Come look at this map," she said, changing the subject as quickly as she could.

"Right." Scarlett dropped it, too, fortunately, and for a mo-ment, she looked as unsettled as Megan felt before her regu-lar demeanor snapped back into place. "You know, I thought maybe you'd have, like, a whole itemized list drawn up with mileage and key facts. It doesn't seem like you to procrastinate."

"I didn't procrastinate. I wanted your input." Megan tapped the map. "I will draw your attention again to my excellent highlighting skills."

Scarlett leaned over to nod at the single line. "A notable start."

"So you are okay with detours?" Megan had been worried Scarlett would want to do this the most direct way possible so as not to spend time in the car with her, and she hadn't wanted to fight about it.

"I thought you were planning to stop at every ass-back-wards tourist trap between here and the border. I've already resigned myself to my fate." Scarlett spread her arms wide. "Hit me with your destinations."

Megan got hesitantly to her feet. Now, faced with the paper map and the permanence of marking something on it, she paused. Her sensible ballpoint pen lay untouched in the mid-dle of the map, resting in a crease.

She couldn't put her dreams aside forever. At some point, she had to start living.

She grabbed the pen and drew a tight circle around New York City. "There."

Scarlett nodded slowly, looking at the circle. "It's a good choice."

"Thanks. I'm glad you approve." Megan couldn't keep the sarcasm out of her voice, but it was just defensiveness without malice, and Scarlett didn't take the bait.

Scarlett waited, her expression expectant. "And what else?"

She might as well dig into the scrapbook. Megan flipped it open with a sigh of resignation. Scarlett was going to see this stuff anyway. If Scarlett made fun of her choices, she could always say that she was allowed to do whatever she wanted since she was paying most of the money, and she kept that excuse in her back pocket.

New York was the first page, so she was able to skip right by that. Scarlett put out a hand as she turned the page, though, and stopped her. "Wait a minute. Let me see." She kept her hand there, holding the page open. "You made this?"

It was just a scrapbook page, decorated with images of the city, photographs and a couple of drawings, the words "New York City" spread across the page. "Yeah." Megan drew back her hand. Scarlett didn't look about to make fun of her, so maybe this was fine. "I like scrapbooking."

"Why'd you leave all these blank spots?" Scarlett asked.

"For my own pictures."

Megan turned to the very front page, the one at the start of this section, where she'd created a sort of vision board for her scrapbook. It had all kinds of inspirational words like "travel" and "dream," which was maybe a bit cheesy but she liked it. The center focal point was a couple of Polaroids she'd taken: one of the beach at sunset that she'd taken over the Gulf of Mexico, and one of a dandelion just starting to lose its seeds to the wind.

"This is really good, Meg." Scarlett sounded genuine. Genuine, and impressed, and *kind*. Oh, suddenly Megan wanted to forgive all the ways she'd been wronged, wanted to tell

Scarlett all her deepest hopes and dreams, wanted them to go back to the way they were.

Instead, Megan clamped her lips shut and nodded once, curtly. Those were dangerous feelings, the kind that got her in over her head. She couldn't get her heart broken again by trusting Scarlett too much.

"Can I look at the rest of it?" Scarlett asked, drawing the book closer to herself.

"No." Megan pulled it out of her hands, more violently than she'd intended, and Scarlett's eyes widened. "Maybe some other time. I just…want to focus right now. On the map."

She added a few easy ones first. Washington, DC, which was a place everybody should visit. Tybee Island in Georgia was the closest one to home that she could circle, followed by Myrtle Beach, South Carolina. That was where Scarlett stopped her.

"Okay, wait a minute." Scarlett held out another hand. "It is February. And you have not one but two beaches on this sheet. Are you unfamiliar with the fact that winter is occurring, right now, in our lives?"

"I know. But I want to go there." Stubbornly, Megan flipped the pages of her scrapbook until she found the page she'd made for Tybee Island. "It's supposed to have the most beautiful sunrises on the east coast."

"So you want to get there for a sunrise?" Scarlett frowned. "That's a far drive, Meg. That's got to be what, four hours?" She pulled out her phone and started typing in something. "Five hours! It's a five-hour drive. Do you have any idea what time we would have to leave in order to watch the sun come up on Tybee Island?"

"Okay! Fine. It was dumb." Megan's skin felt hot, and she quickly drew an X through her previous circle. She should have known this wouldn't be a good idea. It was only five hours away; maybe she could go there on her own. She drew another X over the Myrtle Beach circle. "And we can skip Myrtle Beach, too. I just heard it was pretty." It was easier to give in. Did any of it matter that much, anyway?

Scarlett looked at her. Really looked at her, close enough that Megan couldn't escape that gaze. She was never comfortable with the intensity of Scarlett's full attention.

"Sorry," Scarlett eventually muttered. "Show me your Tybee Island page."

So Megan slid the scrapbook over to her, and Scarlett looked at the magazine picture of grasses blowing against white beach sand, the reddening sky promising daylight. "Fine. We'll go to your beach." Scarlett leaned over and re-circled Tybee Island. "And the other one, too." She added Myrtle Beach to the list with another circle. "I'll freeze my damn ass off, but you can get your scrapbook pictures. Okay?"

"I can go on my own, if you're gonna be a bitch about it."

Scarlett smiled. "Very funny. No, I'll go with you. I'm not swimming or some ridiculous shit like that, though, capisce?"

Scarlett left that night more exhausted than she'd been in a while. Dealing with Megan was exhausting. Had it always been so difficult? Of course not. Not when they were friends. But whatever they were now, it certainly wasn't *friends*, and the tension between them was enough to wear her out and leave her emotionally drained. She had to walk on eggshells around Megan. Megan was so touchy, ready to get defensive about everything, even when Scarlett was totally only teasing.

They'd ended up with a route, though. Scarlett hadn't computed the days of travel, but she was going to have to. The trip had gotten quite lengthy once Megan started opening up about things she wanted to see. Scarlett hadn't added any destinations of her own—this was Megan's trip, after all, and she was just along to do some of the driving.

The worst part of all of this was how much she wanted Megan to have a good trip. She'd let that friendship go, and now she was getting sucked right back into it again. Back when they stopped talking to each other, it had seemed a necessary evil. Now, though, Scarlett missed her, and she missed the friendship they had.

She hadn't missed the fact that Megan was really cute.

She wasn't hot. Megan wasn't a "hot" type of girl. Maybe with a haircut and the right makeup, and a really slutty dress, sure, but Megan as-is had this fresh-faced beauty that Scarlett had quietly mooned over back in high school, and then ignored, because Megan didn't swing that way and Scarlett was terrified of being rejected.

Whatever. The damage was done. She was going on a road trip with Megan Harris in only a few short days, from the looks of things, and she hadn't packed or, hell, even bought that gray velvet suit she'd been eyeing in the mall.

She had a lot to get done. And that wasn't counting all the ways she was going to have to distract herself from her frustrating—and frustratingly cute—road trip buddy.

She pulled into her driveway. Jacen had gone to bed already, or was out with his boyfriend. Good thing she had the place to herself; she needed some alone time to think.

And, as embarrassing as it was, maybe a cold shower.

Megan spent the next day in a flurry of disbelief and worry, vacillating so quickly between the two sometimes that she could barely tell them apart. One minute, this was the best idea she'd ever had, and the next, she was being reckless and irresponsible. There was no middle ground in her mind, not when she was doing something so far outside her comfort zone. But her comfort zone had gotten way too limited, and it was time to shake it up.

Now, with the two of them leaving in just a few days, Megan was in focused efficiency mode. She had tacked a to-do list onto the fridge and checked it again, for the third time today, to make sure she was on schedule. She'd blasted through almost everything on it, but a few annoying items still lingered, and she was going to get them done today.

The next item on her list was cleaning out the fridge, and that was where Matt found her an hour later, down on her hands and knees scrubbing the glass shelving.

"You still going through with this?"

This question again, like he hadn't brought it up a dozen times in the last weeks, either directly or obliquely. Megan rubbed her forehead with the back of her hand, not bothering to look up from her task. "Yes."

"You don't have to do this to prove something to me, you know."

Like she would actually do that. She laughed. "Sure. Shouldn't you be at work?"

"Eh, I don't know if I want to keep that job. They booked me two Saturdays in a row, and there's a concert I want to go see next weekend."

Megan sat back on her heels, pausing, the cold air of the fridge on one side of her face as she looked up at her younger brother. The mixture of annoyance, anger, and disgust rolling in her stomach was making her feel sick, and it wasn't anxiety about the trip. "What the hell are you doing with yourself, Matt?"

"What?" He shifted back, frowning. "You're asking me that? You, who don't know what the fuck you're doing with yourself without the diner?"

She had told herself she'd deal with reality after her trip, and reminded herself of that, tamping down the uncertainty his words evoked. "I paid your share of the electric and cable bills again."

"Thanks." Matt reached past her to grab a can of soda off the top shelf, where she was still cleaning.

"No, not thanks. You owe me a hundred and twenty dollars."

He winced. "Meg, I'll get it to you before your trip. I want to keep a cushion in case I get to go to that concert."

Something snapped inside her, like a rubber band overstretched inside her brain, the parts ricocheting sharply around her mind. "Move out."

Matt laughed. "Soon enough. I'm saving up, you know that. It's way cheaper to live here than at my own place, and my friends aren't responsible like you—"

"No. I mean, this month. Move out."

Matt stopped laughing all at once. "You're serious?"

"As a heart attack." Everything else had vanished in the face of her resolve. She'd put this off long enough, always resistant to putting out the effort, always coming back to the underlying belief that family took care of family, no matter what. Her brother had been taking advantage of her for years, and he was going to keep doing it until she stopped letting him. That moment was today.

"You're kicking me out, just like that?" He pressed a hand to his heart. "I'm your brother."

The calm settled over her like a soft blanket, smothering the anger and frustration that so frequently colored their interactions, and Megan no longer felt sick at all. "Yes. I'll give you thirty days. If you can't find a place by then, you can ask mom and dad to crash with them."

Matt pressed his lips tightly together. She had never drawn a clear line like this with him before, never made him act like an adult, and dammit, she couldn't survive like this anymore. Not today, not now, not with everything else in her life.

"Fine, whatever. You know this trip isn't going to fix anything, right? You're going off with your girlfriend, and you'll come home and be the same girl you've always been. And then you're not going to have me here helping you."

She didn't even want to fight with him over this, didn't need to correct him. He could believe whatever he wanted. She was done. Megan turned back to the refrigerator. "You can get boxes for your stuff at the liquor store."

Matt swore under his breath and walked away, leaving Megan alone with the fridge. She smiled into its depths. He could say what he wanted, but she could feel changes yet to come.

Packing? Packing was a different story.

By all accounts, this should be easy. She liked the methodical precision of arranging outfits and folding them neatly into packing cubes. She had mapped out the predicted weather for the entire eastern seaboard for their trip, as far ahead as the websites would let her, sketching out the next ten days as close to precisely as she could. But she was a Florida girl; temps making it down to freezing was a newsworthy event around here, and where they were headed, thirty degrees was an optimistic high. How many sweaters did a person wear when it was below thirty? She didn't even own long underwear, but was long underwear something a person owned in this day and age, or was that just some *Little House on the Prairie* thing?

With practically the entire contents of her closet spread out on her bed, she flopped down on top of them with a sigh. She had brought the scrapbook into the bedroom with her, and she pulled it closer across a swath of T-shirts to flip through the pages. Scarlett hadn't judged her out loud, but knowing Scarlett, all the judging was happening silently. She turned

to later pages in the book, the ones she didn't share with anyone, the embarrassing ones, and then pushed up into a sitting
position to look at them better. They weren't even that embarrassing. They were just photos she'd found in magazines
of couples doing couple things: walking hand-in-hand on a
beach, cooking together at a backyard barbecue, snuggling
on the couch in front of a fire. The couple themselves didn't
matter; they all looked different, a whole assortment of genders and pairings, and none of them looked like her. None of
her previous relationships had ever felt like the people in these
pictures seemed to feel. The images were all staged, of course,
clipped out of ads for cars or jewelry or cruises, but she could
ignore that part. She wanted that kind of intimacy, but it had
always eluded her. It was easy to tell herself she was unlucky
in love, harder to face the uncomfortable truth she *knew*, the
truth that love required vulnerability and trust and asking
for what you wanted...all things Megan was pretty shitty at.

She didn't do friendships well, either, come to think of it.
She'd never resolved things with Scarlett, and now they were
heading out on the road together for weeks on end.

Megan sighed, then got up off the bed and tossed the scrapbook into her suitcase. At least that was one thing she knew
she could bring along.

Chapter Five

The clock was just ticking over to midnight when Scarlett pulled into Megan's driveway, slotting her own shitty broken-down car alongside Megan's much more reliable Toyota Camry Solara. Now faced with the prospect of spending a week or so in that car, Scarlett had to accept that it was older than she'd remembered. Did Toyota even still *make* the Solara? She had no idea, but this one had to be over ten years old. At least, knowing Megan, it was kept in good working condition. Scarlett's was in such bad shape, the AAA guys knew her by name. But she couldn't focus on that; she had to get Megan actually on the road without having her freak out. Not that Megan had ever been particularly *anxious*, but this was new, and they hadn't spent much time together at all, and now they were going to be trapped in a tiny old convertible for days and days with no company but each other—

Oh, shit. Maybe Scarlett was the one freaking out.

Scarlett unloaded all her bags from the trunk, the two large suitcases she'd packed full of everything she thought she might need for this journey, a backpack to use as an overnight bag, and the tote bag of snacks. Knowing Megan, she wouldn't realize you had to get snacks for an epic road trip, or she'd get really shitty ones like rice cakes.

Megan, of course, wasn't freaking out. Megan was standing behind her car, carefully lining up her bags and appraising the empty trunk space.

"It is way too early for this. Or late." Scarlett walked over to her. "What are you doing?"

"I'm figuring out the optimal way to pack the trunk." Megan put her hands on her hips, then looked from her bags to Scarlett's. "Bring your bags over here. I need to compare all the sizes and see which to put in first."

"Oh, for Christ's sake." Scarlett hoisted her bags into the empty trunk space, ignoring Megan's irritated squawk, and stacked them up. She'd put her backpack in the back seat. "There. Put yours next to them."

"You have no system." Megan grumbled, but she loaded them anyway. "You can't do these things without a system."

"My system is to get on the road on time so we get to your damn island by sunrise, like you wanted." Scarlett stepped back from the trunk, but when Megan struggled with one of the bags, automatically reached for it to steady her. Megan looked up in surprise, and Scarlett stepped away again as soon as the bag was settled. "There. You ready to go?"

"I just need to load the snacks." Megan hoisted her tote bag into the backseat alongside the one Scarlett had already put back there. "You brought snacks, too?"

"Of course. I can't rely on your snacks." Scarlett snatched her coffee out of the car and took another sip. She'd made herself a third cup of coffee to survive the drive tonight, but it was not going to be enough. She hadn't slept well last night, either, always unsettled about the journey ahead and not sure what she was going to do about that unsettled feeling.

"My snacks are fine. It's my coffee I'm not sure about." Megan frowned. "I made some but it's not very good. I don't usually drink it, and the only time I make it is at the diner. I don't think I made it well, but I didn't want to fall asleep while I was driving."

"I've had a lot of coffee. I can take the first shift." Scarlett filed that weird little bit of information away: Megan didn't know how to make coffee other than diner coffee, and she didn't like it. How could anyone not like coffee? Scarlett had started drinking it as a teenager, so maybe she wasn't the best example. "You got everything? Your playlists all loaded up on your phone? Got your chargers? Your atlas? Got your maps pre-downloaded to your phone in case we lose signal? Got your passport?"

"Oh my *god*." Megan held up her hand. "Have you ever tried asking one question at a time?"

"No time for that. We've gotta hit the road. I need to know." Scarlett gestured to the road. "Out there. We've gotta get going."

"How much coffee did you have, Scarlett?"

Scarlett blinked. "I had like two cups before this one. But that's normal. And they were big cups. So maybe a little bit more than usual." She rubbed her hands together. "But answer my questions anyway. I'm not turning around once we get going."

"I have everything we need." Megan's tone was long-sufferingly patient, the kind of patient that meant she wasn't really feeling patient at all. "Except I don't have any playlists, because my Bluetooth isn't working. So I burned CDs."

Scarlett stopped. "Excuse me?"

Megan stared at her. "What?"

"CDs? You didn't fix the Bluetooth?"

Megan shrugged. "Why does it matter? I've got enough music."

"But if I had known, I would have paid to have your Bluetooth fixed. I have so many playlists on my phone, and I'm not gonna be able to listen to any of them." Scarlett paused. "Oh, wait! I have an aux cord." She dug one out of her car.

"I'm still gonna listen to my CDs," Megan said. "I worked hard on those."

"Sure. I'm aching to get some mid-'90s twelve-at-a-time playlists into my life for this next ten days of driving." Scarlett felt a wave of sickness, which might have been either anxiety or too much caffeine. "Let's get on the road before I change my mind."

Driving at night was miserable in the way that it kept you up all night, but way better than driving during the day because there was less traffic. Scarlett didn't mind the night. She was a night owl anyway. And if Megan was going to just keep her mouth shut and stare out the window like she was currently doing, that was fine by her.

"You do this a lot?" Megan asked after a long stretch of silence, after they pulled out onto the highway and started zipping north through the desolate darkness.

So much for silence.

Conversation was probably better than silence, anyway. Silence got her thinking, and she tried to avoid too much of that lately. Scarlett adjusted her grip on the steering wheel. "Do I do what a lot? Go on road trips in the middle of winter?"

"Go on road trips in general." Megan didn't look away from the window, but in her reflection, she glanced up at Scarlett. Scarlett pretended not to notice.

"Not a lot," Scarlett said. "I did one back when—" She

stopped herself, not wanting to bring up anything about college. "Back a few years ago. When I moved to New York."

"When did you move to New York?" Megan shifted in her seat. "I didn't know you lived there."

"A bit after I turned twenty-three, so three years ago. I only lived there a couple of months. It's an expensive city." She didn't want to share more about that time in her life. It wasn't a pleasant time, a time when she felt like she had to run away from everything familiar and start over. But you couldn't ever run from the past, not really.

Megan didn't say anything for a minute, and they drove on in silence. "Why'd you come back?" Megan asked after a few moments.

"I told you. It was expensive." That wasn't the whole story. She'd been too out of her league, up against all her insecurities, unable to hold down a job and frustrated by her own incompetence. She'd come home to lick her wounds. Like hell she'd ever admit that to Megan, though. Megan may not have lived a very adventurous life, but she was always together in a way that Scarlett was scattered. Even in high school, Megan was acing her classes while Scarlett was trying to get away with a C-minus average and lying about it.

Megan made a thoughtful noise and didn't ask her to elaborate. Either she knew Scarlett was lying and didn't want to push, or she thought Scarlett was telling the truth. Or, maybe, she just didn't care.

Better turn the attention to Megan. "So what about you?" Scarlett asked. "You never thought about leaving the diner?"

Megan snorted. "Never crossed my mind. Each time the alarm went off at four, I thought, 'Yes, perfect, I'm living my dreams.' I never considered there was more to life than waiting tables."

"Hey, hey, I'm not criticizing being a waitress." Scarlett

had done that herself, and she'd been shit at it. "I'm just asking. You want to do something else with your life, I thought maybe you'd have done it."

"I didn't do anything. You already know that." Megan's voice was a low mumble. She was apparently touchy about this subject. Scarlett was a lot of kinds of bitches, but not the kind who poked at somebody who was down. Not even someone who'd been previously untouchable, like Megan.

But Megan wasn't untouchable now. Megan wasn't as prim and proper and frustratingly immune to human failings the way Scarlett seemed instead to be entirely comprised of human failings. Megan was a person, and she lost her job and she was going on this road trip for probably a bunch of personal reasons. And the wedding or whatever. But along the way, she wanted to see some of the country, and Scarlett could help.

Maybe this was a terrible plan overall. But they were in it. They were headed for the Florida border in this tiny, mediocre car from 2008 or whatever, and that was that.

This Toyota Camry. Scarlett scanned its nondescript interior with all its boringness and its beige decor, matching Megan's beige house. Everything was the worst color, and Scarlett could not deal with it any longer.

"Why do you still have this boring-ass car, Meg?" Scarlett waved a hand around at it.

That got Megan's attention. "What?" She sat up straighter. "What's wrong with my car? It's a convertible."

"It's old."

Megan seemed to be grasping for how to respond. "Well… it's red."

"Red? Yeah, it's red, but the whole inside is beige. Everything is beige! Why do you live such a beige life?"

Megan shifted even more over toward her, an incredulous expression on her face. "I don't live a *beige life*."

"Yes you do. Your life is so fucking beige it's killing me." It wasn't what Scarlett wanted to say. She wanted to say, *You're so much more interesting than this*, or *You're the most capable person I ever knew*, but those words slipped away in favor of the angrier, crueler ones, the ones that would make Megan actually react.

Megan folded her arms. "Fuck you, Scarlett. My life doesn't require your approval."

Scarlett fumed, because Megan was right and now they were fighting. They were fighting less than an hour into this drive, and it was her fault, because she didn't know how to be around Megan anymore. "I just thought you wanted to make your life more interesting. Like you weren't satisfied with how things were."

"No, I didn't say that." Megan's frown was sour now, more of a pout than a frown. "I said I've never been out of the state and have some places on my goal list."

"Sure. You sounded real satisfied." Scarlett snorted. So much for Megan showing any vulnerability at all. "You're probably totally satisfied with everything. I bet you come every time you fuck, too."

Megan spluttered, obviously shocked out of her words, and her skin flamed up fast with a complete blush. Scarlett never saw Megan blush like that. Then again, they'd almost never talked about sex. A few conversations in high school where Scarlett had tried to get Megan to tell her all her secrets the way Scarlett told Megan hers, but Megan never had anything to share and so Scarlett had eventually stopped asking.

Maybe some things never changed. Maybe Megan was still as shy about sex.

Oh, fuck, maybe Megan was a virgin.

Megan couldn't be a virgin, right? She was twenty-five. Well, there was nothing wrong with being a virgin as long as Megan *wanted* to be one. Like, if she was waiting, or if she was asexual, whatever. But Scarlett wanted to know, and she wanted Megan to tell her. The desire for information bubbled up inside her like lye, burning her from the inside out. And it was one in the morning, and she was overtired, and hell, she wanted to know, so she blurted it out.

"Are you a virgin?"

Megan stared at her, open-mouthed. "You did not just ask me that."

She could probably back away or turn it into a joke. That was likely the best decision. "I'm just fucking around. You don't have to answer that. I just wanted to get a reaction out of you."

"No, no, let's keep going. I love this. First you tell me my whole life is beige, and then you ask me if I'm a virgin. It's a delight. Just exactly the right conversation I want to have at one in the morning." Megan scrunched down into her seat. "I should sleep if you're gonna drive. Unless you want to insult me some more."

"What? That's not an insult. Being a virgin's not a bad thing." Scarlett didn't want Megan to think she was making fun of her. They may not get along well, but Scarlett felt weird inside, thinking that Megan might believe she was being deliberately hurtful. She wanted to get a rise out of her, not make her upset. "I don't care if you're a virgin. It's all right."

"I'm not a virgin," Megan finally said, harsh and sharp and all at once, like it burst out of her. "I've had lots of sex. Okay?"

"Okay. Okay." Scarlett really should not have asked. "I told you, it was a joke. I was joking around."

"Not everything's a joke, Scarlett." Megan turned away fully, and reclined her seat. "Wake me up when there's a rest area."

The interior of the car went silent. Beneath the tires, the road hummed, blending with the purr of the engine. Scarlett glanced over at Megan's reflection, and Megan's eyes were open the first time, but the next time she checked, they were shut. Megan looked all closed up and small on her side of the car.

"You should've brought a blanket," Scarlett said. "You'll get cold."

Megan's reply was mumbled. "There's one in the back."

"Put it on. You're like some sad orphan, sleeping there without a blanket." Scarlett hated seeing her like that, even with her sweater looking cozy and soft.

Megan grumbled, and then turned to grab the blanket out of the back seat. She tucked it around her and then went back again, quiet and solemn and closed-eyed in the passenger seat like she was sleeping. Maybe she was. At least she didn't look like a Dickens character anymore. Scarlett enjoyed the peace and quiet.

Until, of course, she stopped enjoying the peace and quiet. She couldn't sleep, because she was driving, and she couldn't talk to Megan anymore because Megan was sleeping or pretending she was sleeping. So she flicked the radio on and waited for Megan to complain about it.

She didn't.

Scarlett poked through Megan's presets. She had good channels programmed. Megan was always into music back in high school, so it shouldn't surprise Scarlett that she still had good taste. She settled on some pop song and let the music play, tapping along on the steering wheel, humming quietly to herself. Maybe she could do this whole stretch, all the way to Tybee Island. Maybe she could let Megan sleep. She wouldn't have to wake her up and deal with more conversation that she was sure to ruin.

Light snores came from the other side of the car, and Scarlett had to smile. Some people snored like they were terrifying beasts, a dinosaur eating another dinosaur, but Megan sounded like a tiny cat with little purring snores. She was adorable in many ways. That realization was kind of shitty, too. She didn't want to feel like Megan was adorable. It was safer to think of Megan as frustrating, untouchable, stubborn as hell, holier-than-thou.

The pop song switched from whatever was on to an oldie, Joan Jett singing "I Love Rock and Roll," and Scarlett *had* to sing along. She really wanted to sing *loudly*, as the song demanded, but she kept her voice down instead. Megan didn't wake up, so maybe she could sing a little louder. She tried it out. It felt good.

When the song ended, a quiet voice came from the other side of the car. "If you didn't want me to sleep, you could just say so."

Scarlett grimaced. "I thought you were sleeping."

"I *was* sleeping. But then there was a karaoke bar happening next to me, and so I woke up." Megan flopped over, shifting to glare at Scarlett from her other side. "You couldn't have waited until I was awake?"

"I didn't know what kind of sleeper you are. Maybe you're a hard sleeper." Scarlett's face was hot.

"I normally am. But normally, I'm not listening to the greatest hits of Joan Jett and the Blackhearts from two feet away." Megan's expression was still deadpan, but was that a small smile at the corners of her mouth? Did her mouth just twitch? Scarlett couldn't look away from the road long enough to really see. Hopefully Megan wasn't that mad. So far, she wasn't being a very good road trip companion.

Megan shifted back to a regular seated position again. "We should get a book on tape. I don't want to listen to this bullshit for the entire eastern seaboard."

"Are you calling Joan Jett *bullshit*?" Maybe Scarlett would have to reevaluate Megan's taste.

Megan stifled a yawn with her hand. "No, Joan Jett's great. I'm talking about your singing."

It was mean, but the kind of mean with no real malice in it, the kind of mean that made Scarlett laugh out loud. She definitely deserved that. "Go back to sleep. I won't sing anymore."

Megan made another "hmmm" noise and rolled back onto her other side once more, facing the window. She pulled the blanket up to her chin. "Maybe just not so loud," Megan said quietly.

Smiling in the darkness, Scarlett drove onward into the night.

Megan jolted awake all at once, with no sense right away of where she was, why her body felt all stiff and her eyes dry, or what had awoken her. The reality came flooding in along with the cool gray light of dawn slipping through the windows. She was in her car. She'd fallen asleep in the passenger seat. And she'd woken up because they stopped.

"Where are we?" Her voice came out croaky, and she rubbed her eyes, which felt gritty and gross. She shifted to sit up, stretching her neck.

"Tybee Island." Scarlett sounded exhausted.

"Have you even stopped since we left?" Megan said. "Have you just been driving?"

"I stopped to pee about an hour after you fell asleep. You didn't wake up." Scarlett rubbed her own eyes with the heel of her hand. "I stopped at this McDonalds because I thought you might also want to pee."

"Oh." Megan sat up, checking in with her body. "Yeah. Definitely." She pushed out of the car, swinging the door open. The seatbelt tugged her back. Face burning, she unbuckled, Scarlett's gaze nearly tangible on the back of her head. She was probably judging. Megan grabbed her toiletries bag out of the backseat and tumbled out, her legs first refusing to support her and then locking up as she headed for the familiar brick building.

With her bladder empty, she was able to breathe again, and she took time to brush her teeth in the McDonalds bathroom sink and then stare at herself in the mirror. She looked like she had slept in a car all night, but it wasn't too different from the way she normally looked. Her face was creased from the seat headrest.

But she was on Tybee Island in Georgia. She was in a new state.

She'd finally, finally left Florida.

Megan was still staring at herself in the mirror and smiling when the door swung open and Scarlett came in. "Out of the way," she mumbled, heading for the stall and then locking the door. "We'd better get a move on if you want to catch the sunrise," she said from behind the closed door.

"You want to grab breakfast while we're here?" Megan asked.

"Sure. I'll meet you out there."

Megan bought them both sandwiches, hoping Scarlett still liked Egg McMuffins, and was waiting outside when Scarlett finally came out. "I had to brush my teeth," Scarlett explained. "My mouth tasted like the inside of a sock."

"Ew." Megan handed her the bag of sandwiches and the cup of coffee. "I don't know how you take your coffee, so I had them put cream and sugar on the side."

"Thanks." Scarlett took them. "One cream, two sugars."

"What?"

"That's how I take my coffee." She tucked the bag under her arm to dress her coffee. "Cold as fuck out here, huh?"

Megan hadn't really noticed until she said something. "I'm too sleepy to notice. You must be dying."

"It's okay. I've pulled my share of all-nighters." Scarlett stifled a yawn behind her hand. "Let's go, yeah? It's gonna be dawn soon."

"You all right to drive?" Megan asked. Scarlett generally looked put-together, but right now, she definitely didn't. She had her hair pulled up into one big, messy bun at the top of her head, and she was still wearing her traveling pajamas.

"I'm good. Let's go. I want to take you to the ocean." Scarlett climbed in and buckled up. Immediately, she paused, sighed, and closed her eyes. "No. I'm not all right. What about you? Can you drive?"

"Yeah. Better than you. Get out." Megan climbed out of her car and switched seats with Scarlett. "Which way to the beach?"

Scarlett pointed vaguely down the road. "Straight down there."

Megan adjusted the seat and the mirrors and pulled out onto the road. Scarlett was already nodding off, resting her head back against the seat. She looked so innocent when she was sleepy. It was hard to remember that Megan was somewhat intimidated by Scarlett. She drove out toward the water and put that thought behind her.

Megan had seen the ocean before, obviously. She lived in Florida her whole life. She'd spent much of her beach time on the Gulf coast, with its bathwater-warm temperatures and gorgeous sunsets. Once or twice, she'd swum in the Atlantic ocean, crossing the state to Cocoa Beach to brave the crowds and get a dip in the somewhat cooler waters. But she never had done that in the winter. Now, headed toward the shore, the buildings diminished in frequency before disappearing altogether, and she followed the brown signs until she reached the parking lot at the edge of the beach at the edge of the water.

The sky was already turning pink with the rosy tendrils of dawn, and Megan's breath quickened in excitement. She needed to see it from the shore.

Scarlett was snoring, and she didn't care about this beach visit anyway, so Megan might as well leave her behind. She grabbed her jacket out of the backseat, and her instant-print camera, and opened the car door into the blowing wind.

Damn, it was cold. The wind immediately pulled Megan's breath from her lungs, and she zipped her coat all the way up to her chin. Too bad she didn't have a hat. The wind blowing made it feel freezing, and yet she didn't care. She tucked her neck down into her coat, pulled up her hood, and headed down the path toward the shore.

Tall grasses bent in the wind, stretching out as far as she could see, with the small rolling sand dunes guiding her down to the water's edge. The sun was just peeking above the horizon as she stepped from the wooden boardwalk down onto the sand itself, her shoes sinking into the white surface with little grains blowing up over the edges. The air smelled like salt and cold, with the wind in her face still taking her breath away. She loved this. She loved the beach, and she loved the water, and right now, she could be happy even though she was alone.

Megan waited with her camera until the first red gleams stretched long over the water. Film was expensive and she wasn't going to waste it. So she waited, as she always had the patience to wait, as she had been trained to wait over years of photography. In this digital age, it was easy to take a dozen pictures in search of the right one, and she liked to do that as well. But there was also something precious about getting the imperfect shot on actual film. She held up her camera and snapped. The film ejected, sliding out of the slot with a whirring noise, and she cradled the photo while she watched the sun climb past the horizon.

"Would you look at that."

Scarlett's voice behind her made Megan jump.

"I was letting you sleep," Megan said. She wasn't sure if it was out of altruism or because she wanted to be alone, wanted to have this moment without Scarlett making fun of her for it. Another part of her definitely wanted to share this time, this beauty, to have someone who would appreciate it the way she did. "I didn't want to bother you. I know you didn't want to come here."

Megan didn't want to be vulnerable. She may desperately deep inside want Scarlett's approval, but she didn't need it. She could live without it.

Scarlett looked toward the horizon, her eyes going soft. "It's beautiful."

Something eased inside Megan's chest.

Scarlett nodded to the camera still hanging around Megan's neck. "Why don't you use your cell phone?"

Megan had fielded that question a lot over the years. "It's different." She could explain more, but she sort of didn't want to. She wanted Scarlett to understand without being told.

Scarlett seemed to get it. "Something real, right? Not just on a screen."

"Yes, exactly." A trickle of hope blossomed inside Megan. "It's permanent."

"How'd it come out?" Scarlett asked, gesturing toward the photo that Megan was holding close to her hoodie in thin, cold fingers.

"I don't know yet. I'll look after." Megan nodded to the horizon. "I don't want to miss this."

Scarlett turned to the sunrise that Megan was watching and fell silent. They stood side by side in the dawn light, watching as the sun crested the horizon like an orange fireball. There weren't good words for the beauty; if Megan was a poet, perhaps she could capture it, but instead, she was just an ordinary person who didn't write anything except captions on photographs. The colors faded, one to the next, a panoply of warm hues. In front of her, the ocean waves rolled back and forth, crashing on shore, dragging gravel back with each grating pull.

Finally, the sun rose entirely past the horizon. Megan exhaled and relaxed; she hadn't realized she'd been waiting. Finally, she looked down at the photo in her hand. It was not perfect; the colors were never as brilliant as they would be in real life, but it captured that moment of dawn and the crisp line of the horizon. It was the photo she had hoped for.

Scarlett nudged her. "Can I look?"

Megan handed the photo over. Scarlett stared close at it, and Megan held her breath again, trying to come up with some kind of retort in case Scarlett insulted her. "It's a good picture." Then she handed it back. "I never got into photography. I didn't think I'd be any good at it."

"I wasn't good at it sometimes. I don't know if I'm good at it now." Megan looked back down at the shot. "But I take better photos."

Scarlett chuckled. "That probably means you're good at it. Did you used to do it back in high school? I don't remember."

"A little bit. But I got into it in college because my roommate was part of the photography club." Megan paused. It was a reminder that her roommate wasn't Scarlett, but neither of them circled back to that. "I didn't like developing my own film, but I liked shooting photos. Maybe that makes me a poser or whatever. But I'm into Polaroids. I like the rawness of them." She was still holding the picture.

Scarlett nodded, but she didn't comment, and they let it all go.

"You ready?" Megan said at last.

"I guess so." Scarlett shrugged. "It's pretty cold. But this was your stop. If you want to hang out on the island, we can do that."

Megan thought about it. She'd wanted to come here, but she mostly wanted to see the sunrise. She had done that. "I'd like to keep going."

"We're four hours from Myrtle Beach. That's next, right?"

"If you don't mind." Megan didn't want to be a bother. Immediately as she said it, she hated that she didn't want to be a bother. She hated that she was accommodating Scarlett the way she always accommodated others. But it was too late to take her words back.

"It's fine. I've never been there. It's probably all closed up, but at least it'll be a place to spend the night." Scarlett yawned. "I could use a real bed."

"I'll take the next part of the drive." Megan started back to the car. Before she got in, Scarlett caught her attention.

"Hey."

Megan looked up, across the car. "What?"

"Congratulations. It's your first time out of Florida." Scarlett flashed her a beaming smile, and Megan had to return it.

"Thanks." With a warm feeling inside her, she got into the car. She put the camera into the back seat, tucked the photo into a pocket of her scrapbook, and turned on the heat in the car. Onward to the next stop.

Scarlett had thought South Carolina wouldn't be much different from Florida, and as the highway pressed north through endless miles of country...yeah, she was right. The whole southeast was filled with pockets of culture and heritage and beauty, but I-95 was a single tarmac scar on the landscape. They were going to be on this highway forever. At least Megan was driving, so Scarlett could stare out the window and try to get lost in her thoughts.

"Hey, can you grab that CD case in the back?" Megan asked, disturbing her daydreaming.

"What?"

"The CD case." Megan looked over at her. "In the back."

"I still can't believe you have a CD case. Weren't you born in the '90s?"

"Yes," Megan said, her tone sharp and defensive. "We're the same age. Well. You're a little older."

"Thank you for that reminder." Scarlett was four months older, and it didn't matter to anyone after the fifth grade.

"You used to remind me of that all the time when we were in school." Megan smiled, seemingly to herself. "You'd tell me how much older than me you were."

"That was fun when I was ten, and not so fun now that I'm twenty-six." Scarlett wasn't old, and she knew she wasn't old, but being the oldest wasn't a prize anymore. "You'll be here in another couple of months."

"That's right. It was your birthday." Megan sounded like she was just remembering.

"I have one every year."

Megan paused, thoughtful. "I just was thinking how long it's been since I did anything with you for your birthday."

Was she just full of weirdness today? "It's been a while since we hung out, Meg." Scarlett rooted around in the backseat and found the black zipped case. "Any CD in particular?" Scarlett unzipped the case, then immediately forgot her question. "Holy shit."

Megan had filled the whole case with CDs, and they were all labeled in precise Sharpie writing with multicolored markers. "You named them?" Scarlett asked, flipping through, trying to figure out what the system was. The names didn't give any indication of what specific songs were on them, but the moods were pretty clear. They were named things like "Kicking Ass and Taking Names," "Funkalicious Funk Train," and "Screaming into the Void," and those were just some in the first set.

Megan's smile looked impish. "Naming the CDs is my favorite part."

"So what do you want to listen to? You want me to read them all off to you?"

"Nah. Why don't you find something that seems chill and upbeat?"

This was an easier task in theory than practice. Frowning, Scarlett started flipping through the pages until she found one that seemed to fit the bill. "'Hammock Summer Saturdays'?"

Megan's smile broke out across her face like the sun coming out from behind clouds. "Perfect."

As soon as the first song came on, Megan visibly relaxed, her whole body softening. Scarlett hadn't thought about Megan as being particularly lovely. Smart, and sometimes goofy, and quirky, and overly too serious, but not lovely. Scarlett, though, was seeing her a bit differently now. Maybe it was lack of sleep. Today, when they finally got to Myrtle Beach, she was gonna crash so hard into whatever shitty motel bed they managed to find.

Megan hummed along with the song, tapping her hands lightly on the steering wheel, bopping. Scarlett had never seen Megan bop. "Hey," Megan said. "Call and get us a hotel."

"What's your budget?" Scarlett pulled out her phone to search. Surely Myrtle Beach wouldn't be booked. She'd assumed they would just find places to sleep along the way.

"No Hiltons. But like, a Holiday Inn, or even a Motel 6. That's fine." Megan started humming along with the music.

Scarlett started scanning through the websites to look at hotels and motels in Myrtle Beach. Lots of stuff was closed for the season. That made sense; it was February and who in the world wanted to go to Myrtle Beach in February? Megan. Of course Megan would want to go. Not just one beach, but two.

"I found one. It's thirty-five dollars per night."

"Thirty-five dollars?" Megan looked over at her in shock. "Are there actual beds? Or do we have to sleep on the floor?"

"There seem to be actual beds. There are other places in the same price range, so I don't think it's abnormal. I think it's just the off-season pricing." Scarlett clicked through the photos of the Pink Sands Inn. It looked decent enough. "So I take it this is in the budget?"

"Yeah, no problem. Go ahead and book it. Online or whatever." Megan waved her hand. "My credit card's in my wallet." She dug it out of the center console and handed it over.

"You want me to just go poking around in here?" Scarlett opened the wallet.

"Why not? I've got nothing to hide."

Scarlett would be far less nonchalant about letting someone go through her purse or wallet. But Megan didn't care. So Scarlett pulled out Megan's credit card—the only credit card, unlike Scarlett who had about five of them—and called the Pink Sands Inn. Of course the place wouldn't have any kind of online check-in, so she had to interact with a *human*.

"Hello?" A bored male voice picked up on the other end.

She'd at least expected the name of the place. "Is this the Pink Sands Inn?"

"Oh, shit. Yeah. Sorry. I thought I was picking up my cell. What's up?"

Scarlett took the phone away and looked at the screen, like that might give her any kind of answers, before putting it back to her ear. "I want to rent a room for tonight."

"Okay. You can just show up."

"You don't need my credit card or anything?"

"Nah. You're the only one here." The guy yawned loudly. "What time will you be here? I'm probably gonna take a nap."

Scarlett looked at the clock. "Early afternoon?"

"Sure. Sure." He finished his yawn. "Okay. See ya." And then he hung up.

Scarlett stared at the phone again. "What the fuck?"

"He didn't need a credit card?"

"I'm not sure if he even works there." Scarlett shook her head and tucked her phone back into the side-door pocket of the car. "It's like bizarro world."

"As long as we've got a room. I want a bed that won't wreck my neck. I'm so sore from sleeping against the car door."

"At least you got to sleep." Scarlett was not bitter, but she couldn't help pointing it out.

"You slept the whole morning," Megan reminded her.

"An hour. I slept an hour." Scarlett curled up into herself. "You mind if I look through your wallet?"

Megan glanced over. "I don't know why you'd want to."

"Something to do."

"Don't you have a book or something?"

Scarlett had an entire e-reader, and a phone full of mobile games, but she wasn't in the mood for those. "You can just say no."

"Sure, whatever. Knock yourself out."

Megan's wallet was quite neat. Her driver's license was first, boasting a photo that didn't even look bad. "Your driver's license photo looks good."

Megan wrinkled her nose. "Nobody likes their driver's license photo."

"Yeah, but you really look like this." Scarlett tapped it.

"Don't remind me." Megan grimaced, and Scarlett put the card away.

She found Megan's debit card, and put the credit card back

behind it, and then started going through the rest. A medical insurance card. A gym membership card. "You go to the gym?"

Megan paused. "Not as often as I probably should."

Scarlett put the card away. The next item was a membership card for a bulk store. She also carried a gas rewards card. The wallet had a hundred dollars in it in twenties, as well as ten ones and a single five. She had receipts neatly folded in half and tucked back there along with the money. One receipt was for Target, with a number of snacks listed, probably the snacks for the trip. Another was for Sephora. "What did you buy at Sephora?" She couldn't picture Megan there.

"It says it on the receipt." Megan's tone was a little sharp.

There was a whole list of makeup items, but that wasn't the point. "I mean, why did you buy makeup? You don't wear makeup."

"I know." Megan seemed to hesitate, her lips parting in a thought. "I thought maybe I could try." She was quick to qualify her statement. "I've worn it before. For special occasions. I just don't do it regularly. I'm probably not very good at it."

"I could teach you." Scarlett didn't know what she was doing offering, but makeup was one of the few things she did well. "If you wanted."

The silence hung between them.

"Maybe. We'll see." Megan pressed her lips together in a thin line. "Do you want to sleep? I can turn the music off."

Scarlett put the receipt back into Megan's wallet and returned the wallet to its former place. "Leave the music. I like it."

Megan smiled, a tiny curl of her lips, and Scarlett could live with that. She closed her eyes. Maybe she'd be able to doze.

As soon as Scarlett closed her eyes, Megan felt something relax inside her spine. Scarlett made her feel tense and uncomfortable somewhere deep inside. It wasn't a horrified discomfort, or even an unpleasant one. It was hard to describe. She just felt like she couldn't settle when those beautiful eyes were focused on her. Scarlett probably didn't even know how beautiful she was, and that was obnoxious. Her amazing curly hair, her tanned skin dappled with freckles, those big brown eyes? It was ridiculous. Megan could never look that good. It had been a source of tension throughout their high school years, and now that she was away from Scarlett for a few years, those feelings were all crashing back over her again.

Help her with makeup. Like Megan had a *chance* of looking anywhere as good as Scarlett, even with the help of makeup. Scarlett hadn't slept all night and she still looked like she was a tinted lip balm away from modeling in a commercial for moisturizer or something. Megan was always operating about one level above goblin. Without Scarlett watching her, though, with Scarlett's eyes finally closed, Megan let herself relax. The music helped, soothing her bones. She was tired, sure, but she had the open road in front of her and the novelty of her trip still keeping her content.

The highway itself was boring, though, and so was the road she turned onto in order to head toward Myrtle Beach. There was nothing to see this time of year. It was cold, first of all, and all the trees had dropped their leaves, so bare gray branches surrounded the road, except for some misshapen pine trees that didn't have any snow on them. Not that Megan had ever seen snow except in photos and videos, but it would be the better option for these trees. Not this nakedness.

Scarlett thought she was ridiculous for going to the beach, and maybe she was. The beach was going to be more of this austere nakedness. But in winter, the beach had a type of raw beauty that made Megan feel close to something bigger than herself. Scarlett could think what she wanted. Megan was going to get past worrying what Scarlett thought of her. The beach, with its cold beauty and gray, crisp light, was the perfect place to feel like she could find herself.

She hoped to find herself on this road trip. But she was all tangled up in thinking of Scarlett, and not about herself and what she wanted. Maybe with Scarlett sleeping, she could sit on the beach and gather her own thoughts. But they had to get there first.

Chapter Six

By the time they arrived in Myrtle Beach that afternoon, after almost five hours of driving from Tybee Island, Megan was starving and really sick of being in the car. The mediocre McDonalds breakfast sandwich was a long time ago. Scarlett had slept for the whole drive, or at least faked it, and Megan had listened to the same CD three times before switching to the radio and trying to find some likable local station. Eventually, she found a channel playing Led Zeppelin, and it was nearly enough to distract her from her stomach as she drove into downtown Myrtle Beach.

"Hey." Megan slapped Scarlett's arm. "Wake up."

Scarlett jumped and made an undignified noise. "What the hell?" She rubbed her eyes. "Why'd you hit me?"

"We're here. I want to eat." Megan leaned forward to peer more closely at the buildings as they drove by. "Everything looks closed."

Scarlett's voice came out all mumbly. "Somebody's got to be open. A diner or something."

A diner. Megan had spent the last ten years of her life in a diner, and apparently she wasn't going to escape. "Can you find one?"

"Just drive around until you see something," Scarlett mumbled, tucking herself back into her ball.

Irritation flared up in Megan. "I haven't *eaten* and I want some *lunch*."

Scarlett sat back up and blinked owlishly over at her. "My god. You're serious, aren't you?" Grumbling, she straightened herself out and pulled the snack bag out of the back. "Here." She handed her a granola bar. "Eat this. I'll find us some place for lunch."

Megan grimaced at the granola bar, but Scarlett was probably right that she should eat something rather than nothing, and she took it.

"This is your second new state." Scarlett stifled a yawn. "I have to pee."

"We can pee when we get to lunch." Megan had to go, too, but she was determined to get the prospect of food figured out first.

Scarlett directed them to a local restaurant a few blocks over, and Megan pulled in right up front. That was one nice thing about being in a beach town on the off-season: easy parking.

They got a booth near the door, and after using the bathroom, returned to their table to stare at each other across the expanse of table between them. Megan looked around her at the familiar decor.

"Whatcha thinking?" Scarlett asked.

Megan grimaced. "It looks like the Starlite."

"All diners kind of look alike." Scarlett's tone was apologetic, surprisingly. "Too many bad memories?"

"They're not bad memories. Just memories." Megan looked into her glass of ice water like it might give her the answers.

"I grew up there. And now it's going to be a Winn-Dixie expansion. I dunno." She shrugged one shoulder. "I guess things change."

"Things are supposed to change." Scarlett's tone was blunt, like she often tended to be. "You can't hold them back."

"I know."

Megan was saved from having to say more by the waitress's arrival. She looked like every waitress at a local diner in the off-season: bored, friendly because of obligation, distant but professional. "Can I help y'all?"

Scarlett ordered, and then it was Megan's turn. Despite having the menu and having made up her mind a while ago, Megan suddenly had a thought flash to mind. "I'll have...the turkey club, and some fried green tomatoes as an appetizer."

The waitress left. "I've never had those," Megan announced, because she felt like she should. "Fried green tomatoes, I mean."

"Okay?" Scarlett was looking at her like she was being weird again. "Why do I need to know this?"

"You don't. I thought, though, that I should try something new." Megan found herself saying more though she wasn't planning on it. "I feel like I should try something new as often as I can on this trip."

Scarlett stifled another yawn. "You do you, I guess."

She may not care, but Megan did. Making this assertion out loud felt like an important first step. Maybe this was how she learned to do more with her life. Maybe she could step beyond her comfort zone in more ways than just this road trip.

Scarlett didn't need to approve. She didn't need Scarlett's admiration or approval; she just needed to keep moving forward on her own. Fuck approval.

And yet.

And yet.

"Why are you still living in Florida?" Megan asked.

Scarlett looked across the table, her expression shifting from cautious to aloof. "It's cheap. I told you that." She took a sip of her water. Her red nail polish was chipping. It was such a weird detail to notice, a bit of vulnerability, a crack in Scarlett's armor. Megan felt defensive, and she hated feeling defensive.

"Lots of places are cheap," Megan said, pushing a bit.

Scarlett seemed to consider the comment, and then gave a bit of a half-shrug. "I used to think I wanted to get out. I thought there was nothing for me in Florida."

"Is that why you moved to New York?"

Scarlett smiled, but it was a bitter smile, the kind of smile with no amusement in it. She looked down at her chipped fingernails for a long time. "Sure. That was part of it."

Megan wanted to ask about the rest of it, but she knew Scarlett wouldn't tell her. "But you came back."

"I came back." Scarlett nodded. "And I'll probably stay. I think Florida is in my blood, now." She let out a long sigh. "What about you? You ever think about moving away?"

Megan snorted. "Doesn't everybody?"

"I mean seriously. Did you ever seriously consider it?"

Megan had, sometimes, when another stilted relationship left her alone again, when Matt was being a particularly vocal douchebag, when her parents hinted that she might want to do something different with her life…back before they stopped caring or commenting at all. But she'd never done it. She'd never felt like it was worth the effort. Wouldn't every place be the same?

"Now and then. But I don't like being far away from everything I care about." Megan shifted on the slick vinyl of her chair.

"What do you care about?"

Megan looked down at the laminate table, anywhere but

at Scarlett's searching gaze. She cared about her family, of course, even her asshole brother, and she cared about her book group and the gym she didn't attend often enough, but none of those seemed like the right answers. "I like stability," she said. "Maybe I like it too much."

"Nothing wrong with stability."

Megan gave a little half-laugh, thinking of all the ways her life was losing stability by the day. "I threw my brother out of the house."

Scarlett raised her eyebrows. "Really?"

"Yeah." Megan flushed with the emotions running through her, remembered pride mixing with the irritation she still got when she thought about it. "I told him he had until I got back from this trip to move out."

Scarlett whistled. "You think he'll trash the house in retaliation?"

Megan had considered it. "I think he's too lazy for that. I think he'll take the path of least resistance and move in with my parents or one of his friends."

"The path of least resistance is probably just to stay put in your house and see if you're bluffing." Scarlett took a sip of her water. "Unless you've stood up to him before."

"I don't think he'd do that. I think he knows I'm serious." Megan remembered the way his expression had faded from anger to something like resignation and exasperation, portraying himself as a victim in his own mind once again. He always did that.

The waitress returned with Megan's fried green tomatoes, which looked like golden-brown disks sitting next to some kind of pink sauce. She frowned at them. She had never been one for trying new foods, but then again, she'd never been one for trying much of anything. Across the table, Scarlett watched her slice one of them in half.

It crunched in her mouth, breading and then the sour un-
derripe tomato, and it wasn't *unpleasant* but she wasn't sure how
she felt about it yet. She dipped the second half in the sauce,
and that was much nicer. She didn't realize she was smiling
until Scarlett smiled back, tentatively. "What?" Megan asked,
a little flare of self-consciousness rising up inside her.

"I just...like seeing you happy." Scarlett looked away, leaving Megan with weird feelings that she couldn't quite explain.
Megan shoved the dish toward her.

"Here. Eat some of these."

Their conversation was actually pleasant for the rest of
lunch, and eventually, Megan let her guard down enough
to relax. It helped that she was so tired she had a hard time
maintaining her walls. As she ate, she started to feel like she
might even have some affection for Scarlett. Those were dangerous feelings, the kind that got people hurt, and she tried
to rein them in. But when she yawned for what might be the
fifth time since finishing her sandwich, Scarlett smiled at her
across the table, a gentle smile that made a soft warmth spread
throughout Megan's chest.

"We should get a room," Scarlett said.

When Megan blinked a few times at her, Scarlett blushed,
color coming to her cheeks. "Not like that."

Megan smiled lazily, tired enough not to second-guess playing along. "Sure. You're just trying to get me into bed, aren't
you?"

Scarlett flushed more. "You definitely need some sleep. Let
me get the check."

Megan dozed off as soon as Scarlett pulled out of the diner's
parking lot. Scarlett turned the GPS sound down low and
followed the directions to the Pink Sands Inn, which fortunately was only a few miles away. She should probably wake

Megan up, since she wasn't going to be able to sleep for long, but didn't have the heart to do it. When she slept, she looked so innocent and vulnerable. The real Megan was neither. She was sharp-witted and ready to defend herself, like an armadillo covered in heavy plates of armor. Like this, sleeping on the passenger seat of the Toyota, though, Megan might as well be exposing her soft undersides.

Not that thinking about Megan's soft undersides was a good plan. Scarlett's gaze drifted to Megan's breasts, the gentle swell pushing out against her sweatshirt with every breath, and she dragged her attention back to the road before she drove into a ditch. She had to steady her breathing. Maybe it was the lack of sleep, but her feelings for Megan that she could always keep under wraps were *much* more resistant to being kept under wraps right now.

The Pink Sands Inn looked sort of like its website, although it was somewhat less flattering when viewed head-on instead of at an artful angle with the sunset illuminating the stucco, like it had been on the internet. Scarlett pulled into a spot and had a moment's crisis. Megan was going to pay for the hotel, but Megan was asleep. Scarlett could just…take her card and check in, but was that *okay*, or another breach of trust?

She was saved from having to make the decision by Megan jerking awake all at once, startling into alertness. Staring wildly around, she seemed to take a minute to realize where she was before nodding at herself and stifling another yawn. "Sorry. How long was I out?"

"Only about five minutes. We're here. You want to come in with me?" Scarlett jerked her thumb at the front door. "You've got the credit card."

"Right." Megan got out, fumbling a bit with the door as she did so.

The outside air bit into Scarlett's face as she stepped out

into the chilly afternoon. The day was bright and clear, and the crispness woke her up as she led Megan inside. Megan, though, didn't look very awake at all. She had a sort of half-asleep grumpiness that made Scarlett smile. Megan grunted a quiet thanks as Scarlett opened the door for her.

The guy behind the desk looked up as he saw them, putting his book down. "Hi."

It wasn't a very formal way to greet them, so he was probably the one who had picked up the phone earlier, the one who didn't even give the name of the hotel.

"We're checking in," Scarlett said. "I called this morning."

"Right. I remember you." He was probably about their age, in his mid-twenties, maybe working his way through college or just trying to hang on to a summer job through the rest of the year so he could be near the beach when it mattered. He had long hair that looked like it had been bleached before growing out again, shaggy from not getting frequent cuts or just enjoying the surfer look. His name tag said "Jeremy" and his pink polo shirt advertised the Pink Sands Inn with black embroidery over the pocket. He slid a paper registration form across the counter, making a decision between the two of them and settling on Scarlett. "License and credit card, please."

Megan produced the credit card from her wallet and set it on the counter while Scarlett filled out the sheet. "You know my license plate number?" Megan asked, sounding grudgingly impressed.

"Yeah." Scarlett had double-checked it earlier. "So there's really nobody else staying here?"

Jeremy laughed. "It's winter. You try to book this in June, or even on spring break, and we're sold out. We're probably already sold out into the summer."

That was a relief. At least the place wasn't a disaster year-round.

He finished processing their paperwork and slid a pair of key cards across the desk. "You're in room 103." He waved at a display of brochures next to the front door, right beside one of those racks of twenty-five cent candy dispensers. "You can look through there for stuff to do if you want. All the local places are listed." Megan was halfway over there before he added, "But most of it's closed for the season."

Megan turned with a sigh. "Then why did you point it out?"

Jeremy shrugged, unconcerned. "It's part of my job."

Scarlett took the key cards. She was kind of surprised they had key cards at all; this definitely seemed like the kind of place with actual keys on the little plastic diamond keychains. Scarlett bid goodbye to Jeremy and led Megan out to the car to grab their overnight bags.

The door swung open on a somewhat stale-smelling room, but one that was nonetheless clean. Scarlett flipped the light on and surveyed the space, which wasn't nearly as bad as she'd expected, with one glaring exception.

"Oh." Megan, who had stepped in behind her, stared at the one king-sized bed in the middle of the room. "That's not right."

"Nope." Scarlett laughed, but her laughter masked a few other thoughts and feelings. "How do you feel about sharing?"

She was only half kidding, but Megan gave her a withering look, and that was all she needed to know. She took Megan's key card back. "Let's get this straightened out."

Jeremy was back to reading his book again. Scarlett slid both key cards back across the desk, getting his attention.

He looked down, puzzled. "What's the matter? Isn't it clean?"

"We need two beds. Not one." Scarlett glanced at Megan, who was nodding emphatically.

Jeremy turned red right away. "Oh, hell, I'm so sorry. I just thought...never mind." He started typing in the computer. "There we go. Two queens. I'll put you right next door in 104 so you don't have to move your car."

"Thanks." Megan fairly snatched the proffered new key cards from him and led the way back to the new hotel room.

As soon as they were in the room, Megan set her sights on the bed farthest from the door and started piling her stuff on it.

"Wait a minute." Scarlett put her hands on her hips. "Why do I get the murder bed?"

Megan paused halfway through unzipping her overnight bag. "The what?"

Scarlett patted the floral bedspread. "The murder bed. The bed closest to the door."

"Don't be ridiculous. No one's going to murder you." Megan finished unzipping her bag and started rummaging around in it. "There's nobody in this town."

"That's not much comfort." Scarlett wasn't particularly bothered, even if she teased Megan about it. She was too excited to get into an actual *bed* and sleep.

Megan was more methodical about all of this, and Scarlett stopped to watch. First, she folded her pajamas—*folded her pajamas*—and set them down on the bureau. Then she put her overnight bag on the floor *next* to the bureau. Finally, she peeled back the comforter and all the sheets, and she leaned close to inspect the sides of the bed.

Eventually, Scarlett had to ask. "What are you doing?"

"Looking for bedbugs." Megan straightened. "Don't you check for bedbugs? The internet recommends it."

"No." Now that Megan mentioned it, Scarlett probably should.

"That seems like an oversight." Megan had that obnoxious, all-knowing expression on her face.

Scarlett really hadn't gotten enough sleep to have this conversation. "I don't usually stay in places where there are bedbugs. And what about you? You've never stayed in a motel."

"I've stayed in motels."

"And besides! You already put your bag on the bed." Scarlett pulled back the covers of her bed and gave it a cursory glance. "There. No bugs. We're fine."

Scarlett started stripping off her clothes. It took a minute to notice the silence behind her. Down to just her bra and underwear, she turned. "What?"

Megan was staring at her with wide eyes and color high in her cheeks. "You're just going to get naked right there?"

"Yes?" What was wrong with that?

"I'll be in the bathroom." Still flushed, Megan grabbed her pajamas and went into the bathroom.

Whatever. Scarlett pulled off the rest of her clothes. She was too tired to find pajamas. All she wanted was sleep. She got into bed, pulled up all the covers, and closed her eyes.

Megan wasn't sure what woke her up at first, or for that matter, where she was. She jolted out of a sound sleep and sat upright, heart racing, surrounded by darkness. Everything came back to her all at once: the drive, the sunrise, the leg of the journey out here to Myrtle Beach. She'd gone to sleep right after they got here, and now it was—she checked the clock—nine at night. All right, so she had slept for like six or seven hours, and now she was still pretty tired but also *massively* hungry. Her stomach made some unfortunate grumbling noises, followed by something that sounded like...groaning?

No, that part wasn't her stomach. Megan pushed carefully out of bed and walked across the narrow space between the beds to where Scarlett was sleeping, cuddled all the way under the blankets. She was making a sort of low, moaning sound, like she might be in pain, or...or...*not* in pain.

That alternative made Megan stumble back in surprise, sitting hard on the bed. Her immediate follow-up was laughter, and she stifled her giggles behind her hand. Scarlett was either having a bad dream or a really good one, and she was making some noises that gave Megan some *really* inappropriate thoughts. Fucking *hell*. Leave it to Scarlett to be distracting even when sound asleep. How was Megan supposed to focus on anything else now?

At least she was wide awake now, so she might as well do something about getting food. That would be enough of a distraction for whatever the hell Scarlett was murmuring about.

Megan flipped on the light on the nightstand. Maybe it would wake Scarlett up, which would solve the second problem just as easily. But Scarlett kept right on sleeping, so Megan went through the binder the Pink Sands Inn provided about area food and hotel information. The sheets inside with hotel info were slightly yellowed and a bit crinkly to her touch, like no one had updated them in years, and maybe they hadn't. Maybe the Pink Sands Inn knew that tourists were going to pay whatever they asked and not care much about other amenities with the ocean right outside their doorstep.

She settled on Domino's, because they were still open and had an app, so she didn't actually have to talk to a human being. With a large pizza and cheesy bread en route to their hotel, she decided to go for a walk to the vending machine and to get some ice. The vending machine looked straight out of the '80s, with the old-fashioned Coca-Cola logo and the large plastic buttons you had to push with your whole hand. The colors were faded, but she could make out the varieties and chose a root beer for herself. The can tumbled out, thunking into the bottom drawer, its metal surface cold against her fingers. She should get one for Scarlett, too, in case Scarlett woke up. What kind of soda did Scarlett drink? She had ordered sweet tea at lunch. At one time, she'd known what Scarlett liked, but maybe those things changed. It had been a number of years. She got a can of Coke and filled the ice bucket.

Scarlett was still asleep when Megan got back to the room, and stayed asleep even when Megan flicked the lights back on. Megan sat back down on her bed to wait and watch the pizza get closer on the app. Scarlett could sleep through anything, but at least she wasn't making sexy noises anymore. Megan frowned at her former friend. It wasn't Scarlett's fault, so Megan knew it was ridiculous to be irritated at her, but she'd been irritated at Scarlett for years and it felt like habit. Of course, she'd been irritated at the *thought* of Scarlett, not Scarlett herself, and now having the person here complicated all of Megan's pure memory-based irritation. The in-real-life Scarlett was not the monster Megan had been making her out to be. And now, sleeping in her bed, looking innocent and also beautiful, Scarlett was tangling up all of Megan's emotions.

The pizza delivery person knocked on the door, and even that didn't wake Scarlett up, so Megan didn't feel bad going back to her bed with the entire pizza and cheesy bread and turning on the television. Scarlett could sleep, and Megan could eat.

Megan ate nearly half the pizza on her own and was working her way through the cheesy bread when Scarlett woke up. She came awake slowly, first with a few murmurs, and then some shuffling around, and then she rolled over and blinked at Megan. "Is that a pizza?"

Megan had to smile. "Yeah. You want some?"

"Definitely. I'm starving." Scarlett sat up, the blankets slipping down around her hips.

Megan reflexively turned away. "Oh my god! Why are you naked?"

"What?" Scarlett looked down at herself. "Oh. I was too tired to put on pajamas." She reached across the gap between the beds. "Slide that pizza box over here, will you?"

"You're just going to stay naked?" Megan couldn't help the shrill tone in her voice.

"Does it bother you?"

Scarlett's tone was mischievous, and Megan didn't know how to feel about it. She wasn't a prude; she'd seen lots of people naked, had been naked in front of lots of people as well, but something about it being *Scarlett* unsettled the hell out of her. She forced her glance across the space between them, the pizza box held like a shield. *Don't look at her tits.* They were *right there*, though, just at the bottom of Megan's vision, even as she locked eyes with Scarlett like they were in a staring contest. "It doesn't bother me," Megan lied.

Scarlett was still grinning, that little impish smile. "So why do you look so horrified?"

"I'm not horrified." Megan shoved the pizza box across the space. "Take your damn pizza, will you?"

"And cheesy bread?"

Megan looked down at the cheesy bread in the box on her lap, then handed two of the breadsticks across the gap. "There. The rest is mine."

Scarlett laughed. "We'll see about that."

She ate the breadsticks first, then finally sighed. "You want me to put some clothes on?"

"Doesn't bother me. You do whatever you like." Megan might be terribly distracted, but she could fake nonchalance.

Scarlett grumbled good-naturedly and rolled out of bed, walking bare-assed over to her overnight bag and pulling out some clothes. Megan looked up only once to see the golden-tanned curves of her body and then looked away again, focusing on chewing the breadsticks. Scarlett was probably just radiant like that *naturally*, when Megan ended up always looking like someone had kept her locked up in a closet for most of her life. It wasn't like she was ashamed of her body, but if she looked like Scarlett, she'd probably go around naked a lot more, too.

The idea of being hidden in a closet reminded Megan of all the other ways she'd been closeted, back before realizing she was bi, and all of a sudden her feelings about Scarlett crashed through her with a devastatingly simple explanation.

Fuck.

Fuck, no.

"There, is that better?" Scarlett stood in front of Megan's bed, now wearing a nightshirt. It didn't reach her knees, leaving a long expanse of thigh exposed, and Megan swallowed what she was chewing. It went down kind of hard.

"Much better," she forced herself to say, and drank some root beer. "I got you a Coke. It's in the ice bucket."

"You got ice?" Scarlett walked over to peek in the square taupe plastic container lined with a plastic bag. "And soda?"

"I wanted to go for a walk."

"How close is the pizza place?" Scarlett returned to her bed with her soda.

"Delivery."

Scarlett nodded. "Good choice." She stifled a yawn. "I'd normally say this was gonna fuck up my sleep schedule, but honestly, I could sleep another nine hours."

"Me, too. But the hunger woke me up." Megan pushed the box of breadsticks away. "I've been defeated. You can have the rest of these if you want."

"Thanks." Scarlett took them over to her bed. "I was worried I was gonna have to wrestle you for them."

Megan almost retorted, "I'd like to see you try," the words hovering just at the tip of her tongue, but Scarlett would do it. She'd come over here and push Megan down onto the bed and pin her, and…and…

Megan chugged more of her root beer to try and cool the flaming feeling in her body. Scarlett didn't seem to notice. Of course she didn't. Scarlett didn't notice anybody who was interested in her, and Megan shouldn't be interested in her anyway, since Scarlett *screwed* her—and not in the fun way—before they started college. She was still mad.

That righteous anger that had kept her warm for so many nights was fading away into something less righteous, though, and Megan was too tired to fight it. She got up to go brush her teeth again and give herself some space.

When she returned, Scarlett was tucked back into bed, playing on her phone, her eyelids drooping. The pizza box was empty. "We destroyed it." She looked over at Megan. "Good teamwork."

"Right." Megan climbed back into bed. She should probably say something, but didn't know what to say. "I don't care if you sleep naked. I was just surprised."

Scarlett snorted. "Sure. You *looked* surprised. But don't worry. I usually wear clothes to sleep. So you don't have to look at my tits anymore."

"Great." Megan's voice didn't sound as excited about that as she'd hoped to sound. "I, uh, appreciate that."

Scarlett made some quiet noise that Megan didn't hear, and then silence fell between them. Megan scrunched down under the covers again, suddenly heavy with sleep. Across the aisle, Scarlett was rustling around, clearing up the trash from their pizza, and it was just so good to have a friend here. She could ignore whatever unwelcome other feelings for Scarlett were surfacing, and focus on friendship. Friendship was fine.

Chapter Seven

Maybe it was all the pizza, or the fact that she slept for basically twenty hours, but Scarlett awoke the next morning feeling amazing. After the initial uncertainties about where she was or what day it was, she blinked open and sat up, looking around at the room. The heavy motel curtains were still drawn across the windows, and she was about to get up and open them, but then she stopped. Megan was still asleep, curled up into a tiny ball beneath the covers, completely silent. Also, the alarm clock said it was only seven in the morning. Shit, when was the last time she'd been awake at seven when she hadn't stayed awake the whole night before?

Megan could have her sleep. Scarlett felt refreshed and rejuvenated, and she wanted to get *up*. She took her time in the shower, enjoying the limitless hot water of a decent motel, and then got dressed in some comfortable clothes for traveling. Megan still slept on. She would let her sleep until at least nine, and then wake her up if she wasn't awake by nine thirty.

In the meantime, though, Scarlett got some remote data

entry work done, a bit of mindless number crunching that she could do without paying very much attention to it. The Wi-Fi was reliable, at least, and she set up at the round table with her aging laptop and slid the curtain open just enough to let some sunlight spill across her workspace. It was a pleasant place to work. Something about this whole thing seemed pleasantly domestic, with Megan dozing nearby, and Scarlett couldn't let those feelings settle too deeply on her. Megan, after all, seemed to have maintained her irritation toward Scarlett, even if it was interrupted by brief, beautiful stretches of kindness or at least civility.

And then there was that whole thing with the nakedness. It wasn't like Scarlett was a nudist, but she spent a lot of time walking around naked while she was doing laundry or just didn't want to get dressed right away. None of her roommates had ever cared. Megan, though, reacted like she'd never seen a tit before.

Oh god. What if she'd never seen a tit before? Was that even possible? It couldn't be. She had to have seen some PG-13 movies, right? Or a foreign film? Or maybe porn? Scarlett couldn't picture Megan watching porn. Well, actually, she *could* picture it, could picture Megan's little hitching breaths when she got turned on, the way she might furtively sneak a hand down into her pajamas, biting her lip at the indecency of it all...

Fuck. Scarlett shook herself out of that train of thought right that minute. Whatever feelings she'd had for Megan in the past, they were an adolescent crush, and Megan never returned her affection. Whether it was because Megan was straight (likely) or not interested in Scarlett (also likely), nothing had come of it, and then they'd stopped talking after Scarlett didn't follow Megan to college.

She winced at that memory. Way to throw a bucket of cold

water on any latent arousal. Remembering that time of her life brought up so many feelings she had decided to bottle them away, so she didn't have to deal with them. When Megan hadn't addressed the elephant in the room at the start of this trip, Scarlett had decided to ignore it as well. Megan didn't need to know she hadn't gone to a fancy private college the way Scarlett had told her, back when the lie seemed like the only way to save face. Megan didn't need to know Scarlett had done a few semesters at community college before dropping out, that she'd never finished any degree at all. She didn't need Megan's pity, and she didn't need Megan's forgiveness.

Well. Maybe just her forgiveness would be nice.

Scarlett looked over at the sleeping figure in the other bed. If she had an easy way to talk to Megan, they probably could have cleared all this up years ago. At first, it had been self-preservation; she was embarrassed, and Megan was smart and competent and thought all her friends were the same. It was far easier to make up an acceptance at a fancy private college across the state rather than admit that she'd flunked all her placement tests and deal with Megan's pity…or worse, Megan's insistence that she persevere on a hopeless path. By the time Scarlett decided to come clean, after almost a full year of avoiding Megan on school breaks and letting her believe the lie, Megan wouldn't return her calls, and this wasn't the sort of confession you left on a voicemail. So Scarlett had given up. Told herself that Megan had *always* been a bit holier-than-thou, that some friendships weren't worth saving. And when *Megan* had reached out, over two years later, Scarlett had been too proud to return the texts. She was leaving Florida, anyway, getting the hell out for New York, and she didn't need anyone's pity.

Scarlett sighed. These weren't good memories.

But they *were* on this road trip together, with a thousand

miles left to go. Maybe it was time to make amends. Megan had stepped out of her comfort zone for this trip, and she had a whole scrapbook of dreams she wanted to fulfill. Maybe Scarlett could help.

Jeremy wasn't in the lobby when Scarlett showed up there, and only a "We'll Be Right Back" sign gave a vague hint of his someday return. She poked through the wooden display of brochures for places to add to their trip. About ten minutes later, and after a stop at the car, she returned to the motel room with their road maps and all the brochures that seemed relevant. Megan still slept on, and Scarlett began hatching a plan.

By the time Megan woke up, Scarlett had given up on the motel brochures and moved onto internet searches. She knew what detour she wanted to add, but was having trouble pinning down the specifics.

Megan blinked sleepy eyes over at Scarlett. "What are you doing?" she asked, voice a bit slurred.

"I'm checking our route." Scarlett leaned back in her chair. "Making some shifts where we need them."

Rubbing her eye with the heel of one hand, Megan looked even younger than usual. "Why do we need shifts?" Megan asked.

"Just a few amendments." Scarlett waved Megan away. "I already showered. You can have the bathroom."

After her shower, Megan walked down to the beach to get some more photographs, leaving Scarlett alone in the motel room. She'd thought about joining her, but she'd had enough of a beach in the cold with Tybee Island the previous day— had that really just been yesterday?—and was happy to make a few calls and put the finishing touches on the next leg of their trip. By the time Megan returned, she was much more cheerful, her cheeks windblown from the cold. She'd also brought breakfast sandwiches back with her, which made Scarlett just as cheerful. After they ate, Megan took time to place two photos into the "Myrtle Beach" page of her scrapbook, pure satisfaction on her face. "Okay," she announced at last, closing the scrapbook. "I'm ready to go."

That enthusiasm waned once Megan got into the driver's seat and saw the GPS Scarlett had already programmed. "What is this stop that's six hours away? Where are we going?"

"Our first surprise stop." Scarlett couldn't hold back the beaming smile she gave Megan. "Let's go!"

Megan was still frowning as she followed the GPS out onto the highway. "I don't like surprises."

"Of course you do." Scarlett could remember plenty of surprises she'd thrown for Megan. "When we were younger, I surprised you all the time."

Megan sighed. "I didn't like them then, either."

"What?" Scarlett shifted in her seat. "Not even when I bought you tickets for things? All those concerts and movies?"

Megan squirmed in her seat, both hands wrapped around the steering wheel. "I liked going to all those shows. I loved that. But I hated not knowing where we were going or what we were doing. I didn't have any chance to get excited ahead of time. I would rather you just have told me."

Embarrassment burned Scarlett's face, followed immediately by defensiveness. "Well, I'd rather you had just told *me* that you didn't like it. I always tried to surprise you because I thought you liked surprises."

"I didn't want to *tell* you because I didn't want to hurt your *feelings*." Megan glanced over, just a quick moment of taking her eyes off the road, but her expression looked set and irritated. "I thought you might have figured it out when I never surprised you back."

Scarlett had always just assumed Megan didn't know how to plan a good surprise. "You should have told me."

Megan snorted. "And you should have told me you didn't want to go to college with me."

There it was. The silence fell hard between them, like a heavy weight settling into the car, the unsaid thing finally said. The longer Scarlett let this go on, the more painful it was going to be to reveal it. Megan already was mad at her, but Scarlett didn't want her *pity* as well.

But she'd been lying for a long time, and they had a lot of miles ahead of them in this car.

"It wasn't that I didn't want to go to college with you." Scarlett forced the words out.

Megan didn't respond, but she'd gone back to driving with both hands on the wheel, her eyes set straight ahead.

"I flunked my placement tests, okay?" Scarlett stared out her side window at the trees flashing past, anything to keep from having to look at Megan. "My whole first year would have been remedial everything."

Silence again. This time, Scarlett had to look. She turned slowly, just enough that she could see Megan out of her peripheral vision. Megan was still staring straight ahead, but her frown looked more confused than angry. Scarlett seized onto that. She'd started this, so she might as well go all the way.

"I wasn't gonna pass, Megan. So I said no and went to PHCC." Pasco-Hernando Community College had seemed like a better option than failing at the University of Southern Florida. "I figured if I failed, at least it was cheaper."

Silence. She'd hoped Megan would start looking less angry, but Megan still looked irritated and confused and...hurt? The hurt was unexpected.

"I don't see why you didn't just *tell* me," Megan said quietly into the empty space. "I thought I was your best friend."

"And have you know how dumb I was? No thank you." Scarlett snorted.

"You lied to me. You told me you were going off to a fancy private school and made me think I wasn't good enough for you."

"I didn't want you knowing I was a fuck-up."

"You get test anxiety. You've always gotten test anxiety. Did you even tell them?" Megan looked over. If possible, she seemed even more angry. "Did you tell them at USF? Or at PHCC? Did you even tell them about your 504 plan?"

Scarlett had had a 504 plan in high school, where they'd run a bunch of tests on her and identified her test anxiety as a medical issue that warranted some special accommodations. But she wasn't going to take that sort of thing to college with her. "Colleges don't care about that stuff." She folded her hands in her lap. "And anyway, none of it matters."

"None of it *matters*?" Megan practically exploded. She was looking over at Scarlett more than at the road, now, glancing back and forth like a windshield wiper. "Of course it matters! I thought you left me. I thought you didn't care about me anymore, and you let me think that about you! How could you let me think that? How could you go all that time and never *tell me*?"

"I was embarrassed, okay? I didn't want you to pity me." Scarlett folded her arms. She'd thought Megan would pity her now, and somehow Megan was even more angry. "And then I tried to reach out to you and you wouldn't return my messages."

"Because I was mad! And then when I got over it and tried to make amends, you ignored *me*." Megan glared at her. "I left messages."

Scarlett fiddled with the direction of the air vent, wiggling it back and forth, not wanting to look at Megan again. "I was mad you'd ignored me."

Megan let out a long, exasperated sigh. "I can't believe this.

I can't believe you let our friendship end because of your stupid pride." Megan grabbed a half-eaten granola bar out of the center console and shoved it in her mouth. Something about that struck Scarlett as so funny, she had to struggle to repress a laugh. Maybe it was some kind of hysterical giggle, something from the tension of holding these secrets in for so long and then letting them go. Megan talked through a mouthful of food, the first few words indecipherable, and then swallowed so Scarlett could hear the rest. "—no reason to be ashamed of going to a community college. Lots of kids do that. I would have understood. We could have been friends."

"I dropped out of that, too." That part was important, even if she didn't want to say it. "I didn't even make it through the last semester."

"I would have been your friend, Scarlett." Megan crumpled up the wrapper of the granola bar and tossed it back over her shoulder into the backseat, a complete departure from the way she normally treated the trash in her car, which had its own portable trash can. "I would have stayed your friend. Fuck you."

There wasn't much to respond to that. Scarlett laced her fingers together, relieved and upset at the same time, and weirdly overcome by humor. "We're going to the Blue Ridge Mountains," Scarlett said. "I wanted you to see snow."

That made Megan go silent, her mouth falling open in a small O. Taking the advantage, Scarlett pressed on. "I know you've never seen snow before. And one of those scrapbook pages had snow on it. So I thought, maybe you could see some."

"It seems really far out of our way," Megan said, frowning. "Are you sure we have enough time? I could always see snow once we get up north."

"The Blue Ridge Mountains are gorgeous, even in the

winter, and you should get to see them." Scarlett folded her arms. "Just let me show you something pretty, okay? I thought it would be nice."

Megan stared at the GPS, then at the road, silent for an endless few moments. "It...does sound nice. You're sure we have enough time?"

"We have enough time. I promise."

Megan nodded, relaxing a bit. Maybe some fences were mending.

Not that Scarlett was going to ask about those fences, though. If her confession about flunking out of college didn't earn Megan's sympathy, she didn't have a plan B except to be nice and hope they had a pleasant or at least tolerable trip.

She'd have thought, though, that Megan would have more comments or questions about their next stop. It took almost an hour of driving, with Megan quietly humming along to the CDs she had made, before the topic came up again.

"Where are we staying?" Megan asked.

"It's nothing special, just a motel near one of the mountains. I haven't stayed there, but the reviews online were good.

"But you've been to the area?"

"Once, when I was a kid. It was a time-share freebie, where you have to listen to their pitch, but I just remember how pretty it was." Scarlett smiled at the memory of snow falling outside the windows. "It was the first place I ever saw snow, myself."

Megan was doing that weird thing where she stared at Scarlett again, like she wanted to say something but didn't know how. At least when she was talking, Scarlett could respond. Eventually, she couldn't take it. "What? You keep looking at me like a creeper. Look at the road."

"I'm confused as to why you'd do this for me."

Scarlett rolled her eyes. "I saw snow in your scrapbook and

I wanted to take you some place that you might like, and this is an area I know at least a little about. So I figured out the logistics, did some googling, fit this into the schedule."

"We're not going to get there until late." Megan frowned at the clock.

"Not until dusk, no. But it'll still be pretty."

Megan considered. "Are you sure we have enough time to get to Canada? We're still in North Carolina."

"We have plenty of time, you know. We're not going to miss the wedding." Scarlett had done the math. "Would you just trust me for once?"

Megan didn't say what Scarlett feared she'd say, about the broken trust in her past. Instead, she just nodded. "All right. It sounds pretty."

Scarlett smiled.

"Hand me a new CD, will you?" Megan waved vaguely at Scarlett. "Something kick-ass."

Scarlett leafed through the pages of the CD case. "Leather Jacket Life?" She laughed. "Do you even own a leather jacket?"

"Just put the CD in."

As soon as she did, Pat Benatar came through the speakers. Within only a few measures, Megan's loud, clear voice rang out through the car, joining in. Scarlett stared.

Megan caught her eye and stopped singing. "What?"

Scarlett hadn't heard Megan sing…what, since high school chorus? Maybe a solo or two, but nothing noteworthy. "When did you learn to sing like that?"

Megan's freckled face flushed. "I don't know what you mean."

"You're a good singer! You could be on the radio."

"Shut up. Stop making fun of me." Megan was already curling back into herself like an under-watered plant, scrunching down to end up nearly level with the steering wheel.

"Come on." False modesty wasn't Megan's style, and Scarlett knew it. "You know you're a good singer."

Megan sighed. "Yeah. I know I'm a good singer. I just don't do it around other people a lot."

Interesting. "Forget I said anything. I didn't compliment you. Whatever. You're a mediocre singer." Scarlett tried to stifle her grin as she lied, badly and with terrible acting.

Megan laughed. It was just one quick bark of laughter, but she relaxed as well. And when the chorus came on again, she started to sing. Scarlett joined in so she wouldn't feel weird, even though staying on key was not her strong suit.

They sang through the next song as well, a Cyndi Lauper hit, and by the time it ended, Megan had fully relaxed. She let her head loll back against the headrest, a lazy smile on her face. She looked like...

She looked like she'd just been fucked. The thought flashed into Scarlett's mind before she could help it, a sudden image of Megan giving that same lazy, self-satisfied expression when stretched out on a bed, and she nearly choked. She covered the surprise and embarrassment by coughing and then drinking some water. If Megan noticed anything, she didn't comment.

Best to change the subject. "Did you ever think about becoming a singer?"

Megan shook her head right away. "Nah."

"Because you don't think you're good enough?"

Megan hesitated, a flicker of tongue brushing over her lips. "I don't know. Success isn't always about how good you are. Even if I was good enough, and I don't know if I am, it's way too stressful to do it for a living."

The fact that Megan had a thoughtful answer, and didn't just dismiss the idea outright, surprised Scarlett. "What part's stressful? Being up onstage?"

"No. That part's kind of nice." Megan smiled, a tiny sliver

of embarrassed pleasure on her face. "I don't usually do anything where people clap afterward." She twisted her fingers on the steering wheel. "But the music industry is a lot of luck. At least the performing part. I wouldn't want to get involved with that end of things."

Scarlett glanced across the center console. "So what end of things *would* you want to get involved in?"

The song ended, and Megan turned the music off. "It's not important."

"I asked because I want to know." Scarlett didn't mean to sound irritated, but it came out that way, and she softened her tone. "I'm not gonna make fun of you."

Megan hesitated. "I've always wanted—" She paused, then seemed to steel herself to continue. "I've always wanted to have a radio station. Or a podcast or something. Or work as a DJ. I want to be on the radio sharing everything I love about music, curating playlists, living in the music." She got more animated as she spoke, moving her hands before she pulled them back, as if realizing she was getting too excited. "I—*love* music."

Megan visibly waited for her reply, hands quiet on the steering wheel once more. Maybe she still cared about what Scarlett thought, no matter what she said. "You could do it." Scarlett gestured lightly, a quick hand wave to sweep the impossibilities away. "It wouldn't be that hard to get a podcast started. And if you wanted to be a DJ, there's always the local radio station, or maybe you could go somewhere closer to Tampa or Orlando if you wanted more options—"

"Whoa, whoa, I'm not ready for that." Megan closed back in again. "I just got laid off. And I don't have much experience."

"Well, do you have *some* experience? Aside from making mix CDs."

Megan gave a half-nod. "I had a night gig on the radio at the university. I did the midnight-to-two shift on Thursday nights." Megan's annoyed expression softened, her eyes going unfocused as she remembered. "I didn't have any Friday morning classes that semester, so it worked out fine. I think I was the only one listening, probably."

As long as Megan was talking, she wasn't being mad at Scarlett, and that cold gulf between them was a bit warmer. Scarlett would ask more questions. "What did you like about it?"

"Everything." Megan sighed. "It was so immersive. Me and all the music, alone in the sound booth, with people out in the world hearing what I wanted to share. It felt like magic."

This was the Megan that Scarlett had remembered, the one who said things like "It felt like magic" and sighed like a character in love in a Hallmark movie. Not the bitingly sharp, angry Megan from those first conversations after reconnecting.

Megan snorted. "You probably think I'm being sentimental."

"It's okay." Scarlett didn't want her to stop sharing.

"What about you?" Megan asked. "I told you mine. Tell me yours."

"My what?"

"Your dream."

Scarlett folded her hands in her lap. "I don't have dreams."

"Liar." There was no malice in Megan's tone, but the word still stung. Scarlett didn't need to be reminded of her lies.

"Don't call me a liar."

"But you're lying to me right now." Megan still didn't seem angry, though, in that direct way she had. She thought she was being factual. Maybe she was.

If only Scarlett had something to focus on instead of sitting here with her own thoughts. "Can I drive?"

"Why? I've only been driving for a little while." Megan frowned. "Are you getting carsick or something?"

"No, I'm just antsy. I want something to focus on."

Megan pulled off at the next exit, and they switched places. Back behind the wheel, Scarlett started to relax.

But then Megan piped up. "So what are your dreams?"

Scarlett groaned. "Fuck, I thought you might leave that alone once we changed drivers."

"Nope."

Dreams. Her dreams. "I try not to think about that sort of thing."

"That's sad."

A muscle twitched in Scarlett's jaw. Did she want to be pitied by Megan, or hated by her? It was difficult to choose. "I don't want to get my hopes up about something ridiculous."

"What, you want to be an astronaut? A professional figure skater?" Megan teased.

Scarlett whipped her head around to glare at Megan, without any real anger. "If I'm going to become a professional athlete, it would be for shot put or something, not fucking *figure skating*. We're from Florida."

"Don't deflect. Come on." Megan reached across and gave her a nudge. It was the first time she'd touched Scarlett, and Scarlett's brain short-circuited for a moment at that realization. Even the briefest touch had Scarlett hyperaware of how close they were in this car. Then Megan added, "I showed you mine, you show me yours."

Scarlett laughed. "That means something *very* different than you're using it for."

"Words can mean multiple things." Megan shrugged. "Whatever. You don't have to be honest with me."

Scarlett sighed. Of course it would be guilt of some kind. "Okay. Fine. You want to know what I want? I don't know what I want, because all the things I thought I could do are things I failed at."

"You're not being specific."

"Have a healthy relationship?" Scarlett gripped the steering wheel tighter, her foot getting harder on the accelerator as her heart began to race. "That's one. And also have a good career. I thought I'd become a teacher, but high school was hell for me and now we both know how college turned out." She stared straight ahead. "I'm stupid and I'd be stupid to deny it."

They were doing eighty, and Scarlett forced herself to ease off the gas. Megan was silent beside her, as Scarlett had suspected. No way to compete with the truth.

"I think you're smart," Megan said eventually, and the words sounded hollow.

"Don't patronize me. It's more insulting." Scarlett didn't want to look over. Her eyes felt hot, and she tried to blink the feeling away. "Put the music back on."

"No." Megan shifted to face Scarlett. "I'm not going to say I'm not still mad at you for lying to me and abandoning me, because I am. But I'm not going to sit here while you lie *again* and say that you're stupid. You're not stupid. You don't test well, sure, but you did great on projects and essays. And you got through three semesters of college with none of the accommodations you needed. If you wanted to be a teacher, you could do it."

Scarlett shook her head, lips pressed tightly together. She didn't want to hear this, didn't want the hope to spring up only to be crushed again. When she thought she could speak without her voice shaking, she explained more. "I'm not teacher smart. And that's fine. Not everybody is. So I'm making ends meet. I used to hope something would come up that I loved, some job that might fit, but it didn't. And I don't think it will. I'm afraid..." She stopped short, mouth snapping shut.

The silence fell between them again. Scarlett wanted to crack a joke but couldn't find one.

Megan's words came gently into the quiet. "Afraid of what?"

Scarlett didn't need to answer her. But maybe Megan needed to hear it. Maybe Megan needed Scarlett to put her guard down, just a bit, and mend something between them.

Miraculously, her voice stayed steady. "I'm afraid I can't do whatever I set my mind to. I care about things but I don't know if I can achieve them, and that's not something I like to confront."

They sat in the silence again. Damn, it was an uncomfortable silence. Finally, though, Scarlett relaxed, her shoulders sliding back down from where they'd crept up toward her ears. She thought of something meta to say. "Pretty heavy subject for the car ride, right?"

Megan looked over at her, and her gaze wasn't judgmental or pitying. It was thoughtful. "I think it's okay. Car rides are made for heavy conversations."

"How would you even know?"

Megan shrugged. "From movies."

Scarlett relaxed a little more. "I guess it's good to talk about it."

After a few more minutes of silence, when Scarlett was about to change the subject, Megan spoke up again. "For what it's worth, I think you can do whatever you set your mind to. It's one of the things I always admired about you. And I think you'd make a great teacher."

Scarlett flushed and mumbled her thanks. Then she quickly turned the music back on. It was a song from the Runaways, perfect for car singing, and she started humming along. Megan joined in, singing the refrain, and the conversation mercifully ended.

Chapter Eight

Megan shifted in her seat for probably the hundredth time that day. This was only day two of their trip, but it had to be that these seats were growing less comfortable with each passing mile. Bucket seats. Who wanted to sit in a bucket, anyway? If she asked to get out and stretch again, though, Scarlett might throttle her, putting an end to the uneasy peace they'd developed throughout the day after a fairly tense start. Plus, the GPS said they were close to the motel, with a left turn coming up off the town road they'd been driving on for a while now. Scarlett pulled off onto the shoulder next to a turnoff heading steeply upward. She frowned at the GPS for a moment, then the road, then back to the GPS. "I think this is it." She put the blinker on to turn back onto the road, but Megan stopped her with a hand on her arm.

"That doesn't look like a real road."

Scarlett shrugged. "It's paved, and the GPS says turn left. There's a sign of some kind, but I can't really read it from here."

Neither could Megan. "Haven't you ever heard of death by GPS? It's where you follow the GPS, but the GPS doesn't know that some roads shouldn't be driven on, and you end up stranded somewhere and dead."

"If it's not this, we'll turn around before we die, I promise." Scarlett pulled back onto the road and started heading up the hill, which was leading them off into a more wooded area. They were clearly in the mountains, or at least more mountainous than anything Megan had encountered in Florida. Not that that was saying much.

"This is definitely where you end up dead." Megan leaned forward as well, frowning as she looked where Scarlett was looking. "It looks like a place people go to get murdered."

"Nah. We're fine." Scarlett pointed. "Look, that's the motel up ahead."

The Timber Pines motel lived up to its redundant name—everything was surrounded by pines. It was a cute little place, probably a dozen or so rooms, and it was at least newly painted. Megan's fears of being murdered were somewhat assuaged. Despite the gain in elevation, they hadn't seen any snow, but she didn't mind that too much. It was kind of sweet for Scarlett to be so excited about Megan having this first snow experience, though.

Sweet, and a little disarming.

The room itself was simple but clean, with two double beds covered in flowered bedspreads and a back window that overlooked the forest. Scarlett went for a walk, leaving Megan to unpack her bag and have a bit of time alone with her thoughts after the revelations from earlier. She laid out her scrapbook and started designing a new page as she let her mind wander.

Scarlett's explanation for lying made sense, or at least Megan could see how it had made sense to eighteen-year-old Scarlett. She still didn't like it, though; she didn't like the lying, but she especially didn't like empathizing with Scarlett's reasoning. Maybe it was just residual anger from holding this grudge for so many years, or maybe it was something deeper, but she couldn't forgive Scarlett so easily. Scarlett hadn't trusted her with her feelings of inadequacy. She'd rather have had Megan hate her than admit she wasn't as perfect as she'd always acted. And because of that, they'd lost out on years of a friendship, and Megan had had to navigate the biggest changes of her life alone. That kind of betrayal didn't untangle so easily, not with a single confession, not after seven years. Worst of all was how easily Megan could see herself yielding, drawn back into Scarlett's dazzling orbit, captivated by Scarlett's beauty and charm, blinded by her desire for Scarlett's approval. The only path forward was to stay hard-hearted, to remind herself that Scarlett had betrayed her trust and she didn't want to get hurt like that again.

Scarlett came back in a little while later with her cheeks pink from the cold, bringing a gust of the outside air in with her. "I've got good news."

Megan set aside her scrapbook and art supplies. "What's the good news?"

Scarlett nodded at her work. "What are you doing?"

"I'm making a page for this stop." She held it up, already labeled with the Blue Ridge Mountains, spaces for facts she was going to look up on the internet later. "What's your good news?"

"It's supposed to snow tonight." Scarlett beamed. "Not a lot, only a dusting, but the guy at the front desk said he was pretty confident in the forecast."

"Is that going to be bad for driving?" Megan could imagine them skidding down out of control on the steep road they'd taken to get here.

Scarlett waved a hand dismissively. "Nah. The sander just

went by as I was coming back to the room. There's a path down to a river out behind the motel. Maybe in the morning you'd want to go down there and get a picture or two for the scrapbook."

"Thanks." Megan felt a little guilty with her desire to stay hard-hearted in the face of Scarlett's kindness. She forced a smile. "This place is nice."

"It's all right. The price is good, too. Well within the budget." Scarlett flopped down onto her bed. "I assume you already inspected these for bedbugs?"

"Of course." Megan ignored the way Scarlett seemed to find that hilarious. "Any places deliver food around here?"

Scarlett dug some folded pamphlets out of her pocket. "Got some local offerings from the front desk."

They ordered Chinese and watched the local weather on the tiny television while they ate it. Megan was glad to be out of the car, but she couldn't settle. After dinner, she finished the scrapbook page, and then tried to find something to do. She tried to read a few pages out of a novel, but couldn't focus on the words; she fooled around with a mobile game, but quickly lost interest; she folded and refolded the clothes she'd unpacked and then reorganized all the snacks in the snack bag. Nothing held her interest, her attention skittering as her body itched for something physical. She knew what would relieve that nervous energy, and if she'd been alone, she could indulge to her heart's content—some sex toys, a locked bedroom door, and no Scarlett passing judgment. But no, she wasn't alone, and so even that foolproof stress reliever was denied her. Annoyed, she tried pushing herself through some yoga.

Scarlett closed her laptop. "The Wi-Fi here's shitty. I can't get a good signal." She leaned back against the headboard of her bed. "What's wrong?"

Megan grimaced. "I'm restless."

"I can tell."

Megan shifted into Triangle pose, trying not to roll her eyes. "I wasn't trying to hide it."

"Yeah." Scarlett grinned. "So what do you usually do when you're restless?"

Scarlett would be completely floored if Megan told her the truth, wouldn't she? She had thought Megan was a virgin like she'd been back in high school, like Megan hadn't changed at all, like just because she didn't brag about sex meant she wasn't a sexual being. And right now, Megan was unsettled and restless and just about out of fucks to give, so she shifted out of Triangle pose and threw Scarlett a thin smile. "I masturbate, usually."

She was rewarded by Scarlett giving her a slow blink, momentarily speechless, color coming suddenly to Scarlett's lightly freckled cheekbones. Anything that made Scarlett speechless was worthwhile. "Okay," Scarlett said after a long pause. "So go for it."

Megan's stomach dropped. That was *not* what she'd expected. "What?"

"Rub one out." Scarlett's smile was mischievous. "It wouldn't bother me."

"I bet it wouldn't." Megan could feel her own face get hot. She forced herself into another yoga pose just to keep from looking as shaken as she felt. The pose was called Warrior pose, but she didn't feel like a warrior as she did it, Scarlett's attention still on her body. When she came out of the pose, she looked over and yeah, Scarlett was watching her. "Don't you have a book to read or something?"

"What's the matter? Haven't you ever had a wank in front of one of your boyfriends?" Scarlett's eyes were sparkling. She was enjoying this, damn it. She was enjoying Megan's discomfort.

Two could play at that game. "My boyfriends, no, but I have done it in front of some girlfriends." She raised an eyebrow. Scarlett's increased flush was gratifying. Knocking her off-balance was a delight.

Scarlett's embarrassment didn't last long, though. "Megan Harris." She folded her arms. "Why didn't I know you weren't straight? Why am I finding this out now, in a mountainside motel in North Carolina?"

"Because you've been too proud to talk to me for seven years, and because I didn't know it myself until college. So there." Megan sat down on the floor and stretched forward, in part so she didn't have to keep looking at Scarlett's face. Her words came out muffled. "Now you know."

Silence fell. Eventually, Megan had to stop stretching. Scarlett had started doing a crossword from the book she'd brought, and she didn't look up. Apparently the conversation was over, and Megan still wasn't sure where anything stood. She might as well take a shower and get ready for bed.

By the time she came out, much later, Scarlett had turned off all the lights except the little nightstand one. She was under the covers in her bed, rolled onto her side and facing the door. Maybe she was asleep. Megan got beneath her own covers and flicked off the one remaining light, plunging the room into darkness.

The restlessness in her body would not go away. She flipped from one side to the other, and finally lay on her back, staring up into the darkness, her heart beating too quickly against her ribs, her mind too full of Scarlett.

Quietly, barely loud enough for Megan to hear, Scarlett's voice came through the darkness. "I really don't care if you want to get off."

Megan couldn't deny she'd been thinking about it. "It doesn't bother me, but I don't want it to be weird for you."

There was another part of it, too, that she might as well say out loud. "I don't want you to think it means anything."

Scarlett's quiet, breathy chuckle floated over to her. "It definitely doesn't have to mean anything. Does that go both ways?"

Megan's heart was racing, now. "Of course," she made herself say. Because it didn't. She'd done this sort of thing in front of partners before, or alongside them. Like other types of sex, mutual masturbation didn't have to mean anything. But she'd never done it in the same room as someone who she wasn't actively sleeping with. She'd definitely never done it with Scarlett.

The first soft, hitching breath from the other side of the room brought her whole body to attention at once. Oh, god, Scarlett was touching herself. She wasn't making a show of it, but if Megan listened—and she did, she *strained* to listen—she could hear the quicker intake of breath and the muffled soft, wet noises. She might have been rubbing her clit, or dipping her long fingers inside herself…

Megan bit her lip to keep from gasping as she reached down to touch her clit. The spasm of pleasure overtaking her was sharper than usual, less controlled, and she sucked in a ragged breath. Scarlett was going to hear her. She was going to listen, and she was going to hear Megan come. Every touch, she thought of Scarlett, thought of her doing this exact thing only a few feet away. This simple act, this shared intimacy, had never been so erotic. Megan had to fight to keep from groaning aloud. She made herself slow down and savor the moment as near her, Scarlett's breathing grew faster, her noises less muffled. She wanted so badly to hear Scarlett come, had never wanted anything like she wanted this.

The bed near her went silent for a moment, and then a long, deep exhale, with the barest hint of a moan at the end. Megan couldn't hold back. She gasped out loud as she came, pleasure overtaking her like a force of nature, and she shuddered her way through an endless, perfect climax.

Afterward, silence filled the room. Megan caught her breath. She had done that. They had done that. Was…was that it? She carefully reached over to the nightstand for some tissues.

"Not so bad, right?"

Scarlett's voice made Megan freeze for a moment before she forced herself to relax. This was fine; this didn't have to mean anything, just like sex never had to mean anything. "No big deal," Megan said, even though her heart was still racing. "I can probably sleep now."

Scarlett laughed quietly. "Good night."

She shouldn't think too deeply about this. Tomorrow, they'd be on the road again, and whatever had happened in the darkness would be just another memory.

Megan did not want to get out of this bed. The crisp air on her face was enough to tell her that outside of this bed, it was cold, but her whole body was toasty-warm under layers of blankets. It was still dark out, or at least the gray pre-dawn twilight that indicated the sun wasn't quite up yet, and she could easily fall back asleep. But someone was shaking her, and so she resentfully opened her eyes.

Scarlett was looking down at her with a look of pure excitement on her face. "Megan! Come see the snow!"

The events of the previous night came flooding back to Megan all at once, but Scarlett didn't seem to care in the wake of the apparent snowfall outside. Her excitement was contagious, and so before Megan was fully awake, she had pulled on a bunch of layers and shoes and her glasses and followed Scarlett out into the freezing cold.

It was still snowing, light flakes drifting slowly down onto the parking lot. They hadn't gotten much snow, but it was enough to cover the ground, and Megan suddenly understood Scarlett's enthusiasm. The sky was lit just enough to illuminate the snow, which in turn reflected the light, and sunrise would probably dazzle the entire landscape.

"Come back here." Scarlett took her by the hand and tugged her through a walkway that passed to the back of the motel, where the trails lay, and out into the forest. Megan tangled Scarlett's cold fingers with her own and laughed as her footsteps crunched on the newly fallen snow. Snow was already dotting Scarlett's curls and melting into water droplets, and it was surely doing the same on her own hair. Scarlett released her hand, and Megan reached down to try to gather up some of the snow in her numb fingers. The cold seared her skin as she crunched it wetly into a misshapen ball, but oh, she didn't care. Her face hurt from smiling.

Scarlett squealed indignantly at the first snowball Megan lobbed at her, and then returned the favor. The snowballs came mixed with leaves, since there wasn't really enough snow to make good snowballs, but none of it mattered. The snow stuck wetly to Megan's hoodie, soaking through immediately. She got in another good throw, this one hitting Scarlett right in the back, before Scarlett got her in the head with one and it started dripping down the back of her neck. Laughing and screeching in equal measure, she tackled Scarlett down to the snow, trying to shove some under her collar. Scarlett was way too strong for her, though, and quickly flipped her over, pinning her down on the soaking wet ground.

They stopped moving immediately. Scarlett's smile faded, leaving something else in its wake, an expression of surprise and then...desire. Oh. Megan opened her mouth to speak, but no words came out, her own smile fading with the sudden surge in her blood.

Scarlett stood up quickly, getting to her feet and offering Megan a hand. "We should get dressed before we both freeze," she said, brushing snow out of her hair.

Megan nodded, too shaken up to say anything else, taking Scarlett's hand to get up. Snow had soaked through her layers. "Yeah. Let's...let's go change."

She let Scarlett have the first shower and used the time to gather her thoughts and take a few pictures of the snow. Then it was her turn for the hot water, which blissfully melted away not only her chill, but also her shakiness about this morning and last night. By the time she got out of the shower, Scarlett had the maps spread out on the table and was poring over them. Whatever moments they'd had—last night in bed, this morning in the snow—were gone, shifting into the past, and all they needed to focus on was the road trip.

Scarlett looked up from the maps wearing an eager, expectant, but nervous look on her face, the look she got when she wanted to say something but didn't know how.

"What do you want to convince me of?" Megan asked.

Scarlett's hesitation melted into a smile. "You can still read me."

"Of course. You wear your thoughts all over your face." Megan let a touch of irritation through in her voice. Best that Scarlett didn't think she was completely forgiven yet. Nothing was forgiven yet, not even if Megan spent time in the shower thinking really inappropriate thoughts about Scarlett's hands and lips all over her skin. She swallowed the lump in her throat. "You always have that expression when you're about to try to convince me of something."

"Well, I was thinking." Scarlett traced her finger in a circle over a spot on the map. "We're all the way out here. How about we keep going west?"

"We're going to *Quebec*." Megan pointed up. "That's North."

Scarlett shook her head. "Not west forever. Just as far as Nashville."

"Nashville, Tennessee?"

"No. Nashville, Wisconsin. *Yes*, Nashville, Tennessee." Scarlett made a face, but then immediately got that wistful look in her eyes again. "The Grand Ole Opry records tonight. It's five or so hours away. If we leave now, we could get there in the afternoon, see the city, go to the Opry at night." She bit her lip. "What do you think?"

Megan had never thought about going to Nashville before; it wasn't in her scrapbook, wasn't on her plans, but she loved the thought. Nashville was one of the holy places of music, and the Grand Ole Opry was legendary. "What happened to no more than two hours either direction of I-95?"

Scarlett shrugged. "You're really into music. You should get to go to Nashville."

That was unexpectedly sweet, the kind of sweet that made Megan melt a bit and then immediately try to un-melt. She was staying hard-hearted. She would not be hurt.

"What does it do to our Quebec arrival?" Megan asked.

"Another day delay, but we've got the time."

"Let's look at the route." Megan joined Scarlett over by the map. She found their current location in Western North Carolina, then the city of Nashville further west. It didn't look that far on the map, but nothing looked that far when zoomed out to this scale. Five or six hours, Scarlett had said.

Megan traced an alternate route back with her finger. "If we go out to Nashville, we could head back east on 40, and then pick up 81 in…" Switching to the Tennessee state map, she relocated their route. "Dandridge. In Dandridge, Tennessee. 81 will take us all the way back to…" Back to the country map. "Well, we could take it all the way up through Pennsylvania, or we could switch to 66 and head through Virginia…"

It didn't seem like Scarlett was listening to her anymore, and Megan looked up to catch her eye. "Are you even paying attention to this?"

Scarlett nodded a bit too quickly. "Sure. Route 66 through Virginia. And Route 66 is famous, so that's cool."

Megan looked back at the map and did some quick calculations. "It might mean we cut another stop, though, if we want to get to Quebec on time."

"We don't have to cut anything." Scarlett started ticking off days on her fingers. "Nashville today. Full day's drive to DC tomorrow. We stay over in DC. Drive the next day up to New York City. A day in New York, then we drive up to Salem. A day in Salem, then up over the border all the way to Quebec. Plus we've got some wiggle room because we were planning to spend a couple of days in Quebec."

She was right; they did have enough time.

And Scarlett had planned this trip just for her, just so Megan could see something Scarlett knew she'd like.

Outside the window, the snow had stopped, and the sunshine was already melting it into sparkling dampness, promising clear roads. "All right. Let's do it."

Chapter Nine

Megan took the first stretch of driving, leading them down out of the mountains and toward Nashville. She was in a really good mood, and Scarlett could get used to seeing her that happy. Maybe it was the snow, or the new plan for Nashville, or maybe it was because she'd gotten off last night. Scarlett would be replaying that memory for a long time, that soundtrack of Megan's desperate breaths as she tumbled over the edge into climax.

She distracted herself from that by digging through the CD case for some traveling music. Megan had a CD labeled "Tumbleweed Feels," which she slid into the drive. Some country music could prep them for Nashville. The first song, though, was "Life is a Highway," the old Tom Cochrane version and not the country Rascal Flatts version.

"Is this the 'Tumbleweed' CD?" Megan asked.

"Yeah. What is it? I thought it would be country."

"It's songs about traveling. I think there's some country on it, though." She looked over at Scarlett. "You wanted country?"

"We're going to Nashville. It seemed appropriate."

The next song was John Denver's "Take Me Home, Country Roads," which they both sang along to. After that was a country song Scarlett didn't know about highway sunrises. The miles rolled on, and Scarlett had just about managed to put memories from the previous evening out of her mind when Megan interrupted her thoughts.

"So I guess I've tried my next new thing."

Scarlett could not believe she'd just come out and say it like that. "What, you mean last night?"

Megan gaped, then laughed. "I meant the *snowball fight*."

Scarlett had to laugh as well. "Oh my god. I'm sorry."

"Nah. It's all right. That was new, too, I guess." Megan tipped her head to the side, far more relaxed about this than Scarlett had expected. "New with you, I mean."

Scarlett considered her. "I'm starting to think I don't know you as well as I thought I did."

Megan gave her a tiny, satisfied smile. "Good."

"You like being a mystery?"

"I don't need to be a *mystery*, but I don't like feeling like someone knows everything about me. Especially when they formed all those conclusions based on me as a teenager."

Scarlett turned to stare out the window. "I sometimes think it would be nice to be totally understood."

"Then be honest with people."

Scarlett glanced back, hurt flaring up in immediate response, but Megan's expression was placid. She probably wasn't intending to be hurtful at all. Scarlett let it go.

The drive west to Nashville was more pleasant than Scarlett had imagined, especially after the uncertainty of the morning, but even with her love of road trips, the reality of so many hours in this car was starting to wear on her. Even Megan's extensive CD collection wasn't helping, although they did sing along to a few songs as the miles rolled past, moving from "Tumbleweed Feels" to "Summer Thunderstorms" in the CD case.

"Stop squirming."

Megan's command shook Scarlett out of her reverie. "What?"

"You're squirming all over the place. Stop it." Megan glanced over. "You want to drive?"

"I'm just tired of being in the car."

"There's a lot more road trip ahead." Ever the voice of logic, Megan wasn't saying anything Scarlett didn't already know, but hearing it was still grating. "You want to drive?'

"I don't know." Scarlett wasn't sure driving would help. "You want to play a game?"

"What, like the road sign game or something?"

God, the road sign game. "No. Not that. Something else."

"Truth or dare?"

Megan seemed like she was kidding, but the idea sounded great to Scarlett. "All right."

Megan made a face. "Really?"

"Sure. Why not?"

"Because we're not at my twelfth birthday party." Megan stared fixedly ahead. Wait, had they actually played truth or dare at one of Megan's birthday parties? Surely, Scarlett would have remembered. Although even *she* didn't get up to much trouble at twelve.

"I'll ask first." Scarlett shifted to look at Megan. "Truth or dare?"

"Truth."

"Are you just gonna pick truth every time?" Nothing ruined a truth or dare game like someone who wouldn't do any of the dares.

Megan sniffed and raised her eyebrows. "Is that my question?"

"No. That's not your question." Scarlett considered. "How many people have you slept with?"

Megan paused, and it took Scarlett a second to realize she was *counting*. "Eight. And I would have just answered that question if you asked."

"Eight?" Scarlett had been expecting three or maybe, *maybe* four, after the slow reveals she'd been getting about Megan's past.

"Eight." Megan's expression was still carefully neutral. "Does that offend you?"

"Nah. Just surprised, that's all." Scarlett *really* didn't know this girl. "Your turn."

"Truth or dare?"

"Dare."

"Okay. Um..." Megan trailed off.

"You suggested truth or dare and you don't have any dares in mind?" Unbelievable.

"Shut up! I'm thinking." Megan glanced over at her, then back at the road. "Wave enthusiastically at the next five cars we pass."

"You have to go fast enough to pass someone first."

Megan made another face. "Shut up. Just because I don't drive like I want us to die in an accident."

"You drive like you want us to die of old age."

Megan laughed at her own roast. "Fuck you."

Maybe to prove Scarlett wrong, she accelerated enough to pass another car on the highway. Scarlett rolled down the window to wave, giving an enthusiastic thumbs-up at the car they were driving past and the very confused driver, who waved back after a moment. Megan moved back into the slow lane after that and settled back to something near the speed limit, leaving Scarlett in no immediate danger of having to wave to anyone.

"Truth or dare?" Scarlett asked.

"You haven't done your five."

"And I'm not going to do my five until you drive faster."

Megan sighed. "All right. Dare."

"Sing along to the next song on your CD."

"I've been singing along with the CDs. We both have."

"But just you. Full voice. Whole song." Scarlett wasn't really sure why she was asking for this, when it wasn't like it was challenging for Megan or anything. Maybe that's why she was doing it.

Megan made another confused face. "Okay. Fine."

The next song was "Kill Me Deadly" by Lita Ford, and Megan leaned into it without any hesitation from that opening high note and onto the wailing, punk rock chorus. Damn, she was good. Scarlett could listen to her all day. Maybe that was the reason behind all of this. Maybe she just wanted to hear Megan sing.

The song ended, and Megan let the CD keep playing, but turned the volume down. Instead of asking Scarlett "Truth or dare," she stayed quiet. "I like hearing you sing," Scarlett said at last to break the silence.

"Thanks." Megan's neutral expression didn't change.

"You looking forward to Nashville?"

At that, Megan's lips twitched up. "Yeah. It was a good idea." Then, after a pause, she added, "Thanks."

Scarlett smiled out the window, and Megan sped up to pass another car. Scarlett waved enthusiastically to the confused driver as Megan laughed, and they headed on to Nashville.

Nashville. Megan was nearly vibrating with excitement as her old Camry rolled through the city, with its distinctive architecture and music culture thrumming through every aspect of the space. She had never thought about going here, never really put it on her list of places, saw it as something distinctly different from herself.

Her excitement was almost enough to help her put aside the unsettling realities of her feelings for Scarlett. Sex of any kind had always been fun, always a good way to pass the time, even if she always felt like she was holding part of herself back in bed. Somehow it was different to fool around with *Scarlett*. Not that she'd been fooling around *with* Scarlett...but she'd been thinking about it pretty much nonstop since they'd gotten on the road. At least now she'd have Nashville to distract her.

Their hotel room was a chain hotel, which had at least the reliability of a standard name. It was good to be out of the car, and Megan flopped facedown on one of the beds and let all her muscles relax.

"You can't sleep now!" The bed dipped as Scarlett sat next to her, and Megan's pulse quickened at the touch of her hand on Megan's back. Scarlett rubbed a gentle circle first, then shoved her affectionately. "We've got to go eat and head to the show."

"We have time, right?" Megan rolled over to lie on her back instead, which was a mistake. Scarlett was now propped up over her, leaning across her prone form.

Maybe Scarlett was thinking the same thing, because her gaze dropped briefly to Megan's mouth, and Megan remembered being pinned down in the snow this morning. But then Scarlett grinned and gave her another shove, this time from the side. "Not a lot of time. The curtain goes up at six, and I want to eat something other than fast food."

Megan made a face. She didn't want to get up off this bed, but she was excited about seeing the show. "Okay. Okay, fine. I'll get dressed."

Elia Winters

Megan hadn't brought a lot of clothing on this trip, anticipating getting to do laundry at some hotel along the way, but she had a couple of nice outfits in addition to the dress she planned to wear for the wedding. She selected an emerald green sweater dress from her suitcase. She was normally more of a jeans kind of girl, but this dress made her feel cute, and it felt very Nashville when she paired it with some knee-high boots. She gathered up her clothes and undergarments and headed for the bathroom.

When she left the bathroom, Scarlett was pinning up her curls into two buns up near the top of her head. It was one of the cutest hairstyles she wore, and one that always made Megan wish for something other than her own super-straight brown hair. Scarlett looked away from her hair when Megan entered the room, her gaze skimming down Megan's body in a way that made Megan burn up inside.

Before Scarlett could say something, whether it was going to be a compliment or not, Megan blurted out, "I don't know what to do with my hair."

Scarlett tapped her lips, studying her like she was an interesting painting. "You want me to curl it?" Scarlett asked.

"My hair doesn't curl." Megan had never had any luck with that. "It's too fine."

Scarlett tucked the final bobby pin into her own style and walked over to Megan, running her hand through Megan's hair. The contact sent a chill all down Megan's spine. Oh, she wanted Scarlett to keep touching her like that.

"It's pretty fine." Scarlett gathered up a bunch of Megan's hair in her hands. Megan shivered. Hopefully Scarlett wouldn't notice the shiver. "It would curl if you didn't wash it so much. You need it to get dirty."

Megan laughed, and it sounded breathless coming out. "I don't really do dirty."

Scarlett still had the hold on her hair, and she tipped Megan's head back to look at her. "You sure about that?"

The unspoken *after last night* hung in the air between them. Megan sucked in a breath, her lips parting, and their gazes locked. Then it was like Scarlett had suddenly realized what she said, and she slid her hands out of Megan's hair and backed away. "Your hair is cute just like it is. You don't need to do anything to it." She turned toward the mirror again and fumbled with her makeup bag. Was it Megan's imagination, or were Scarlett's hands shaking? "You, uh, ever think about cutting it?" Scarlett asked.

Megan was still rattled and warm all over. It took her a moment to process Scarlett's words. "Oh. Yeah, actually. Sometimes I think about a pixie cut. Cutting all of it off. But I get nervous."

"It's a big step. But you've got the perfect heart-shaped face for it." Scarlett glanced over, then back at the mirror. "If you ever want to do it, there's probably a million great salons along our road trip. Could be a fun change. And it grows back."

She was talking fast. Megan was having a hard time thinking. "Yeah. Maybe. I'll...do my makeup."

She had the new makeup from Sephora to try, and while it wasn't her area of expertise, she put together what she hoped was a good look—not super fancy, but she didn't end up looking like a clown, either. When she returned from the bathroom, Scarlett was done.

"What about lipstick?" Scarlett asked.

"I'm wearing some." Megan resisted the urge to touch her lips in reflex.

Scarlett frowned. "Nude?"

"It's light pink."

"You need a bold lip. Something really red. It would bring the whole look together."

"I don't have anything really red." Megan stuck with all light pinks whenever she got makeup, which wasn't very often. Red was showy and ostentatious, and she wasn't the type of person to try to get noticed.

Scarlett rummaged in her bag and pulled out a lipstick. "Here. Let me." She touched Megan's chin, gently tilting her head back, and then began to apply the lipstick with focused precision. Megan tried not to shiver as Scarlett held her face perfectly still, her attention locked onto Megan's lips. When she finished, they held that pose, and desire flared up in Megan like a flashover. She wanted to lean forward and ruin that perfect lipstick against Scarlett's berry-red mouth.

Scarlett stepped back hastily, like she could read Megan's mind. "There." She fumbled the cap back onto the lipstick. "That looks great."

The effect was striking. Megan's mouth looked so full and lush, like a ripe fruit. She looked like she'd been kissing someone instead of just imagining it.

"Hang on to it," Scarlett told her, handing over the lipstick. "To reapply."

They went to a little barbecue place not far from the hotel so they wouldn't have to walk far to get to the Opry. Conversation was mostly about food and music, light topics, and the tension underneath Megan's skin had nothing to do with the conversation but about all the things they weren't saying. She knew she was still upset with Scarlett, but the reasons for that anger felt more nebulous the farther into this trip they went. By the time they were seated at the show, it was hard to latch onto anything but her own excitement and the aching desire now settling into her bones like it had always been there. Maybe it had.

Then, the big red curtain went up, and Megan's focus shifted to something far more immediate and transporting.

When the first performer began singing, Megan's breath left her. Why didn't she go see more live music? Why didn't she do this all the time?

"She's incredible," Scarlett said breathlessly when the first song was done and the audience applauded. "And she's the opener."

"I've never seen anything like this." This place felt holy, even with the riotous applause and the loud music, the experience resonating in Megan's body was like when she used to go to church concerts as a little kid with her grandmother and feel the music shake her down to the core. Tears filled her eyes, even though the songs weren't sad. She wanted to hold Scarlett's hand. She wanted to dissolve in this music. She wanted to lose herself and never find herself again.

By the time the show finished, hours later, Megan was wrung-out and exhilarated. Her emotions bounced all over the place, and she struggled to hold the camera steady to photograph the big guitar in front of the building. As she watched the image develop, Scarlett asked her how she was doing. She ended up shaking her head, struggling to articulate her feelings. "I...never get to hear music like that. It's so consuming. It's the way music should be." Being here, listening to people who had devoted their lives to this art, evoked a longing inside Megan like a tangible ache. At the same time, she felt transported and transcendent.

"You gonna be okay?" Scarlett asked, nudging her.

"Yes? And no. That was amazing." Megan felt giddy. "I can't go back to the hotel and sleep right now."

"Good." Scarlett pointed down the street. "There's a bar a few blocks over doing karaoke, and we're going. All right?"

Megan nodded, still a little dizzy, and tucked the photo carefully into an envelope in her pocket. She wouldn't say no to anything right now. "All right."

★ ★ ★

Ah, damn, Megan was drunk. Okay, it wasn't like it was an actual surprise; she'd planned on getting drunk the moment Scarlett had mentioned karaoke. Maybe, if she was honest, she had planned on getting drunk ever since the morning when she'd realized she was going to have to deal with her feelings for Scarlett and whatever weird form they were taking. Maybe knowing they were coming to Nashville was enough of a reason. But even if all those things hadn't been true, they'd gone to a bar, she'd sung some songs, and she'd had several very strong drinks. Bar snacks hadn't done much for absorbing the alcohol, and even with a few waters in her, she was going to feel it in the morning.

But right now? Right now, the judgmental side of her brain was blissfully quiet, and it had warmed up enough that the night was pleasantly cool rather than bone-chillingly cold, and she and Scarlett were walking very close together down a sidewalk toward a beautiful and well-lit park. They kept bumping against each other as they walked, and Megan wanted to grab Scarlett's arm to steady herself, and so she did. She didn't stop herself from giggling. She didn't blame it all away on the alcohol, either, even though Scarlett would probably think that's what it was.

"Are you even drunk?" Megan looked up at Scarlett, who was only an inch or so taller but sometimes felt larger than life, and tried to tell from her eyes. Ha! Like she'd be able to tell in her own inebriated state. Scarlett's gentle smile indicated that she was thinking just such a thing.

"I wouldn't drive, that's for sure. But I don't think I'm as drunk as you." Scarlett gave her a little nudge with her elbow.

"I don't get drunk that much. It's nice." Megan's smile felt lazy. The dichotomy in her body warranted further investigation; on one hand, she was alert and alive, all her nerve endings firing like she was hyperaware of her senses and her surroundings. But on the other hand, she was sleepy, slow, lazy, not worried about anything. "What about you? Do you drink a lot?"

"Not anymore." Scarlett looked like she had thoughts about that, and Megan didn't want her to stay quiet. They'd reached the park, and they stopped beneath a streetlight, not willing to sit but still lingering.

"You did but you don't much anymore. Tell me." Megan faced Scarlett and took both of her hands. They should really get gloves. Her hands were freezing.

Scarlett looked at their hands together like she didn't know what to make of them, her brow furrowing. She stared without speaking for a long time before looking back into Megan's eyes. "All right. You want some honesty? Here you go. I drank a lot while I lived in New York. It got to be a shortcut for relaxing. I was first drinking with people, then I was drinking alone. One night I woke up passed out in a subway station with no memory of how I got there, so I stopped drinking."

Megan felt a trickle of soberness return to her, the icy realization of truth pushing a bit of her fog away. "I'm sorry. Do you... Should you have done it tonight?"

Scarlett smiled gently. "It's fine. I'm not an alcoholic. I can drink in moderation. I just needed to get it out of my system to get some new habits. Now I have new habits, and if I drink, it's okay."

"I don't do anything fun, Scarlett." The words were tumbling out before Megan could stop them. She even slurred a few, and god, maybe she was too far gone for this. Scarlett might not even think she was in her right mind. "I don't. I work and I come home and I don't do anything. I don't go anywhere. I fuck people and I don't let myself open up to them. I put everybody else first and I don't know how to do anything different. My whole life is shit."

Scarlett's laugh broke the quiet of the night.

"Don't make fun of me!" Megan pulled her hands back.

"No, you just don't swear a lot. It's sweet."

Megan was annoyed by that, too. "Don't call me sweet! It's patronizing." It took her two tries to get through the word patronizing.

Scarlett was still smiling, but apologetically now. "I'm not making fun of you. I like it." She paused like she was going to say, "I like you," but she didn't. She bit her lip instead. That full, plump lip, that Megan wanted to feel against hers.

Megan surged forward in a clumsy, impulsive movement, leaning up, reaching for Scarlett's upper arms to get some leverage as she attempted to kiss her. She needed to do this fast, before she thought too much of it, and the adrenaline pulsed through her body and urged her onward.

"Whoa! Easy." Scarlett easily ducked back, holding a hand out to push Megan away. It was a definite push, a definite refusal. She wasn't smiling anymore. Her eyes looked wary and she didn't want Megan to kiss her. Oh, fuck, she didn't want Megan to kiss her.

Megan felt her whole face burn up with embarrassment. Wasn't this okay? "I don't—" she began, but she didn't know what to finish that with. "Like last night. It doesn't have to mean anything."

"Not like this." Scarlett's tone, gentle and soft, was nearly worse than her refusal. "Not when you don't know what you want."

Hot tears welled up in Megan's eyes, the shame of being rejected bubbling up through her and burning her skin. "Let's just go back."

Chapter Ten

Scarlett wished she'd slept better as they loaded up the car the next morning. For how drunk Megan had seemed last night, she'd woken up without a hint of a hangover, but that didn't mean she was chipper. Scarlett had taken steps to prevent her own hangover, like aspirin and a lot of water, but still felt tired as they finished packing the car and grabbed breakfast at the utilitarian breakfast place attached to their hotel. Megan was a person of few words as she ate her meal, avoiding eye contact and making small talk only about the decor in the restaurant. But she apparently wasn't going to bring up trying to kiss Scarlett, and they couldn't spend ten hours in a car together today without clearing the air at least a little.

"Do you want to talk about last night?" Scarlett asked.

Megan froze, then shook her head, her eyes locked on the glass of orange juice in front of her. "It's fine. I shouldn't have done it. I was hoping we could forget it ever happened."

"I don't need to forget it ever happened, but maybe we could talk about what you want?" Scarlett tried to keep her tone gentle, because Megan looked like she was going to bolt. "You haven't done a lot of talking about that."

Megan stared down at her juice, then drank more of it. "Can't we just forget it and move on?"

Forgetting it would mean it never happening again. Scarlett wasn't sure that's what she wanted, either. "I thought you were still mad at me."

"I am."

"And yet the other night—" Scarlett began, but then the waitress came by to clear their plates and deliver the check, and she had to stop. When the waitress left again, Megan jumped in.

"I can get physical with somebody without it meaning anything." Megan finished her juice and set the glass down. "I thought we were both on the same page about that."

"It's not like I mind." Scarlett didn't mind at all. "But I'm not going to fool around with you if you're drunk."

"Okay. Got it." Megan looked at where the waitress had disappeared only moments earlier. "Why isn't she back yet?"

"Give her time. Look. Megan." Scarlett waited until Megan looked over at her. "There's nothing to be embarrassed about."

Megan snorted. "I don't want you to think I was only coming onto you because I was drunk."

Scarlett's heart skipped, a momentary hope flaring up inside her. Maybe Megan was going to forgive her. Or admit she had feelings. "Then why?"

"Because." Megan stared, and Scarlett held her breath waiting for the rest of this confession. Finally, Megan shrugged. "Sex is fun. Getting off is fun. I thought we'd broken the ice about that."

Oh. So this was just about getting off, then. Scarlett ignored her own twinge of disappointment. "Maybe when we're both sober."

The waitress came back then, though, and Megan signed her credit card receipt and then bolted for the car.

The GPS led them out to the highway, and Megan accelerated to a more aggressive speed as they headed along the road. Scarlett watched it happen for a little over a mile, and then finally cleared her throat. "Hey, so what's the matter?"

"What?" Megan asked, like she hadn't heard.

"Well, you're staring at the road like it wounded you, and you're going—" she leaned over to check the speedometer. "—seventy-five miles an hour."

"You go seventy-five when you're driving," Megan pointed out.

"And you barely go the speed limit. So that's how I know something's wrong." Scarlett folded her arms.

"Fine." Megan sat up straighter in her chair. "Truth or dare?"

Oh, so apparently they were playing this again. It wasn't exactly the best way to talk like adults, but at least it would make Megan talk.

"Truth."

"How many people have *you* slept with?" Megan asked.

It wasn't an unfair question, especially after she'd asked Megan the same thing, but she couldn't be sure of Megan's motives. It might not be curiosity. Still, she'd long since passed shame about her sexual history. "Fourteen." Scarlett looked back over at her. "Does that shock you?"

"Nope." Megan clicked the cruise control on and relaxed back. "Seems pretty normal for someone like you."

Scarlett's mouth fell open. "Excuse me?"

"Someone people want. Someone beautiful."

Megan said it so matter-of-fact, like she was stating the weather or the miles they still had left to go. Scarlett was left reeling, not because Megan saw her that way, but because it was clear Megan didn't see herself the same way at all.

"You don't see yourself as a catch, do you?"

"I know I'm smart." Megan's tone sounded cautious, but Scarlett couldn't hear deceit in her voice, only hesitation. "And I'm friendly, and I'm capable. I think I'm a good conversationalist. But I'm not *beautiful*. I'm not somebody that beautiful people want."

Oh. "Would you believe me if I told you that you're beautiful?"

Megan laughed, high-pitched and surprised. "No. I'd think you're just trying to convince me." She didn't look away from the road, but she held up her hand to stop Scarlett. "I don't need any 'everyone is beautiful' bullshit. I get that there are different tastes for everybody. But I'm not conventionally beautiful and I don't need to be. It's fine."

Scarlett's sudden flash of anger was surprising, along with weird feelings about the wrongness of everything Megan was saying. "I think most people aren't conventionally beautiful," she began.

Megan interrupted her immediately. "You are."

Scarlett stopped, heat creeping up her face. "I—I have my own issues. With my looks."

Megan looked across the car at her, really *looked* at her, before turning back to the road. "I don't know why. You look like somebody I'd see in a magazine."

She wasn't trying to compliment Scarlett, either. She sounded like she actually believed that. It was flattering, and also kind of fucked up. "Thanks. I don't see myself that way. I think a lot of us don't ourselves the way others do." There was a whole industry devoted to getting women like them to hate themselves, but that was a separate issue. "You're too hard on yourself. I could tell you everything that's attractive about you, but you probably wouldn't believe me. You're not hot in the sultry, magazine model way, but that doesn't mean you're not attractive."

Megan was quiet, tapping her thumbs on the steering wheel. Finally, she said, "Thanks," in a quiet voice.

"If the people you're sleeping with don't make you feel like they're the luckiest people in the world to get to have you, then fuck 'em." Scarlett shook her head. "I mean, *don't* fuck them. They don't deserve you."

Megan laughed, a bit of relief trickling out in the sound. "Okay."

Scarlett probably shouldn't add this, but she was talking before she could stop herself. "And if you're feeling restless again this trip, well, you're always welcome to relax with me."

Megan kept her gaze on the road. "... Thanks." Her tone was hard to decipher.

Silence fell, and the increasing awkwardness might just kill Scarlett if it continued. "You want to play more Truth or Dare?"

Megan hesitated. "Not really. I'm afraid of what's going to come out."

"Do you want to just talk some more?"

"What do you want to talk about?"

Might as well go back to basics. "Well, I'm starting to re-alize I don't know you as well as I thought. So...what's your favorite color? Is it still purple?"

Megan smiled a tiny bit. "It's still purple."

"Do you still hate horror movies?"

"Yes." Megan was starting to relax, her shoulders easing down from where they'd been up around her chin.

"Still get seasonal allergies?"

"These are some pretty crappy questions, you know." Megan was really relaxed now, though, and even laughed.

"Okay. So…" Scarlett didn't want to bring it up again, but the words came to her lips before she could stop them. "Are you ever going to forgive me for lying to you?"

Megan was quiet in response to that. Maybe that was all the answer Scarlett was going to get. Finally, she said, "I'm hurt that you didn't trust me."

Scarlett fiddled with the cuffs on her shirt. "I was embarrassed."

"You know, I always looked up to you. I thought you were so damn perfect." Megan wrapped her hands more tightly around the steering wheel. "It would have been nice to know you weren't."

"You wanted me to fail?"

"I wanted you to be human."

Silence again. Scarlett wanted to get defensive, but parts of Megan's accusation rang true in uncomfortable ways. She did always hide her vulnerabilities. To her friends, she was the one with everything put together, and even if her life was a mess, she would be an unstoppable force. "I'm sorry I didn't trust you. I didn't think you'd understand, because you've always been so good at school."

"Well, it doesn't seem to have done me any good now, right?" Megan snorted. "My life is a train wreck."

"You're moving forward, though." Scarlett waved a hand to the road in front of them. "Literally, at least."

That got a small smile out of Megan. "What am I supposed to do after this?"

"What about that podcast, or radio show? You said that's your dream. You could pursue it."

Megan made a noncommittal noise. "We'll see."

Another mile or so of quiet between them. Scarlett didn't want the quiet. She wanted conversation. She wanted something tangible to build on, something that they could construct in the quiet closed space of this car. "I want to be friends with you again. Can we do that?"

Megan's eyebrows went up. "I thought that's what we were doing."

"You keep going between casually friendly and politely neutral." And whatever she was the other night when she'd gotten off while Scarlett had breathlessly listened in the midst of her own pleasure. "I don't know where you stand."

Megan made a thoughtful noise. "Will you promise not to ghost me again? To actually stay and talk through whatever's hard, instead of running away or going silent?"

New York came to mind. "Running away is kind of my thing, you know."

"I know. That's why I ask." Megan looked pointedly across the center console at her before returning her gaze to the road. "I won't be friends with you if I can't trust you to be here when things are tough."

"Okay. And what about you?" Scarlett needed something in return for this. "Are you going to make fun of me for the places where I fall short?"

Megan frowned. "Sarcastic humor is kind of *my* thing."

"You can give me sarcastic humor, but not about being dumb, or flunking out of school." Scarlett's voice was steady, even if her innards trembled at that assertion.

Megan's eyebrows went up, and her lips formed a little O of surprise. "I wouldn't do that."

"You think I'm bulletproof, and I'm not. Not about those things." Scarlett wasn't bulletproof about anything, actually. "I think you think you can't hurt me, but you could."

Megan's gaze softened. "Okay. I promise."

Then it was Scarlett's turn. "I promise not to run away."

It felt like a vow, and Scarlett wasn't sure that she liked the similarities. They made her feel all unsettled inside.

"I now pronounce you friends," Megan said gravely, with a dead serious expression on her face. Scarlett broke out laughing, but something eased inside her chest. It wasn't everything; it wasn't dealing with whatever sexual tension seemed to ebb and flow between them. But it was something. It was a start.

Megan pulled up the collar of her new winter coat and tucked her face into the protective fleece-lined fabric, wind whipping past her skin as she gazed up at the Lincoln Memorial. The marble statue of the president himself stared out into the middle distance, larger than she had expected, looming over her and Scarlett as they stood at his feet.

"It's bigger than I thought." Scarlett had her coat collar pulled up over her chin as well, muffling her words.

Megan laughed. "You've said that for all of them."

"They're all bigger than I thought." Scarlett shrugged.

Megan took her hands out of her pockets long enough to tug her hat down over her ears. Even with gloves on, she was happier with her hands tucked inside the fleece-lined jacket pockets than out in the wind. She was glad for the millionth time today that they'd started their DC visit by buying some proper winter layers. "I can't believe you've never been here."

"Why not? *You've* never been here."

"I've never been anywhere. You've at least travelled." It was easy to see Scarlett as worldly, with the experiences she'd had, but apparently there were a few gaps in her travel history.

"I haven't traveled all that much. It's only in comparison to you that I've seen a lot." Scarlett nodded up at the statue. "And I've never come to the National Mall. Never seen a reason to. But you've clearly got a reason."

"I think everybody should see the monuments."

"Patriotism and all that?"

Megan considered, staring again up at the bearded figure in

the giant marble chair. "I'm not really patriotic. I think maybe it's that sense of being part of things. Seeing them with my own eyes and not just in photographs."

"Except the photographs you take."

The irony made Megan smile, especially since she was already pulling out her camera. "That's different. That's to remember after I've already been somewhere." She sized up a photo of Lincoln, trying to get the inscription above his head in the shot as well.

The slight crinkle around Scarlett's eyes indicated her smile, even with her mouth covered. "It's neat to see it all. I wish we'd come in high school like every other school seems to."

"I wish I'd done a lot of things in high school." Megan said it without much thought, the words slipping out unbidden. Not that it was untrue. She had put off so many things for so long. Even now, finally doing things she wanted just because she wanted to do them, her thoughts revolved heavily around what she had missed out on.

Scarlett shifted from foot to foot, and then turned to gaze out over the reflecting pool. "What's next?"

"This is the last stop." Megan wasn't sad about it, though; her feet ached from walking, and her cheeks were frozen with cold. It wasn't even that cold out, but being outside for most of the day had taken its toll. At least she'd gotten a good night's sleep in the hotel last night. After a long day of driving from Nashville, they'd both collapsed into their beds with no further innuendo about restlessness or its cure. Megan wasn't quite ready to let go of the possibility of fooling around with Scarlett, but the time hadn't been right…and maybe it wouldn't be again.

Scarlett pulled out the guidebook she'd taken from the hotel that morning, now curling up at the edges from being rolled and stuffed in her pocket all day. "You sure you don't want to hit any of the Smithsonian museums we missed?"

"We did Air and Space, and Natural History. Those were the two big ones I wanted to see." Megan could have gone through all of them, obviously, and spent a lot longer at each of the ones they did see, but this was a survey. Not a full trip. "We've got miles left to go before Canada."

The little trolley burger shop where they ended up for dinner had great reviews online, but Megan was skeptical until she started eating.

"This is fantastic." She sighed in happiness. "It's so nice to be warm."

"Didn't the layers help?"

"Yeah, that's why I'm not frozen to the steps of the National Mall." Megan could get used to the warmth of thermals, especially being outside in temperatures far below a typical Florida day. "But it's not the same as being warm inside."

The food was amazing, and as she finished the last of her fries, Megan settled into a contentedness that only good food after a long day of walking outside could allow. She could ignore whatever physical tensions had arisen between her and Scarlett, and just enjoy their rekindled friendship. Any complicating factors were just because of her own newness to having a friendship with Scarlett again, and the forced proximity of their time together.

Scarlett had an odd expression on her face by the time Megan stopped her train of thought and brought it back to the table where they were eating. "What?" Megan asked.

Scarlett glanced at the clock on the wall. "It's a little after six. How are you feeling?"

What was this about? "I'm a little tired, but I'm okay." Megan was getting to recognize Scarlett's expression as one that led them into mischief. "Why do you ask?"

"If we left now, we could be in Manhattan by midnight. Or earlier. It's only four hours."

Four hours of driving, now, when she was tired…but then to be in New York City *tonight*. They hadn't gotten a hotel for tonight yet, deciding to play their DC plans by ear and find something afterward if need be. "Where will we stay tonight?"

"I could find us something in Manhattan. Some place with a parking garage." Scarlett was already pulling out her phone and typing. "It won't be cheap, but I know it's one of the stops you're most excited about. We could get there tonight." She held up her phone to Megan, showing her a list of hotels on some booking app. "Look. I could book something for us right now."

"Are you just saying this for me?" Scarlett was being really selfless, if she was willing to drive another four hours just to get Megan to the city earlier than they'd considered.

Scarlett's eager expression shifted to something more hesitant, and she turned aside, biting the inside of her cheek. "I think you'd really like the city. I got excited to show it to you. And I kind of miss it. I haven't been back since I moved away."

Megan wasn't going to say no to that. "Then let's do it."

After the traffic of DC, the highway rolled out ahead like blissful relief, and Megan's tension eased away as they drove north in the growing darkness. Scarlett seemed in good spirits, too, humming quietly to herself in the stillness of the car as she steered them north. Maybe Megan could get some of the answers she'd been hoping for.

"Hey, Scarlett?"

Scarlett made a noise.

"Why'd you move to New York?"

Scarlett stayed focused on the road for a long moment, maybe trying to decide whether or not to answer. After all, she had very recently shut down this line of questioning altogether.

"I ran away."

Megan waited, but Scarlett didn't elaborate. "I think if you're twenty-three, it's just called moving," Megan said.

Scarlett smiled, thin and without teeth. "My life sort of went to shit all at once: I got laid off from my retail job, my roommate told me she wasn't renewing the lease, and I discovered that my new boyfriend was actually married. So I ran away. I answered a Craigslist ad for a sublet in Queens, sight unseen, threw all my stuff in a U-Haul, and moved to New York."

Megan looked down at where Scarlett's arm lay on the center armrest, inches away from her own. She wanted to touch her, itched to press her hand to Scarlett's and squeeze. Swallowing, she put her hands in her lap. "What did you do for work?"

"Anything I could. I tried waiting tables, but I was really bad at it. Couldn't do the barista thing, either. Ended up doing third shift loading cargo for a trucking company." She smiled. "I think the boss just felt bad for me, because I was bad at that, too. Anyway, I kept it up for a while, but it wasn't like I was happy or anything. The city was great, but it wasn't for me. Eventually my mom called and convinced me to move back home."

Megan had always liked Scarlett's mom, who was young and kind and endlessly patient. "I'm glad you did."

Scarlett smiled, a little bigger, a little more relaxed. "Yeah, me, too."

"Why didn't you tell me this story before?" It was unfortunate, but it wasn't like Scarlett had done something terrible.

"It's one more dumb Scarlett thing. An impulsive, rash decision that turns out to be a terrible idea." Scarlett sighed. "I feel like my whole life is a string of terrible ideas brought on by being too impulsive."

"I could use some of that impulsiveness." Megan seldom did anything without a pro/con chart. "I've become boring."

Scarlett snorted, surprising Megan into looking over. "You're not boring," Scarlett said. "You're methodical, yeah, but not *boring*."

"It's been less than a week since you said I lived a beige life."

Scarlett shrugged one shoulder. "So, I was wrong. I've learned a little more about you since then. Like, you take beautiful photographs and put them in beautiful pages in your scrapbook. And you're terrible at snowball fights."

"You fight dirty!" Megan objected, but Scarlett just kept going.

"I've learned that you're a real asshole when you haven't eaten, and you like paper maps better than the GPS. And you name your mix CDs."

"None of these are particularly not-beige things," Megan said.

Scarlett looked over at her, eyes twinkling. "Okay. You want the not-beige things? I've learned you sing like a professional, and everybody in that karaoke bar wanted to go to bed with you." As Megan tried to object, Scarlett talked over her. "Also!" She reached across the space to press a finger to Megan's lips. "Also! I've learned that you've slept with eight people and aren't at all as straight as I thought you were."

Scarlett's finger pressed into the soft skin of Megan's lips, and Megan's heart began to race. When she opened her mouth again to speak, Scarlett's finger brushed the soft pad of her inner lip, and Megan had to resist the urge to chase that fingertip with her tongue. Adrenaline seared through her. "And," Megan said, speaking before she could let herself think, "you know what I sound like when I come."

Scarlett pulled her hand back, her gaze snapping over to Megan, and then smiled an absolutely filthy smile. "That's not very beige at all, is it?"

Megan's skin felt tight and hot. "No, it isn't."

Scarlett made a thoughtful noise, a low "hmm" that went right to Megan's clit. "You know, a little impulsiveness is good for the soul, now and then."

"I suppose." Megan licked her lips and wished they were Scarlett's.

"Truth or dare?"

Megan pressed her hands into her thighs. "You wanna do this now?"

"If I weren't driving, I'd do a lot of things right now." Scarlett's grin was wide, teasing, tempting, and Megan knew they were crossing into uncharted territory.

Right now, Megan would do nearly anything. "Dare," she said.

"Take off your bra."

Megan tried to laugh, but it was hard to breathe in this car. "Just the bra?"

"That's up to you."

Megan would normally never do something like this, but it was dark out, and she was feeling reckless, and so she pulled her sweater and shirt off all in one smooth, fluid motion. Scarlett's gaze stayed fixed on the road ahead, but her lips parted slightly, giving Megan a surge of satisfaction. If this was some kind of game of chicken, if Scarlett was expecting her to wimp out, Megan wasn't going to do it. But she needed a moment to get her bearings, sitting here beside Scarlett nearly topless.

"You need help?" Scarlett asked.

"You're gonna help from over there?"

"Sure." Without another word, Scarlett reached behind Megan and flicked the clasp of her bra open with one deft hand.

Megan let the bra slide down her arms, onto her lap, and she was sitting there naked from the waist up. The cold air brushed across her skin like a phantom touch, and it might have been that air or the tension that hardened her nipples into sensitive peaks. "Truth or dare?" she asked, forcing her voice to stay steady.

Scarlett exhaled shakily. "Okay. You win. I take it back. If you don't put your shirt back on, I'm gonna drive off the road."

Chapter Eleven

Scarlett knew she'd have memories rolling back into New York City, but the moment they crossed over the bridge into Manhattan, some neurons in her brain lit up like a fireworks display. It had been almost three years since she'd been here, but the memories flooded back so fast it stole her breath.

"You all right?" Megan asked from the passenger seat, watching Scarlett in that intense way she'd developed during this trip. Or maybe she'd always looked at Scarlett like that, and Scarlett had just never noticed it.

She'd done the whole stretch of driving from DC, which had given her something to focus on other than thoughts of Megan's round, perfect breasts, their peaks seemingly begging to be nibbled and kissed. For the whole first part of the drive, she'd been gripping the steering wheel with intent just to keep from reaching across the space between them and touching everything she wanted to touch. Now, though, with Manhattan spreading out around them like a dazzling tapestry of light, she could think about something other than Megan: the traffic, the one-way streets, the GPS guiding them to their hotel in midtown. Normally, Scarlett would have tried to find something cheaper, maybe down in the financial district or way up in Washington Heights, but midtown would make it easy for sightseeing. Less easy, however, for driving.

There were a few benefits to arriving near midnight, though, and one was the way the traffic had eased from totally horrific to just terrible. She never drove in the city when she lived here, only on the rarest of occasions, and only a few blocks reminded her of why that was the case.

Megan, though, was rapt. She had her face nearly pressed to the windows, gaping at all the lights, trying to see up to the top of the skyscrapers. "This is nuts," she breathed once, quietly but loud enough for Scarlett to hear, and her face was all alight.

Their hotel had a parking garage next door, and they got checked into a room on the tenth floor. "I can't believe there are fifteen floors of this hotel." Megan threw open the gauzy curtains and stared out at the city. "I've never stayed in a hotel with more than two floors before."

"That's not a New York thing. That's a cheap motel thing." Scarlett smiled anyway, flopping down on her back on the bed closest to the door. She'd take the murder bed, *again*, so Megan could look out the window. Megan had taken off her backpack, but she was still fully clothed and wearing her shoes, like she was ready to run outside even though it was nearly midnight and they'd been driving for four hours *after* walking around DC in the cold all day. She looked wide awake, breathless with happiness, her eyes sparkling in the reflected light from outside.

Scarlett didn't even have to think hard to make up her mind. "You know, we could go out if you wanted."

"What, now?" Megan bit her lip, but her eyes betrayed her eagerness even as she frowned. "It's late."

"This is the city that never sleeps, though." Scarlett forced herself to get up, because if she stayed in bed, she was going to fall asleep. "Or it can wait until tomorrow if you're still tired."

Megan hesitated. "I want to shower."

"Me, too. We can go out after."

"You really don't mind going out late?"

That was enough of an answer. Scarlett smiled. "Go hop in the shower. We'll head out after."

They were only a few blocks from Times Square, so they walked. Megan carried her instant camera tucked into a pocket but hadn't yet taken any photos, instead staring all around in endless wonder. Even at this hour, there was a crowd, a fact Megan commented on immediately. Scarlett took Megan's hand so she wouldn't lose her.

They stopped next to the "same day tickets" booth at the center of everything, and Megan turned in a slow circle to take it all in. "What do you think?" Scarlett gave her a gentle nudge, speaking loud enough to be heard over the noise. "Everything you expected?"

Megan nodded, her smile as bright as these neon billboards. It was enough for Scarlett to watch Megan instead of Times Square. She'd seen the billboards, spent enough time pressing through crowds to last a lifetime. Now, she'd walk through all those crowds again to see Megan this happy.

Eventually, Megan sighed and turned that thousand-watt smile to Scarlett. "You must be so bored of this after living here."

"It's all right." Scarlett didn't need to tell her that all New Yorkers avoided Times Square except with visitors they really liked.

She didn't have to say anything, though, because Megan saw through it. "You hate it."

"It's *all right*." This time, Scarlett had to laugh. "It's all right because you're here. I'm glad you like it."

Megan pulled her camera out of her pocket and looked down at it, then up at all the lights. "None of these pictures are going to come out, are they?"

"I don't know. You're the photographer."

"I hardly think this qualifies me as a photographer." Megan held up the little instant camera and made a face. "But I think everything will get washed out. This doesn't have any manual settings."

"So take one and see. You've got a ton of film in your bag."

Megan snapped a shot of the billboards and then frowned down at the image as it slowly developed. Scarlett could kiss her. She could kiss those sweet, soft lips, currently downturned in a worried expression, feel the cold of Megan's nose press into her cheek, lose herself in the warmth of her mouth. She wanted to know what Megan tasted like, wanted to feel the sweet press of her mouth and the way her body moved against Scarlett's when their tongues tangled together.

"It's no good."

The words snapped Scarlett out of her daydream, and for a minute, she thought Megan had read her mind. "What?"

Megan held up the photo, with its distorted colors and too-bright, blurred billboards. "The shot. It's no good."

"Sort of artsy, though, right?" Scarlett squinted down at it. The blur could look purposeful.

Megan hesitated, then her expression brightened. "Back up."

"What?"

Instead, Megan backed up. "Never mind. Stay right there." She held the camera up and looked through the viewfinder.

"What are you doing?"

"Look up and to the right. Look at that billboard." Megan

waved her hand vaguely toward where she wanted Scarlett to look, but she was already lining up the shot. Scarlett did as she was asked, staring up at a billboard advertising some movie she didn't care anything about, until Megan called her over.

They watched the shot develop, and then there was Scarlett, lit by the red glow of some advertisement nearby, smiling off at something unseen. The photo was beautiful. Scarlett didn't normally like pictures of herself, but Megan had captured something unique in that shot.

"I like this one." Megan slipped it and the camera back into her pocket.

"But you don't have any of the actual Times Square!"

"This is enough." She looked up at Scarlett, and something in Scarlett's chest plummeted with need and longing and anxiety all in one bundle. Again, she looked down at Megan's mouth, and they were so close. It would be so easy to lean down and kiss her. Megan must have known it. She stayed in place, her lips parting softly, eyes widening almost imperceptibly. But neither of them moved.

And then a taxi honked nearby, they both jumped, and the moment was gone.

Scarlett felt dizzy and breathless, like she'd just run up several flights of stairs. "Do you...do you want to get some cheesecake?"

Megan checked the time. "It's after midnight."

"So? Junior's is open late."

Megan smiled and nodded, and it wasn't a kiss, but it was something else, something sweet. Something Scarlett could reasonably handle without getting in way over her head.

Two in the morning was a time ripe with the potential for bad decisions, and yet knowing that did not stop Megan from standing all too close to Scarlett on the elevator back to their room. She could blame it on sleepiness, but it wasn't sleepiness. Her whole body tingled with excitement and adrenaline and the overtired manic energy that softened all the edges of her vision and made the world seem beautiful and unreal.

"You okay?" Scarlett gave her a nudge, and Megan jolted out of her daydream to see the elevator doors open and Scarlett holding them open with her foot. "Too much cheesecake?"

"The perfect amount of cheesecake." Megan preceded Scarlett out of the elevator and down the hallway to their room. She fumbled the door key card once before letting them in, and immediately went back to the window to look out at the city, leaving the room lights off.

Behind her, Scarlett chuckled. "You should get some sleep. We've only got the room for one night."

"But I got us late checkout." Megan was grateful she'd had the foresight to ask at the front desk. "We can sleep in."

"You don't sleep in."

"I *might*." Megan turned her back to the window, looking in at the room and the way the lights of the city reflected off the metal fixtures gleaming on different surfaces. "I don't know if I can sleep at all."

Scarlett sat down on her bed. She was not as relaxed as Megan, holding herself tense throughout her shoulders and back. The dim light from outside cast her into shadows. "Too much excitement for one day."

"Is it, though? What's wrong with too much excitement?" Megan walked forward, her legs carrying her a few steps toward Scarlett without her making the conscious decision to move them. She knew what she was doing. She'd known since the car, even if she hadn't wanted to read too much into her own desires. This was something chemical, something physical, and she had to deal with it or she would burn up from the inside out. "What if I want more excitement instead?"

Scarlett's expression changed. Her eyes brightened, first, and she licked her lips, a quick flicker of tongue that made Megan's knees wobble. Then, though, Scarlett frowned, and she bit her lip, a tiny crease appearing between her brows.

And because it was two in the morning, and they'd driven across several states and nothing felt real, all Megan's inhibitions had retreated to the back of her brain and were, blissfully, silent. "I'm a little restless." Megan's legs weren't even trembling anymore, and she began to unfasten her jeans with Scarlett's eyes fixed upon her. "What about you?"

Scarlett audibly sucked in a breath as Megan undressed in front of her. "Yeah. Definitely—definitely restless. Getting, um. More restless."

Taking the lead in this moment made Megan smile. How seldom Scarlett was flustered. She wanted to slide her fingers into Scarlett's hair and cup the side of her face, wanted to kiss her. But she couldn't be sure she'd stay detached with Scarlett the way she was with her other partners. She couldn't be sure she wouldn't lose herself and end up hurt again. In this, at least, she could have some control. Scarlett's attention as she undressed made her body feel like it was on fire.

How strange for her mind to be quiet in all this, to not be analyzing or assessing everything alongside the slow reveal of her skin, especially with Scarlett's gaze roaming across her body. Was it just days ago she'd hesitated at the thought of this kind of vulnerability? It felt like a different person, a different world, like she had been dreaming. Or maybe she was dreaming now.

In the half-light, Megan climbed onto her bed in front of the window and lay back on top of the covers. Scarlett still sat on her own bed, watching Megan, her lips parted and chest rising and falling rapidly. Megan slid her hand down her body, over its planes and angles, through the tight curls at the juncture of her thighs, down to the wet folds around her clit. Scarlett sighed, nearly a moan, never looking away. Scarlett kept watching the entire time she stripped off her own clothes until she was sitting naked on the other bed, still watching, her breath loud in the quiet of the room.

Megan had been watched in moments like this before, but it never felt like she was going to catch fire. She'd never felt so *seen*. Looking away seemed impossible, especially as Scarlett dipped her hand between her own legs.

"Fuck." Megan breathed, the word slipping out of her lips at the sight. They watched each other, fingers moving over their own bodies, the moment frozen and unreal and captivating.

Megan didn't even realize she was coming until her body seized up, stealing her breath, pleasure rocketing through her like a force of nature. Her eyes slammed shut in reflex, and distantly, Scarlett moaned. It went on far longer than she'd expected, the feelings too sharp and consuming, the kind of orgasm that wipes away everything. When she finished, she collapsed back and opened her eyes. Scarlett was frozen, head back, thighs clamped tightly around her own fingers, mouth open in a silent scream. She was *beautiful*.

Scarlett sagged, her hand falling away from her body. She took a deep, shuddering breath, and looked at Megan. They stared silently at each other as if trying to figure out what to say. Megan's throat was too tight for words, the tangle of emotions too much to parse.

Scarlett finally gave a delicate half-smile. "I'm less restless now."

Megan laughed, all her breath escaping at once. "Yeah. Me, too."

She could lie here and look at Scarlett all night, and that was dangerous and too much like something else she didn't want to name. So instead, she got up and started rummaging around in her bag for clothes. "I should sleep. I'm exhausted."

"Right... Right." Scarlett also rolled off the bed and disappeared into the bathroom.

Away from Scarlett, Megan could catch her breath. She pulled a nightgown down over her head and sat back down on the bed. The room smelled like sex, like their bodies, an intoxicating combination. In a few minutes, she'd go brush her teeth, and then crawl between those sheets and sleep. In the morning, maybe she'd be ashamed, or worried. For right now, though, all she felt was content.

Maybe that should worry her most of all.

"Where are you taking me?"

Scarlett waved off Megan's request and checked her phone again. "It's just another half a block. I promise you. Best bagels in the city."

"All the bagels are probably great." Megan trailed after her, not quite able to keep up when Scarlett was moving at full city-walking speed. So far this morning, Megan hadn't said anything about last night, but she also hadn't been awkward or weird about it. In the grand balance of things, Scarlett would consider that a win. She'd fully expected awkward, weird Megan, full of regrets and excuses. Instead, she had this chill, friendly person, who didn't seem to think what they'd done last night was at all significant or life changing.

Not that it was either of those things. It was just sex—not even sex, not really—and it didn't have to be any kind of significant. Scarlett smiled bitterly to herself. She could only lie to herself for so long. She never had emotionless sex, never fooled around with anyone she didn't then fall for to some degree. That's just who she was; she got attached and stayed attached, and she got hurt. That was life. And if she kept fooling around with Megan, or near Megan, or whatever it was they were doing, eventually she would get hurt.

The bagels were as phenomenal as Scarlett had remembered, and Megan grudgingly admitted it was worth the long walk in the cold. "So where now?" Megan asked, leaning back in her chair and sipping her tea.

"I was going to take you on Scarlett's patented landmarks tour, where you can see the Chrysler Building, the Empire State Building, and the New York Public Library." Scarlett ticked off the items on the list. "Then, Battery Park to ride on the Staten Island Ferry and see the Statue of Liberty. Chelsea Market for lunch. That's as far as I've gotten."

Megan sipped her tea. "Sex shop?"

Scarlett nearly spilled her coffee. "What?"

"Can we go to a sex shop?"

Scarlett stared. Megan was going to keep surprising her, wasn't she? Scarlett regrouped quickly. "You want to go to a sex shop."

"Yeah. It's New York. There are some good ones." Megan shrugged. "Unless it makes you uncomfortable."

"No, I just…it's not something I've ever done."

"What?" Now it was Megan's turn to look shocked. "Really?"

"I don't have any of that." Well, that wasn't entirely true. "An old girlfriend of mine got me a toy once, but I didn't really like it." Somehow, Scarlett felt embarrassed admitting that. How the tables had turned.

Megan's mouth fell open. "You're missing out. Oh my god. We've got to go now. There's a really well-respected one down in Soho, from what I read. Maybe we can go there at some point today?"

If Megan was going to take her to a sex shop, there was no way Scarlett would say no.

Megan was an eager audience to all of Scarlett's New York facts and figures, some of which she was pretty sure she was getting wrong, but Megan listened attentively anyway and didn't question her. By the time they got onto the ferry, Scarlett was happy to sit down, and Megan was still bright-eyed and excited. When they got within view of the Statue of Liberty, Megan raced out onto the freezing cold deck to take a photo, leaving Scarlett in the warm interior of the ferry without dragging her along. Megan was happy, and Scarlett was getting addicted to seeing Megan happy.

"Do you know," Megan said, coming back in from the cold red-cheeked and windblown, "that this is the first ferry ride I've ever taken?"

"Another first." Scarlett stretched her arm out along the back of the hard plastic seats.

They watched the tiny photograph develop, the statue resolving from a blur to a crisper-edged figure against a light blue sky. From this close, Scarlett could smell the clean scent of Megan's hair, and she leaned in a bit to inhale more.

Fuck, she was in trouble.

Getting taken to a New York sex shop by Megan wasn't as much of a distraction from her attraction as Scarlett had hoped. The brightly colored toys on nearly every surface didn't seem to faze her a bit. She left Scarlett standing in the middle of the large, well-lit space and wandered over to the wall to turn on one of the display models of something, holding it with easy familiarity.

Scarlett made her way to Megan's side after assuring one of the friendly salespeople that she was fine and no, did not need any help.

"But you probably do need help, right?" Megan watched the clerk walk away. "Why'd you send them away?"

"I don't know if I need help. And I don't really want to answer questions." Scarlett thrust her hands into her pockets.

Megan looked her up and down and gave a cheeky smile. "Are you shy? Is this making you uncomfortable?"

"*No.*" Scarlett emphasized the word. "I told you, I just haven't done something like this before. And what about you? What stores like this have you been going into in Florida?"

Megan set down the vibrator she was holding and moved on to a medium-sized dildo, which she turned over in her hand absent-mindedly. "There was this shop near the college that I went to a few times when I didn't want to deal with mail order. Nothing as nice as this, though." She happily surveyed the space around them like it was a damn flower shop, still holding the dildo. "So what do you want to get?"

"I don't need anything." Scarlett still had her hands in her pockets.

"Come on. You've gotta get something, right? This is the best sex shop you're going to see in a while." Megan set the dildo back down on its plinth. "You want a recommendation?"

Scarlett's face was already warm and growing warmer. What the hell. "Sure. Hit me."

Megan smirked, turning purposefully toward a display of paddles. "You sure?"

Scarlett winced. "Okay, poor choice of words."

Megan smiled, tapping her lips with one fingertip, and then immediately led her over to a display at the end of the wall. "One of these." She waved her hand at the display. "They all do kind of the same thing."

Scarlett picked one up and frowned, turning it over in her hand. There was a small round silicone nozzle at one end of the oval-shaped plastic body. "What do you do with this?"

"It sucks your clit."

Scarlett raised her eyebrows. "What?"

"Yeah. This nozzle right here, it fits over your clit. And then it sucks it. I mean, it blows air over it. Sort of feels the same." Megan was grinning, clearly enjoying every minute of this. "Life changing."

The world of sex toys was definitely a lot different than when Scarlett had last gotten that mediocre vibrator from a former lover. She turned this miraculous device over in her hand and turned it on, then pressed it to her palm, the little jets of air tapping against the skin like a delicate finger. Yeah, that would definitely feel good. The price on the box was... ouch, more than she was planning to spend, but her curiosity won out.

And maybe Megan would want to watch her use it sometime.

Scarlett looked up from the box and spotted Megan a few feet down the row, examining a collection of dildos. The unashamed, meticulous focus with which she scanned the rows shouldn't have been sexy, but damn, it was. Megan wearing a harness wasn't something Scarlett had ever thought about much, even in the fantasies that she kept quietly hidden back in high school, but seeing her gripping a curvy silicone cock was enough to get Scarlett's blood pumping.

Megan looked up and caught her eye, and Scarlett hastily looked back to the task at hand. Out of her peripheral vision, she could see Megan smiling.

Were they headed toward something more...physical together? Last night was different than two friends quietly ignoring the other's midnight dalliances. Last night felt like a tease, like a promise, like extended foreplay, but Scarlett couldn't get her hopes up that it was anything other than just a way of "curing restlessness." Hoping for things had never worked out very well for her. Instead, she was better off living in the moment, taking life the way it came, keeping her head down and busting ass to pay bills. She wasn't a planner like Megan, or smart like Megan. Whatever courage she had was tempered by the unfortunate side effects of being fairly impulsive. And now? Now, she had a fun, teasing encounter with Megan that was enjoyable for both of them, and it maybe wouldn't be repeated.

Megan interrupted that line of thought by showing up with a dildo in one hand and a harness in the other. "You ready to check out?"

Scarlett stared. "What are those?"

Megan looked down at what she was carrying. "It's obvious, isn't it? Thought I'd get some things to round out my collection. I won't be able to find good quality stuff like this as easily back home." She gestured at the box Scarlett was holding. "What about you?"

Scarlett held up the box with the too-expensive clit sucker toy in it. "I'm taking your recommendation."

"Good! I think you'll like it." Megan gave her a broad smile before walking over to the register, leaving Scarlett unsure what the hell was going on.

Chapter Twelve

Megan had expected to fall in love with some of the places on her trip, but she nearly cried as they drove out of New York. Well, first, she almost cried with fear a few times watching Scarlett weave in and out of traffic trying to get them out of Manhattan, but then after that, her only feelings focused on the loss of the city and all the adventures they *hadn't* had. Scarlett had been the one to push about heading north that night, rather than spending another night in the expensive midtown hotel, and Megan had reluctantly agreed. After all, there might be more things to do, but even if they stayed another night, Megan would still be reluctant to leave. They had eaten some of the best food of her life that day, too, and she could probably spend a year in New York just eating, but they had more road tripping to do.

Maybe she could convince Scarlett to stop in New York on the way home, too.

The way home. She hadn't given much thought to the fact that they had a whole return trip ahead of them. In her mind, everything ended in Quebec and the world beyond that was a vague uncertainty that she'd been steadily ignoring. The wedding was creeping up on them, though, and she should probably think about the after…but that could wait. For after. Her mental gymnastics made her smile, even if it was a bit of a self-deprecating smile.

"What?"

Scarlett's question brought Megan out of her reverie, and she blinked. They were steadily heading north in light traffic. "What?" Megan asked.

"You looked like you were smiling about something."

"Just thinking." Megan could have been smiling about a lot of things. "It's been a good day."

Scarlett's shoulders relaxed. "It has, hasn't it?" She returned Megan's smile.

Megan had been worried that last night would change things between them, but it didn't have to. It was just mutual masturbation. Rubbing one out. Whatever euphemisms she might use. The fact that Megan wanted *more, more, more* was about her overactive hormones, nothing else. Sure, so she had a bit of a crush on Scarlett. Long before she even knew she wasn't straight, and therefore didn't know it was a crush, she'd had a tiny crush on Scarlett. Maybe that's why she had been so pissed off, all those years ago.

"So this is Connecticut." Megan looked out at the darkness surrounding the car. "It's pretty much the same as all the others."

"That's only because it's dark." Scarlett sat up like she was giving a lecture to a room of students. "Connecticut is a very small, pretty state. And they all drive like maniacs."

"You drive like a maniac." Megan gestured at the dashboard. Without traffic, Scarlett had accelerated up to over seventy-five miles per hour again.

"Because I'm in Connecticut." Scarlett gave her a knowing look and turned her attention back to the road.

Megan smiled. Lots of Scarlett's comments were making her smile today, even the dumb ones that would have probably made her roll her eyes a week ago. This tolerance must be some side effect of being stuck in a car together.

The unquenchable hormones were another side effect.

A few more songs in the CD later, Scarlett broke the conversational silence. "I'm sorry we had to leave New York so quickly. I know you were having a good time."

"Just me?"

"Yeah, me, too. But this trip is much more about you than about me." Scarlett shrugged. "If I wanted to, I could come up and go to New York anytime."

Imagine just picking up and driving across the country *without* several weeks notice. It boggled Megan's mind. "You'd do that?"

Scarlett snorted. "Well. Clearly not, or I'd have done it. But it's more about not wanting to go back to New York than not wanting to travel spontaneously."

"But you had a good time on this visit." It wasn't a question. Megan needed to confirm, to hear that Scarlett wasn't having a miserable time just for her.

The smile Scarlett gave her back was crooked, affectionate. "Yeah, I had a good time. Turns out it's different coming to visit when you aren't running away from a bad breakup and drunk off your ass."

Megan twisted her fingers together in her lap. "Have you had a lot of bad breakups?"

Scarlett made a motion with her shoulders that wasn't quite a shrug. "Hasn't everybody?"

"I haven't." Megan's breakups had all been pretty amicable.

Scarlett looked over, giving Megan an appraising look, before turning back to the road. "Well, you're lucky, then."

"I don't get attached."

Scarlett snorted. "Then you're doubly lucky."

Megan wasn't sure why she felt like she should apologize for never having had bad breakups, like it was a sign of something bad. "Anything recent?"

"A recent breakup, but not a bad one. Pretty mutual. I was seeing this girl Gwen for a while, but we broke up after New Year's. We were just bad for each other, and I think we always knew that." Scarlett sighed. "Sometimes you hold on to something bad, just because being alone seems too scary."

Megan played with the CD case, flicking the zipper back and forth. "I think I'm more likely to stay alone because the alternative seems too scary."

"What, being in a relationship?" Scarlett glanced her way. "What's scary about that?"

"Getting hurt. Getting left behind. Letting somebody in, and then they leave you." Megan hadn't known Scarlett was dating someone so recently, someone who hadn't been good for her but who she probably missed. "Were you in love with her?"

"Who, Gwen?" Scarlett tipped her head to the side. "I don't know. Probably. I seem to fall in love with everybody."

Megan's stomach twisted. "You're kidding."

"Nah. I fall easy and fast. It's not like I'm the one-true-love kind of person. Or nobody's been that for me. But to say I haven't been in love with all of them?" Scarlett frowned. "That feels like it's unfair to me. And them."

Megan tried to wrap her mind around that. Falling in love so easily, without any kind of commitment in return. And then ending things. "How do you keep your heart from breaking?"

Scarlett rested her head back, giving a sad smile to the windshield in front of her. "It breaks all the time. I mend it up and keep going."

Megan turned to look at Scarlett, her beautiful light brown curls pulled up into a messy bun, the loose clothes she'd put on in the hotel bathroom for the drive, the tanned skin still gleaming even without makeup. "That's the worst plan I've ever heard."

Scarlett burst out laughing. "What?"

"Break your heart over and over again and keep going? That's horrible! You should stop doing that." Megan knew this was ridiculous advice, but she couldn't help it.

"You're sweet." Scarlett reached over to squeeze her hand. "But trust me. Not everything is as easy as a friendly wank in a New York hotel. Feelings get involved, and then hearts get broken. It's normal." She put her head back and started to sing, loudly, and not entirely on key. "'It's the CIIIIIIIIRCLE of LIIIIIIIIIFE...'"

Megan waved her hand frantically. "That's enough of that." Scarlett may find all of this funny, but the disquiet settling into Megan's stomach was real. "If you fall in love with everyone you date—"

"Well, not *everyone*," Scarlett interrupted. "I was exaggerating. And sometimes I fall in love with people I'm not dating. But go on."

"If you fall in love with *almost* everyone you date, and people you aren't even dating, how do you expect to have any relationship last?"

Scarlett pursed her lips. "It's about choice. Eventually, if I find someone who wants to be with me, and I want to be with them, I'll choose to be with them."

"What if you fall in love with someone else?"

"That doesn't matter. Because I won't choose to be with them."

It sounded way too complicated for Megan, and she said so, making Scarlett laugh. Then Scarlett turned the music up, and passed some other Connecticut driver, and Megan watched the dance of headlights outside as they headed north to their next stop: Salem.

They'd warned the Witch Way motel in Salem that they

wouldn't be arriving until after midnight, but there wasn't even a front desk clerk when they arrived. Instead, a little envelope with Megan's name waited on the front desk. In it were two room keys and a note to check in officially the next day.

"Seems like they trust people," Scarlett said, letting them into their room at the end of the upstairs hall.

"I can't do these late nights forever." Megan tossed her bag onto the floor and collapsed down onto one of the beds. "It's past my bedtime," she said, words muffled into the comforter.

The bed dipped as Scarlett sat down next to her. "That isn't what you said last night."

Megan rolled over onto her side to look up at Scarlett, who was grinning. "Last night was different. Tonight, I need a good night's sleep." She wouldn't be opposed to more of that some other time, but it couldn't be now, no matter how her body responded to Scarlett's proximity.

Scarlett still studied her, though, not getting up off the bed. "Do you want to stay in Salem an extra night instead of making the push to Quebec?"

Megan mentally started doing the extra math. "That gives us less time in Quebec before the wedding."

"We could see about moving our hotel reservation and stay a few days after the wedding instead." Scarlett shrugged one shoulder. "We've been doing a lot of late-night drives. If we try to make it all the way to Quebec tomorrow night, I think we'll be exhausted."

The idea of *not* driving anywhere tomorrow was enticing. Megan nodded. "Let's call the Château Frontenac tomorrow and see what they say."

Scarlett had never been to Salem, but even if she had, it would probably have felt like the first time again when looking at it through Megan's eyes. "It's probably even better in October,"

Scarlett said as they walked down a cobblestone street between shops, Megan's glance darting from window to window.

"This is fine. No crowds." And truly, there was barely anyone in the town at all, just a few pedestrians to contend with. They'd slept in, successfully called and moved their Quebec reservation, and had a quick breakfast before hitting the downtown area, where Megan wasted no time finding all the "witchy" shops. They were the kind of tourist trap places that clearly thrived in a place like this, and Scarlett was having a hard time not being cynical about their authenticity, but Megan seemed delighted by it all. Finally, after the second witchy bookshop, Megan stopped and addressed her directly. "You don't have to come with me, you know."

Heat rose up in Scarlett's face. "It's fine. I'm having a good time."

"No, you're not. You think all this is dumb."

"A little, maybe." Self-conscious, Scarlett scuffed her toe on the step. "But it's still fun."

"I agree. You don't have to believe in it for it to be fun."

"Do you believe in it?"

"What, witchcraft? Wicca? All of that?"

Hearing her say the word like that made Scarlett feel silly for asking. "Sure."

Megan shrugged one shoulder. "I don't know. I know people practice it as a religion. I know there are things in the world I don't understand. This might be just one of those things. And the possibility is interesting." She tucked her hands into her pockets. "I like possibilities."

This whole trip was nothing but possibilities. It was appealing to be optimistic rather than cynical for once. "I like possibilities, too."

The next shop was different than the rest: smaller, less decorated, situated on a less-populated side street rather than one of the main streets. In the window was a hand-lettered sign that read "Custom Spellwork done here." Scarlett had been expecting something dark and eerie from the look of it outside, but the shop itself was bright and cheerful. It was just small. The young woman behind the counter looked up from her book when they walked in. Scarlett tried to see what the book was, but it was leather-bound with no clear visible title. The clerk herself looked a few years older than them, maybe, with a streak of bright blue in her short black hair. She smiled warmly and adjusted the glasses on her nose. "Hi! You folks looking for anything special?"

Megan walked over to the desk. "Could you tell me what custom spellwork is?"

The woman leaned forward and rested her forearms on the counter. "Well, it depends on what you want it for. It could be some incense to burn, or a candle that's been engraved, or something to put under your pillow, all kinds of things. What are you interested in?"

Megan hesitated. She glanced toward Scarlett, who immediately knew she wasn't wanted in this conversation. A little stab of disappointed pressed inside her stomach, but she ignored it. "Why don't you talk it over, and I'll just go down the block?" Scarlett offered. "I'll go to a coffee shop or something. You can text me when you're done."

Megan's smile was filled with gratitude and relief. "Thanks."

"Give us a half hour," the clerk chirped, and Scarlett walked out despite the nagging temptation to eavesdrop.

The cold February air hit her as she walked out onto the street. She definitely didn't want to stay outside long. She could find a coffee shop, but Megan's words about possibilities made her want to try something else. A little door a half block down was advertising Tarot readings. That could be interesting. She opened the door and went in.

The shop was small, smaller than the others, with only room for a counter and a few displays of books for sale and some Tarot decks. The guy behind the counter was startlingly handsome, with a few strands of silver mixed in with his black hair, but a face that couldn't have been more than thirty or so. "Hi," he greeted. "Are you looking for a Tarot reading?"

"Maybe?" Scarlett wasn't about to say what she was thinking, which was that she'd been expecting an old woman with a lot of scarves. "Are you the one who does the readings?"

He smiled, his eyes crinkling at the edges, and maybe he was a little older than she'd thought. "You were probably expecting someone else, right?"

"Well, no, I mean... I just..." Scarlett floundered for words, but he just laughed and waved a hand.

"It's okay. I get that a lot. But it's really me. My name's Gaelen." His grin was infectious, knocking down all her defenses and concerns. "I promise, I'm an actual Tarot card reader."

"Is that a profession? Did you go to school for that?" She was flirting a little, maybe, but that was her default in new situations.

He folded his hands together. "Actually, I learned Tarot from my grandmother. My degree is in archaeology, but it turns out that it's really hard to get a job as an archaeologist these days. So, now I read Tarot in Salem. And word on the street is that I'm pretty good at it." He pulled a deck of cards out from below the counter, one that was worn around the edges, and held it up. "My rates are reasonable."

Scarlett wasn't going to be called back to meet with Megan for a while, so what did she have to lose, right? "What's the dollar amount on 'reasonable'?"

A few minutes later, she was sitting at a small table behind a curtain in the back of the shop, with Gaelen shuffling cards across from her. This was ridiculous, and she knew it, but she hadn't expected the way her cynicism and amusement melted away as he set the cards down in front of her and instructed her to cut the deck. She did, and Gaelen finished the cut and began to flip cards out in a spread like the ones she'd seen on the internet and movies. He studied the whole layout, and then smiled at her.

"Good news. You're not going to die tragically today."

He startled a laugh out of her. "Was that something I should have been worried about?"

"Nah, but I like to break the ice." He swept his hand across the cards, gesturing to the whole spread. "Some people use Tarot to tell the future, or at least anticipate future events, but I find it helpful to give people a reading of where they are now, and what is standing in their way of the dreams they want to achieve."

"Okay." The cards laid out before her were colorful, with striking images, but they didn't make any sense on their own. "You're going to explain that to me, then?"

"I am." Gaelen folded his hands, and his attention was on the cards as he spoke, tapping certain ones to indicate where he was getting his information. "This part here, it's the current situation: where you've come from, where you are, what you're facing. These cards indicate you've got a lot of missed opportunities in your past. You have run away from things instead of confronting them. And you're at a crossroads right now."

Scarlett wanted to jump in with a rude comment about everyone being at a crossroads of some kind, but she quelled her own inner defensiveness and let Gaelen speak. It was easier to look at the cards than at him, so she focused on those bright pictures. Maybe she could see her story in them.

"It's all starting here in the center. The card that represents you, is a card of someone fleeing or escaping. And the one on top of it, that's what you're up against right now. For you, it's this one." Gaelen held up a card with a tall stone tower being struck by lightning, people leaping from its windows.

"Great. I'm facing plummeting to my death?"

Gaelen smiled. "Not necessarily. The Tower is one of the Major Arcana cards. Those are the most significant in the whole deck. The Tower is change and upheaval. The lightning is the force of change, which isn't always pleasant or fun. What's on the other side is going to be different from what came before."

Discomfort settled on her skin like a prickly blanket. Sure, maybe everyone was at a crossroads in their lives at every point, but the giant burning tower was a hard sign to ignore. Was this about her career, or something else? "Okay. So what does that mean for me?"

Gaelen steepled his fingers. "Well, from what I can see on the table, you've spent your life avoiding and running from periods of major change like this. And now, you have to decide if you're going to run away from this one, or confront it."

Scarlett leaned back in her chair and folded her arms, needing the way it seemed to bar her from what lay on the table before her. "What does it mean to confront change? Change happens."

"I don't know what your situation is, specifically. I'm not a mind reader. I read the cards. This part of the spread here, this is the staff." He tapped the vertical column of four cards alongside the cross. "The staff is the context for your current situation: your hopes and dreams, your suggested actions, the possible outcomes, depending on how you confront these challenges."

"What do those say?" Scarlett leaned in, drawn in despite her attempts to pull away.

"Right now, in your spread, these four cards are all about relationships." Gaelen passed his hand across the whole staff. "Some of them are subjective, but it implies that your actions and outcomes are intertwined with the people in your life. That might also be your challenge. I don't know."

Scarlett focused on the card at the top of the staff, one of two people drinking together from matching goblets. "Is this about romance?"

"Usually, yes, but it can also be a deep intimate friendship." Gaelen looked up from the spread, hesitancy in his expression. "Does one of those explanations make more sense than another?"

Scarlett laughed. "If I knew that, lots of other things would be clear."

"Well, whichever it is, your outcome and path are not solitary." Gaelen shook his head slowly, scanning the cards. "You need people."

"Everybody needs people, Gaelen."

"And yet you run from them." He met her eyes, and the hesitancy was gone. "You can't run forever."

Scarlett tried to smile, but it felt twisted on her face. This wasn't fun anymore. With her heartbeat ratcheting up in her chest, she felt that familiar drive to escape, to flee. The irony of feeling it right now wasn't lost on her. "Gotta tell you, Gaelen, this is way less enjoyable than I was expecting."

"You shouldn't have expected it to be enjoyable." He smiled, though, softening his words. "But is it helpful?"

Scarlett stared at the cards. She could fill in the gaps. "I guess." Hearing her failings reflected so accurately by this stranger was unnerving, but also oddly liberating. Regardless of how much she might want to complicate her own dilemmas, they boiled down to this particular challenge: confront her feelings, and be vulnerable, or avoid and run away? "I don't like it, though."

"Lots of people don't." Gaelen smiled apologetically. "I think maybe I'd be more popular if I lied to people."

Scarlett laughed. "Turns out, that doesn't work out so well, either." She rubbed her jaw, staring down at the cards again.

Looking at the whole spread made her feel lighter. There it was. All the cards on the table, literally. "Is it weird that I feel better?"

Gaelen began gathering up the cards. "No. That's normal."

The cold air stole her breath as she walked out of the shop a few minutes later, a paper shopping bag dangling from her fingertips. The sky seemed grayer. There was no snow on the ground, but a look of snow about the air; she remembered the gray tinge to the sky and the smell of snow from her time living in New York. Come to think of it, she hadn't checked the weather at all in a few days. Was it supposed to snow?

She was just pulling out her phone to check when Megan's text came through, saying she was done. Tucking her phone back in her pocket, she headed back to the little witchy shop.

Megan smiled as Scarlett entered, holding her own purchase in a similar paper bag. "What'd you get?" Megan asked, gesturing to Scarlett's bag.

"Tarot deck." Scarlett held it up. "You?"

"Hand-carved candle." Megan looked bright-eyed and happy. She'd been happy like that a lot lately, on this trip. It made Scarlett want to kiss her, and she resisted the desire by stepping back away. She fumbled her phone to check the time.

"We should go if you want to catch the show at the museum." Scarlett nodded to the door, and then they were on their way, and she could put these feelings aside. There were still many miles to go, and big emotional confessions were not a great idea for long car rides. She could ignore these feelings as long as she needed.

The cards in her bag pulled on her fingertips. Maybe she couldn't ignore her feelings forever.

Megan's candle was on her mind all day. She still wasn't sure how much of all this she believed. Liz, the woman working at the witchy shop, had been a completely non-judgmental listener as Megan unloaded all her complicated feelings. It had started with a few questions, and then Megan was pouring out all her history as Liz listened. Liz had suggested an engraved candle for direction and clarity, and Megan had agreed. For the next half hour, Liz had carved a tall orange candle while Megan had continued to brain dump about her dilemmas, her fears, her uncertainties. Now, sitting in a small restaurant in Salem, she couldn't quite remember everything she'd said to Liz, but the candle sat beside her waiting to be burned, a physical manifestation of...something.

"You okay?" Scarlett interrupted her reverie, and Megan came back to herself with a start.

"What? Yeah, I'm fine." She turned her attention back to the menu spread out in front of her, again looking but not really seeing. The candle weighed on her mind like she hadn't expected. Liz had told her that once she started burning it, she should burn it every night, keeping it lit each time until the top was entirely melted, and to be open to whatever form direction and clarity might take. She hadn't expected to feel this connected to a simple hunk of wax, and maybe that was a sign that she wasn't sleeping enough or something. It took all her focused attention to choose something to eat and then order it when the server came by.

Scarlett started frowning at her phone when the server left. "We're making the last leg of the trip tomorrow, right?"

"Right." It was a six-plus-hour drive, first up through the scenic white mountains, then over the border into Canada, and finally the last few hours to Old Quebec.

Scarlett made a face. "How do you feel about moving that up a bit?"

"What?" Megan was looking forward to another good

night's sleep in the hotel. "What do you mean, move it up a bit? We just moved it back a day to get some sleep."

Scarlett turned her phone around. The image on the screen was an image of mottled blues and purples superimposed on a map of the northeast. "Is that snow?" Megan asked.

"Yeah. That's for tomorrow."

"When tomorrow?"

Scarlett looked back at her screen. "Afternoon, it looks like."

With a six-hour drive, if they left early enough, they should be able to cross the border and be in Quebec before the worst of the snow was falling. And she'd just gotten new tires for her car, so she should be fine, right? The mechanic had told her that with front wheel drive, she shouldn't have any problems if they ran into snow. "Let's leave really early, then."

Scarlett nodded. "I'm really not up for doing that drive to-night."

"Plus, we've already paid for the second night at the hotel here. I don't want to pay twice." This was a good decision. They'd get up early, get on the road before the snow, and cross into Canada in the morning. With any luck, they'd be in Quebec by lunchtime.

"I like this plan." Scarlett put her phone away. "You ready to see your first new country?"

The border crossing felt like the culmination of their trip, even though they were planning to spend some time in Que-bec. Once they crossed into Canada, things would change. They'd be heading for the wedding, turning their attention to Juliet, and getting a break from the car. Megan wouldn't mind getting out of the car, even if it meant the end of her one-on-one time with Scarlett.

"Ready."

Chapter Thirteen

Scarlett did not like this sky. She couldn't stop looking up as they loaded the car, at the sunrise turning the horizon bright red despite the gathering clouds. *"Red sky at morning, sailors take warning."* She'd known the rhyme since childhood, spoken often by her grandfather, a commercial fisherman off the Florida coast. He swore by those rhymes, and he would have told her that these weren't skies for easy fishing. But they weren't in Florida, they were driving north out of Salem, Massachusetts, and the snow was already starting to sift lightly out of those gray-washed clouds.

"I thought you said it was supposed to start in the afternoon." Megan frowned out the window at the skies, eating a muffin from the hotel's sparse continental breakfast spread that had been even sparser at six in the morning. "It looks like it's starting now."

"I see that." Just what they needed. Megan talked the previous night about how she was pretty sure her car would be all right in the snow, but front wheel drive or not, Scarlett wasn't excited about driving through a blizzard. At least it wasn't supposed to be a full blizzard. A squall, probably, maybe a few inches, and they'd probably keep the roads clear. They were on a highway the whole way. The state department had to prioritize clearing the highways, right?

Megan had been pretty quiet since last night overall. Now, with Megan staring out the window, Scarlett had to physically grip the steering wheel with both hands to keep one hand from drifting over to rest on Megan's thigh. Anything to touch her. Anything to keep this physical contact.

"So we'll be in Quebec by the end of the day," Scarlett said, breaking the silence. "It's the end of the trip."

"Well, the end of the first half." Megan laced her fingers together in her lap. "We've still got to drive all the way home."

That was true. "Do you still want to drive straight home directly? Anything we missed on the way up that you want to do on the way back?"

Megan opened her mouth, then paused, a few expressions flickering over her face. "I wouldn't mind going back to New York. It's on the way." She looked down at her hands. "You're probably going to want to get back to your normal life soon."

Scarlett snorted. Like she had anything resembling a normal life. "Easier said than done. I have no idea what things are going to look like when I get back."

Silence. Scarlett kept replaying her conversation with Gaelen; she was at a crossroads, and the way she responded to that could either be like she'd always done—running away—or something totally different. She could interpret that any number of ways, but this lifestyle of eking out a meager existence from piecemeal data entry jobs and gigs was not going to sustain her forever. "What about you?" she asked, needing to not think about her own situation for a few minutes. "What's on the docket for you when you get back?"

Megan shrugged. Her gaze had drifted to the window again, watching the snow that was now falling steadily. "I haven't thought past this trip. Matt will be moving out, and I don't know about anything else. I don't have a job. I guess I have to get one." She didn't sound too pleased, and before Scarlett could suggest a different topic, added, "I don't want to talk about after."

"Okay." Scarlett understood. This world of the car and the open road had become its own haven, a separate existence from reality. She was none too keen to return to reality, either. When Megan started digging around in her album of CDs for another selection, relief replaced her anxiety. They didn't have to talk about what came after. They could live in the now.

After about three hours, though, the "now" had become a lot snowier. Scarlett looked back at the GPS, which had continued adjusting their time of arrival based on road conditions, the hours moving later and later in the day.

"How are you doing?" Megan asked, concern dotting her brows. "How are the roads?"

The roads were shit, but Scarlett didn't want to worry her. "I just have to pay attention." The car wanted to slide everywhere on the untreated slickness, especially now that they were rolling through the white mountains of New Hampshire. At this elevation, the snow was steady and heavy and terrifying. Scarlett just wanted to get through it.

"Do you want me to drive?" Megan's frown indicated that she didn't think it was a good idea, either.

Scarlett resisted the impulse to laugh. "No thanks. I've got it. Once we're out of the mountains it should be better."

It wasn't. After another two hours, they had crossed over from New Hampshire into Vermont, crawling north on I-91, as driving had become downright treacherous. She'd long since turned off the music to concentrate better. She didn't feel safer going more than thirty, and the entire highway was crawling along with the few people dumb enough not to have gotten off the roads already. People like them. The way she saw it, they had a few options. Megan could drive, and they would likely end up off the road in minutes. Scarlett hadn't driven a *lot* in the snow, but Megan had *never* driven in the snow, and northern Vermont wasn't the place she wanted to teach her. Another option was to press on, but Scarlett was probably going to have a nervous breakdown before they arrived, especially as the GPS kept moving their arrival time later and later.

The third option was to find some place to stay and wait for the storm to blow over.

"Megan, do you have cell service?"

Megan pulled out her phone. "For now. It's been going in and out."

"I think we should find a place to stop for the night."

Megan's shoulders relaxed. "Good. Me, too. You want me to look for something online?"

"Yeah. Maybe somewhere with some food." Scarlett had been checking the exit signs and not seeing a lot.

The car fell silent again, and Megan's attention stayed focused on her phone for what felt like a really long time. "Well?" Scarlett asked, after about ten minutes of silence.

"There's a couple of options. There's a Holiday Inn, an EconoLodge, and if we get off at exit 26, we're not too far from a ski resort."

At least a ski resort would be prepared to weather a snow storm. "Ski resort. Give them a call, will you?"

Megan made an irritated noise. "I just lost cell service."

Shit. "Well, pull out those maps. Let's see if we can get there analog-style."

"What do you mean, no vacancy?" Scarlett leaned heavily on the reception desk at the ski resort lodge, looking at a very apologetic reception clerk who was frantically typing into his computer. "How can you possibly be sold out in this snow-storm?"

"I'm so sorry, miss. It's a busy week anyway, with school vacation, and a lot of people booked when they heard about this storm." He looked like he expected Scarlett to hit him, and the way she was leaning forward with her wild hair and the visible stress of a lot of snowstorm driving, Megan was pretty sure she understood the fear.

"It's school vacation? Who has a vacation in February?" Megan hadn't been in school for a while, but weren't those spring breaks in March or April?

"Most schools in the Northeast, actually." He continued typing on the keys as he spoke. "I'm reaching out to all the overflow lodges and inns in the area, and it looks like there's a room available at one of them just a bit down the road from us. It's less than a mile, and there's even a shuttle bus from there to this lodge if you want to go skiing. Is that okay?" His eyes pleaded for them to say yes.

Scarlett was already nodding, but she glanced back to make sure Megan was in agreement. "That good by you?"

"How much is the rate?" Megan asked.

The amount he quoted wasn't nearly as high as Megan expected. "What's the catch?" Scarlett asked. "That's not bad at all."

The clerk shook his head, scanning his computer screen. "It's their standard rate. I don't know. The reviews online are good if you want to read them."

Scarlett waved her hand. "After driving through that storm, I'd be willing to sleep in your lobby."

"Technically, miss, that would be against the rules of our lodge—" he began, but Megan jumped in.

"Just please, can you have them reserve the room for us? We'll be right there."

Thank goodness it was only a half mile down the road from the resort, because even that half mile was treacherous. Megan could feel the car slipping, no matter how much Scarlett said the roads "weren't that bad," and she could tell from the way Scarlett sagged in relief that she was happy when they finally pulled into the parking lot. "This place is cute," Megan observed, peering out at the little stand-alone lodge building. It was way too small for what she had expected, though. "Where's the rest of it?"

"I think...there?" Scarlett pointed past the building at a bunch of A-frame stand-alone cabins. All of them had lights on in the windows except one. "I think those are the rooms."

Megan frowned. "I always wanted to try camping, but this isn't exactly what I had in mind."

"Well, I'm not sleeping in the car. Let's go." Scarlett opened the door and stepped out into the driving snow without waiting for Megan.

After filling out some paperwork at the front desk and receiving an entire folder of instructions to go through, Megan followed Scarlett up the snow-covered path to the one non-illuminated A-frame cabin in the bunch. At least they were bigger than Megan had at first thought. They had looked like glorified tents, but now that she was standing next to one, they were definitely a good fifteen feet tall at the peak. Scarlett jimmied the frozen lock and then pushed into a little foyer for them to take off their snowy layers. They pulled off snow-covered shoes and jackets before finally getting inside and finding a light switch.

Megan leaned back against the closed front door and scanned the entire space. It wasn't large, but it was completely open except for one door to their right that led to the bathroom. They were standing in a tiny eat-in kitchenette, and past that was a living room with a couch and armchair, both facing a woodstove that had a giant pile of wood stacked alongside in an iron rack along the wall. The entire back wall of the cabin was made up of huge, floor-to-ceiling windows, overlooking a forest and then, past that, the ski mountain. Megan walked over to those windows in her stockinged feet, looking out at the snow glimmering in the dim light.

Except something was missing. "Where's the bedroom?" Megan asked, turning, but Scarlett was already pointing to the staircase running along one wall up to a loft.

"Can we figure this out first?" Scarlett pointed to the woodstove. "I'm going to freeze to death."

Megan started leafing through the paperwork from the front desk for the woodstove instructions. It was the second sheet in the packet, and she scanned it. "This doesn't look that complicated."

Scarlett held up her hands. "I'll help if you want, but you and I both know that you're way more mechanically inclined than I am."

She wasn't wrong. Megan knelt down at the front of the iron beast and began to follow the step-by-step instructions. Scarlett's gaze stayed on her, resting like a physical touch on the side of her face, and Megan kept struggling not to lose her place as she lit some newspaper and tucked it between the logs like the instructions said. Within a few minutes, the woodstove was aflame, and she closed the door, making sure all the other levers matched the diagram.

"I'm impressed." Scarlett folded her arms and nodded. "You look like you know what you're doing."

Megan held up the sheet of instructions. "It's all written down here."

"But still. You were always the more competent of the two of us. Building things, fixing things, getting through school, all of it." Scarlett went over to the windows and looked out.

She always said things like that, tossing out disparaging remarks about herself and then moving on like nothing happened. Megan hadn't fully come up with a response before Scarlett added, "It's really coming down out there. You think somebody will bring us a pizza?"

Megan laughed. "Probably not, but we could get delivery from the restaurant at the ski resort. The info pack says they'll walk to any of the surrounding inns, and we're on the list."

Although Megan had been hoping to be in Quebec that night, eating ribs from the barbecue restaurant in front of a woodstove was a pretty good second choice. The snow was still falling heavily outside, with no signs of letting up, and Megan was perfectly happy to finish her meal in relative warmth and comfort while the storm continued outside. At least the Château Frontenac had been gracious with their changing the reservation again, and had told them that the snow had affected a lot of people's arrival plans.

"It's really something." Scarlett returned to the window to look outside once their dinner dishes had been cleared away. "There has to be half a foot out there already."

"You think it's that much?"

"Got to be. That lump out there was a bench, I'm pretty sure."

"Have you checked the weather yet?" Megan had been too preoccupied with food to do any internet sleuthing once they'd gotten settled, and now that she was curled up in the armchair, she didn't want to get her phone across the room.

Scarlett pulled out her phone and settled into the couch. "Good thing this place has Wi-Fi, because there are zero bars of cell service." She frowned at the screen, which reflected a blue glow back at her face. "Fuck."

That wasn't a good sign. "What?"

"Local weather has this continuing for two more days."

Megan's stomach dropped. "What do you mean, two more days?"

"I mean, two more days. It's supposed to stop on Friday. They're calling it a ten-year storm or something." Scarlett flopped her head back onto the back of the couch. "What a nightmare."

Megan was quickly doing math. "The wedding's on Saturday. We can still make it, right? If the snow stops Friday?"

"I mean, yeah, if they dig us out in time." Scarlett grimaced. "Do you even have a snow broom?"

She didn't. "We can borrow someone's."

"Sure." Scarlett's expression indicated she didn't think that was likely. "At least we won't starve. We've got snacks, and the cabinets are stocked with some dry goods. Plus we've got the restaurant."

It wasn't ideal, but being snowed in anywhere wasn't ideal. Megan tried to think on the bright side. "It's not a bad spot to be stuck."

"No, I guess you're right." Scarlett looked around them. "Close quarters, though."

The idea of being stuck in this small cabin with Scarlett for a few days didn't inspire frustration as much as it inspired a bunch of other emotions. They'd fooled around together, and it was fun. It wouldn't be the worst thing in the world to do it again, right?

Before she could suggest anything, though, Scarlett got abruptly to her feet. "I'm gonna take a shower. Let me know if this place has any board games or anything to do when I get out."

With Scarlett in the shower, Megan took time to fully explore the small cabin. She'd peeked up into the loft earlier, but now she climbed the stairs all the way and checked out the one bed. Of course it would be only one bed, with their luck. Maybe she could sleep on the couch. Or maybe Scarlett would volunteer. The cabin was warm, at least, so they wouldn't get cold…

Megan swallowed. She definitely wouldn't get cold in bed with Scarlett.

Fuck, what was she even doing? She shouldn't get mixed up with Scarlett, not when she couldn't be sure that her feelings for Scarlett were purely platonic. What if she got too attached? She didn't want her heart broken like Scarlett's apparently always was.

Megan went back downstairs, treading carefully on the smooth wooden steps, her heart beating far too quickly. The bookcase did have a few old board games and a puzzle, but those weren't going to keep her distracted from what she actually wanted.

What *did* she actually want?

Megan pulled her candle out of its bag and held it, examining the way the intricate carvings shone through the tall glass jar in which it was set. All those carvings had meaning. She hadn't lit it yet. She'd been planning to wait until she got home, but she wanted direction and clarity, right? She wanted answers. While stuck here in this cabin for the next few days, she might as well take advantage of all the resources available to her.

When Scarlett emerged from the shower a little while later, Megan was sitting on the couch with the candle on the coffee table in front of her, the orange wax just beginning to gather around the edges of the flame. Scarlett wore a pair of pajama pants and an oversized sweatshirt, and she was towel-drying her wet hair. "Is that your candle?"

"Yeah." Megan looked back down at it. Suddenly, she wasn't ready to be in the same room as Scarlett again yet. "Can you watch it? I'm gonna take a shower. Don't blow it out."

"You don't have to, like, sit with it or anything?"

Megan smiled. "No. It just needs to burn. I lit it, and that's enough, apparently."

"Right." Scarlett's attention was rapt on the flickering flame, and Megan could look at that intent expression on her face forever.

She gathered up her clothes and quickly went into the bathroom before she did something stupid.

Chapter Fourteen

Scarlett was going to do something stupid. She and Megan were here together in this tiny cabin for at least a couple of days, and there wasn't going to be much to do, and so there wasn't a good reason *not* to sleep together.

Well. Actually. There were *several* good reasons not to sleep together. While Megan was finishing up in the shower, Scarlett made the list to herself. One: Megan didn't actually want a relationship with Scarlett. Megan might be used to emotionless sex, but Scarlett wasn't emotionless about anything. One of them was going to get their heart broken, and it was probably Scarlett. After all, they'd gone from a seven-year fight to whatever fragile friendship rekindling in a week, and continuing to have sex would ruin it. She should make that item two. She amended the list in her head. Two: continued sex could ruin their fragile friendship. Three: they still had several days to go in this cabin, plus their time in Quebec, *plus* the entire drive back to Florida, and sleeping together was going to set a precedent that would surely muddy the waters between them.

Four…there had to be an item four, right? Scarlett couldn't think of one, but the top three were really strong. She should listen to those.

Her body, though, wanted to do something stupid. That desire rekindled when she climbed up to the loft and saw the one bed they were going to have to share. It wasn't a large, spacious king bed where each of them could have her own space and not have to touch. This was barely a queen, probably more like a double, and Megan was going to be so close to her that all that soft, sweet-smelling skin would be inches away.

She should sleep on the sofa.

Scarlett went back downstairs and stretched out on that sofa, facing those big windows, trying to get comfortable. The couch was lumpy. They hadn't exactly put the nicest features in this building. Frowning, she shifted onto her side, and a spring poked right into her hip. No, that wouldn't do. Maybe she could put a blanket underneath her for softness? When she tried, it muffled the springs a bit, but she couldn't imagine sleeping here.

The better solution was to share that bed with Megan, and keep her damn hands to herself.

Megan came out of the bathroom in some fuzzy socks and a nightshirt that grazed her knees. Had she always been this cute, or was this another case of Scarlett's hormones getting the better of her? She'd attributed their one-night dalliance in New York to experimentation and a platonic educational experience, but there was nothing platonic about the surge of hormones running through her body. Megan wasn't even wearing anything sexy. Something about her wet hair and her innocent vulnerability juxtaposed with the sex toy maven Scarlett had witnessed made all of Scarlett's buttons go off.

"Did you see a hair dryer in any of those cabinets?" Megan asked, running her fingers through those wet locks.

Scarlett shook her head. "I didn't look. I don't usually blow dry mine." Her curls were finally starting to dry in the heat from the woodstove.

Megan took her brush and a pillow and sat in front of the woodstove to brush her hair. "I feel like a Jane Austen character, brushing my hair by the fire." Her smile beamed up at Scarlett, who was very glad she was sitting several feet away on the couch so she didn't lean in and kiss that smile. "Although I think they probably brushed each other's hair."

"I'll brush your hair," Scarlett offered before she could stop herself. Shit, what a terrible idea. Worse still was when Megan held out her brush, and so Scarlett *had* to go sit behind her in front of the fire, *had* to move close enough that her knees brushed Megan's hips. Megan's hair was perfectly straight, unlike her own curly, unruly tresses, and it glided through the brush effortlessly. "My hair would never submit to being brushed like this. I'd have a poof like a poodle at the end of it."

"It feels nice," Megan said softly. In the reflection on the back windows, Scarlett could see her eyes were closed. She tried to focus on the rhythm of the brushing, the methodical, rhythmic movement, and not on the way Megan's shoulders relaxed as she leaned into the touch like a cat. The woodstove cast overwhelming heat on her right side as she worked, mirroring the heat running through her body. She was going to combust. She wanted to drag Megan back by a handful of that hair, stretch her out on the floor, kiss her like she couldn't get enough. Instead, she brushed her silky brown hair and tried to think of anything else.

Megan pulled away before her hair was all the way dry, scooting an inch farther from Scarlett. "I think I'm going to fall asleep on the floor if you keep doing that." She took the brush, and her face was pink, probably from the heat of the fire. "There's only one bed. I can sleep here on the couch if you want."

"It's a lumpy couch. I don't think you'd be comfortable." Scarlett swallowed. "I can share if you can share."

Megan averted her eyes. She was still that same rosy color of pink, all over her face and down the curve of her neck. "Sure. That's fine."

The orange candle still burned on the table, a pool of melted wax gathered on its surface. Megan walked over to inspect it, nodded once, and then blew it out.

It was *not* a very big bed. Scarlett had estimated it to be small, but she hadn't appreciated *how* small until Megan climbed in on the other side and pressed right up against her. Megan's laugh sounded breathless. "Not a lot of room in here."

"Right." Scarlett was normally a side sleeper anyway, so she rolled away from Megan and tried to take up as little of the available space as she could. Every time Megan moved, she brushed against Scarlett's back, and Scarlett's heart sped up for a moment before settling down. They lay there, back to back, frozen in stillness, until Megan sighed loudly.

"This is ridiculous."

Scarlett opened her eyes. "What's ridiculous?"

"Trying not to touch you. The bed's barely big enough for both of us."

More shifting behind Scarlett, and then Megan curled up all along her back, slotting into place like spoons in a drawer. Scarlett's breath caught. Megan's arm snaked over her side, then curled up toward her chest, nestling right beneath the swell of her breast.

Scarlett could think of this as just a practical move, just making good use of the space, if it weren't for Megan's breathing. Like a clear tell in a poker game, Megan's breath was coming rapidly, brushing Scarlett's neck in shallow puffs, and her fingers twitched below the curve of Scarlett's breast.

Yup. Scarlett was going to do something stupid.

"It's okay," Scarlett breathed, barely a whisper into the silence.

Megan's hand slid up to cup her breast.

The touch ignited the rest of Scarlett's resolve and burned it away in a moment. One light brush of Megan's palm over the peak of Scarlett's nipple, even through her shirt, and Scarlett's hips twitched. "This is a terrible idea," Megan said, echoing all the thoughts Scarlett had carefully cultivated throughout the evening, a list that was even now going up in smoke.

"Do you want to stop?" Scarlett asked.

"No."

Thank God.

Scarlett rolled over into Megan's arms and pinned her down to the bed, covering her mouth and kissing her hard. Megan always seemed so frail and delicate, but she wasn't, and she arched up to kiss Scarlett back with the same ferocity. They both wanted this. They both wanted this, and they should stop and talk about what it meant, but Scarlett had no intention of doing what she *should* do. She wanted to kiss, and touch, and lose herself in this moment, and explore every inch of Megan's body.

Megan pulled on Scarlett's top, lifting the hem, and the next moments passed in a flurry of undressing. Scarlett nipped the ridge of Megan's collarbone, making her arch up, and then held her hips down with her free arm while she did it again. Megan made a desperate noise, wriggling beneath the touch, like even just this much was enough to drive her mad.

"Tell me what you want." Scarlett kissed lower, down to the valley between Megan's breasts.

Megan moaned, sliding fingers into Scarlett's wavy hair. "I want to fuck you."

Scarlett hadn't expected that at all, and she froze, her lips barely brushing Megan's tender skin. "What?"

Megan tugged Scarlett's hair, gently, just enough to get her to lift her head. In the dim light, her eyes were sparkling, pupils wide with desire. "I want to fuck you. Please."

Not a lot of things made Scarlett blush in bed, but the heat traveled up her spine and scalp and her whole body jumped a few degrees. "Okay."

Megan slid out of bed and rummaged around in her bag while Scarlett propped herself up on her elbows to watch as Megan got her harness and the new dildo she'd purchased. She also had a bottle of lube that Scarlett did not remember seeing her buy. Maybe she brought it with her.

Scarlett's blush was not going away anytime soon.

"Have you done this before?" She'd seen Megan buy the strap-on, sure, but she somehow hadn't thought Megan had had *experience* in this arena. Between this and her extensive knowledge of sex toys, Megan was turning out to be more of a surprise than Scarlett had imagined.

Megan nodded. "A couple of times." Now that Scarlett's eyes were adjusted to the light, she could see how pink Megan's cheeks were. She was blushing, too, and it was an enticing sight alongside the dark straps of the harness against her peach skin and the thick, curved jut of her silicone cock. "What about you?"

Scarlett shook her head. "Nope. With girls, I've always been more of the...you know." She waved a hand. "The equipment I'm born with."

"You don't mind this?" Megan rested her hand gently on the cock, fingers lightly curling around it like it was part of her body.

Mind? Scarlett had to laugh, because she was already filing these images away, planning to replay them endlessly in the future. "I definitely don't mind."

The warm weight of Megan's body pushed Scarlett down into the mattress. The dick pressed between them, and Scarlett pulled Megan in for a kiss, lifted her hips automatically, wanting more, wanting this, wanting to go wherever Megan was about to take her. She rocked up, her clit pressing against the underside of the toy, wringing a gasp from her lips.

Megan broke the kiss, breathing heavily, her smile a flash of white in the darkness. "Eager?"

Scarlett nodded, too turned on to be self-conscious. "How do I— What do I do?"

Megan sat back, kneeling between Scarlett's spread legs, her slender shoulders rising and falling with each breath. Scarlett's eyes closed reflexively as Megan's thin, delicate fingers slid down over her clit and lit off fireworks throughout her body. "Oh," Megan breathed, barely loud enough to hear, and Scarlett forced her eyes open because she *had* to watch as Megan pressed those perfect fingers into Scarlett's pussy. Scarlett moaned, the sound slipping out of her at that first beautiful sensation. Megan's expression was so very focused as she began to move her hand, pressing perfectly like she knew all of Scarlett's sensitive spots by instinct.

"Please," Scarlett gasped, because she didn't want to be teased, didn't want to be warmed up. "Come on."

Megan smiled again and reached for the lube.

Scarlett gripped the bedsheets at that first moment of thick blunt pressure, almost too much, and then her body opened up around the fucking *amazing* length of Megan's cock. She'd had a lot of sex, with all genders, and she couldn't ever remember *this* feeling, that sense of losing control, of being taken over by pleasure faster than she could catch her breath. Megan's movements began slow, gentle thrusts in and out as she found her rhythm. Then she bent one of Scarlett's legs back at the knee, and *oh, fuck*, pressed even deeper, the motion wringing a cry out of Scarlett.

Immediately, Megan froze. "Are you okay? Did I hurt you?"

"Fuck, no, don't *stop*." Scarlett scrabbled for Megan's hips, reaching down, trying to pull her in deeper. "Fuck, fuck, please don't stop."

Megan didn't stop.

Scarlett slid a hand between them to find her clit. This was exactly what she needed. She could lose herself in this, could forget the reasons this was a terrible idea, could ignore the way everything in her begged for this to go on forever. When she came, she came with her lips pressed together to keep from crying out Megan's name.

And then, she flipped Megan over and worked her way down her body with kisses, unsnapping the harness to give her access to the places she wanted most to touch. Megan arched up and cried out when Scarlett's mouth found her clit, writhing on the bed so Scarlett had to hold her in place. Megan tasted like the ocean, salty and perfect, her whole body squirming and writhing even while she begged Scarlett *"please, please, please"* in a high-pitched, desperate, beautiful voice. Scarlett focused all her attention on that tiny, tender bud until Megan began to keen and gripped Scarlett's hair in her fist. Megan came with a scream, curling in on herself, pulling Scarlett's hair so hard it brought tears to her eyes, and then collapsed like all the strength had gone out of her at once.

They caught their breath side by side on the bed, both a complete mess. Scarlett was winded and satisfied and exhausted. Megan moved first, groaning with effort, and tossed the harness off onto the floor. "I'll clean that tomorrow," she mumbled, and tugged her nightshirt over her head.

Scarlett smiled, but sleep was calling to her, and so without even getting dressed, without letting regrets settle in, she pulled the covers up and let herself drift away.

Maybe all Megan had really needed was to get off again. She felt way better the next morning, none of the pent-up frustration and irritation from the drive yesterday, and she whistled to herself as she built up the fire in the woodstove. The cabin was stocked with oatmeal and coffee, so she prepared both while waiting for Scarlett to wake up.

She could have stayed in bed a little longer. She'd woken up with Scarlett wrapped around her, soft skin and curves, and immediately resisted the dangerous impulse to go back to sleep. Last night had probably been a bad idea, but that at least was just sex. Cuddling felt like an entirely new echelon that she wasn't prepared to deal with. It was easier to climb out of the warm bed into the frigid morning air than confront that desire for closeness. She straightened up from the night before and cleaned the sex toys before getting coffee going.

Oatmeal was just finishing when Scarlett came downstairs, a bit bleary and mussed, dressed in the pajamas she'd thrown aside last night. "Is that coffee?" She walked over to the kitchenette.

"Coffee and oatmeal. Help yourself. I think I made them okay."

Megan was already settled on the sofa with a blanket and her own breakfast when Scarlett joined her, taking the armchair instead of sitting beside her on the sofa. Together, they watched the snow continuing to fall outside the window in the gray light.

"It's coming down lighter than yesterday, right?" Megan was sure the flakes were tinier than the fat heavy ones that had splattered their windshield on the drive.

"Yeah, but that just means it'll last longer."

"There's already a foot out there." Megan had never seen so much snow. Her excitement warred with the practical realities of having to travel in a few days to make the wedding. She couldn't imagine digging out the car, but she also wanted to go play in it.

Scarlett's smile indicated Megan wasn't hiding her feelings as well as she thought. "Want to go skiing?"

"What?" Megan frowned. "No. That sounds terrifying and dangerous. I don't want to end up with a broken leg for the wedding."

"It's not really dangerous when you're learning," Scarlett said, but she didn't sound all that convinced, either. "I only went once. I fell down a lot."

Megan shook her head. "I don't want to spend my whole day falling in the snow. Plus I don't have the right clothes for it."

"Oh, that reminds me. There's laundry at the front building, if you want to wash your stuff today. I've got quarters."

That was a good idea. Megan had washed some underwear in the sinks of a few motel rooms, but it would be nice to actually do some laundry. She agreed, and then they continued to sit there, finishing breakfast and letting the silence settle between them.

Scarlett didn't let the silence settle for very long. "So about last night."

Here it came. Megan braced herself for Scarlett to talk about what a terrible idea it had been, or try to make it mean something big and significant for their friendship. Megan didn't want to deal with any of that; last night could be a fun time with no repercussions, if they were both smart about this. "What about last night?"

"Are you okay with all of that? Is everything all right?"

Scarlett bit her lip. She looked legitimately concerned, like something terrible had happened and she didn't want to break the bad news.

Megan nodded. "I'm fine. Why? Didn't you have fun?"

Scarlett relaxed a bit. "Yeah. It was great. But I thought we should talk about it."

"What's there to talk about?" They had wanted sex, they'd had sex. Looking into Scarlett's eyes, though, Megan's stomach clenched. Best not stare too deeply, not so soon after sex; those warm, happy feelings of closeness were far too much like intimacy for her to want to deal with. She swallowed them down.

Scarlett, who was studying her face intently, eventually shrugged one shoulder and looked away. "I don't know if this changes anything between us."

"It doesn't have to." This was what Megan had been telling herself in the shower, and in bed. It was just sex. It didn't have to change anything. Just like that first night, getting off in their separate beds, pretending the other person wasn't there...or, in Megan's case, fantasizing wildly about Scarlett's hands and mouth on her body. *But then there was that night in New York...*

Scarlett was still looking out the windows. "I know. I didn't know how you felt."

"I had fun." There, that was a huge oversimplification, but Megan could stick to "fun" in her definition of last night. Not the whole truth that it was mind-blowing, the best sex she'd ever had, the fulfillment of endless fantasies, but just "fun." And she should be cured of those desires now, the itch scratched, rather than the way she was currently feeling: desperately wanting more.

"I had fun, too." Scarlett nodded once, curtly. "Do you want to go play in the snow?"

It was a blatant subject change, and Megan didn't mind at all. "Definitely."

Playing in the snow was everything Megan had hoped for, way better than playing in that dusting back in North Carolina. They made a misshapen snowman, threw snowballs at each other, made snow angels, and eventually just flopped in the piles of snow and looked up at the sky. It was really freaking cold, and Megan's new layers were not as waterproof as she'd have liked, but she lasted over an hour before the wet snow and cold air sent her back inside with chattering teeth.

"I'm freezing." Megan tried to thaw her numb hands in front of the woodstove, which was warm but not nearly as warm as she wanted to be. "Dibs on the shower."

Scarlett made a face. "I was literally just about to go shower."

"We could share," Megan offered. She wasn't serious, not really, but Scarlett's eyebrows shot up immediately in surprise before her expression turned guarded.

"I, um..." Scarlett began, and turned her head aside as she rubbed the back of her neck.

"I was just kidding," Megan added quickly, just to save the moment. "You can go first."

"No, it's fine. It's fine. You go first." Scarlett was pink, the way she'd been pink last night, the way Megan was starting to realize she liked seeing her. Flustering Scarlett had always been so difficult, and now, it seemed her blush was only a moment away. In bed, Scarlett let her guard down and let Megan see her vulnerable and open and needy, and last night, Megan had done the same.

Last night should be no big deal, a fun encounter like playing outside in the snow, destined to be another pleasant memory and nothing more. But beneath the hot water of the shower, Megan kept replaying the memories. Scarlett writhing beneath her, lifting her hips, digging her nails into Megan's back. The soft, wet press of Scarlett's lips and tongue on Megan's clit, getting her off effortlessly, like she knew Megan's body as well as Megan did. She shivered, and it had nothing to do with the temperature of the water.

She wanted to do it again.

For the rest of the day, she struggled to put the desire aside in favor of mundane, simple tasks. First, it was laundry, carrying backpacks of dirty clothes and using the coin-op washers and dryers. Megan took the opportunity to clean out the car while she could still get into it, even with the snow piling up on the roof and around the wheels, clearing trash and bringing in the rest of the snacks to cobble together lunch. She and Megan did a jigsaw puzzle together on the coffee table, a 500-piece woodland scene that miraculously still had all its pieces, and even played a few hands of rummy with the deck of playing cards. The television only got a few stations, so they checked the local news and weather (yup, still snowing). Megan also spent some time adding her latest photos to the scrapbook. Later, they walked to the ski lodge for dinner, then back again afterward while the snow continued to pile up outside.

"How are you doing being trapped here with me?" Scarlett asked from behind her laptop, where she'd settled with some vague words about "work to do" an hour earlier.

Megan, for her part, had been unsuccessfully trying to read an ebook. "I can't focus. But it's not about you," she added quickly. "I keep thinking about the wedding." That was a lie; she kept thinking about the way Scarlett's long hair felt in her hands and the way Scarlett's lips felt on her skin. She kept her gaze turned away lest Scarlett see right through her. On the coffee table, her candle burned above its pool of melted wax. Direction and clarity. The only place she was being directed was into bed with Scarlett. Last night had been intense, and even though it was just sex, just some getting off between friends, Megan still couldn't stop thinking about it.

"I hope it all turns out okay. We should be fine to drive out tomorrow night. The storm is supposed to stop by afternoon." Scarlett bit her lip, pressing that plump flesh with her teeth, and Megan wanted to lick that spot. It took her a moment to realize Scarlett was still talking. "—early in the morning," she finished.

Megan asked her to repeat herself, trying not to let on what she'd actually been thinking about.

"I said, worst-case scenario, we leave early Saturday morning. It's only a few hours, and the wedding's not until Saturday evening. We can do it if we have to." Scarlett typed something into the computer, nodded, and then closed the laptop screen. "I've been messaging with Juliet. She knows we're delayed and said she's sure we'll make it in time."

"I'm glad."

"You don't sound convinced." Scarlett set the laptop aside on the coffee table next to their completed puzzle.

Megan wasn't about to tell her that the reason she didn't sound convinced was because she was still distracted at the thought of climbing into that bed. "Just got a lot on my mind, that's all."

"You tired?"

"I think I'll probably go to bed, yeah." Megan couldn't look at Scarlett. If Scarlett saw her eyes, she would know what Megan wanted. She'd see right through her.

"I won't be too long. Save room for me."

"Yup." Without making eye contact, Megan got up and hurried to get ready for bed. She paused only to blow out the candle.

The gods were not smiling down on her, because despite her desire to be asleep by the time Scarlett came to bed, she was still wide awake.

"You asleep?" Scarlett whispered, the bed dipping down behind Megan as she slid beneath the covers.

She could feign sleep. "No," she said instead.

"I was thinking. Last night was pretty intense for me." Scarlett's voice trembled a little as she spoke.

Hearing Scarlett admit it, just come right out and say the thing Megan had been thinking, made Megan freeze up. She didn't want to interrupt, and held her breath.

"It isn't normally like that for me," Scarlett finished. She sounded honest, and vulnerable, and needy, and Megan had to roll over and face her.

Suddenly they were only inches apart. In the darkness, Megan didn't feel as afraid about making eye contact anymore, and a gleam from the window caught Scarlett's gaze. "Me neither," Megan finally said. And then, because Scarlett was right there, because her lips glistened wetly in the low light, and because Megan apparently had no self control, she leaned over and kissed Scarlett again.

Megan wasn't expecting Scarlett to laugh against her mouth. The sound rumbled through her, tickling her lips, and Scarlett's mouth twitched upward. "Are we doing this again?" Scarlett murmured.

"Do you want to?"

Scarlett kissed her back. "It's a bad idea."

Her smile was infectious, and Megan returned it. "Then stop kissing me."

Another kiss. "I don't want to."

Megan chuckled. "But it's a bad idea."

"Yeah." Scarlett slid her hand into Megan's hair, fingernails scratching over the scalp. "I'm full of bad ideas."

Those bad ideas had Megan flat on her back in minutes, naked and moaning as Scarlett teased her open with long, deft fingers. When Megan was dripping wet and going out of her mind, Scarlett brushed the dildo against her, gentle pressure without ever quite pushing inside. Lying alongside Megan like this, cock in hand, Scarlett seemed content to take her sweet time and watch Megan's reactions. "You want more?" Scarlett murmured, her lips tickling Megan's ear as Megan swore and arched her hips up. "Tell me you want more."

Megan nodded, throat tight, twitching at each brush of her clit. "Please," she breathed, and then moaned in relief as Scarlett worked the length inside and then began to gently thrust.

"Look at you." Scarlett brushed the hair off Megan's forehead, staring down at her, giving Megan nowhere to escape as she began to rub the heel of her hand across Megan's clit with each thrust. Megan wanted to look away; she was too vulnerable, too exposed, her desire leaving her open, and she closed her eyes as the pressure built inside her.

Then, Scarlett *stopped*. Megan's eyes flashed open and she saw Scarlett grinning, enjoying every moment of this.

"Fuck, Scarlett, don't *stop*!" She thrust her hips up, the climax slipping away. "What the fuck?"

Scarlett laughed, pressing a kiss onto Megan's neck. "I just like seeing your face."

Megan threw an arm over her head, laughing despite her sudden frustration, that laugh quickly turning to a gasp as Scarlett began to steadily fuck her with the toy again. Scarlett was a complete tease, and wonderful, and Megan was going to fall apart in moments.

"Don't worry." Scarlett kissed her on the sensitive spot just below her ear and started to fuck her again, rubbing against her clit with each perfect thrust. "I'll never leave you hanging."

Megan groaned again as the pleasure built to an unbearable peak and then took her over the edge.

Megan was so fucked.

Scarlett was so fucked. If Megan wasn't so amazing in bed, she could blow this off as a simple dalliance. But now, body weak after coming three times, *hard*, she stared up at the peaked roof of the cabin and counted how fucked she was. She'd known it was a terrible idea to sleep together again, but Megan had been right there, eager, willing, so soft and sweet, and the next thing she knew, she was coming for a final time with her legs draped over Megan's shoulders.

There was no good way back from this.

This was not going to get rid of her crush at all. And she was still calling it a crush, even though she knew the truth as surely as she knew anything; she was in love with Megan. She was in love with Megan the way she fell in love with so many others—entirely, consumingly, completely, and yet also with the deep knowledge that unlike everyone else, she *knew* Megan. She'd known her for her entire childhood, and after the hiatus in between, had grown even closer to her during this trip. She couldn't move on from Megan the way she might move on from another failed relationship.

Best not to let this become a relationship at all. At least then, she could prevent this heartbreak from getting any worse.

Right?

Megan had been clear with her feelings on sex, and how she didn't need it to mean anything. Scarlett had had plenty of dalliances with those same parameters. This could have been fine, but no; she had to go and fall in love with Megan. Like always.

Megan was already dozing off next to her, sex toys forgotten on the floor to be cleaned in the morning, and Scarlett couldn't imagine falling asleep anytime soon. She waited until the breathing next to her evened out, until Megan seemed to be completely asleep, and then carefully extricated herself from the bed and pulled her pajamas back on.

The night seemed less dark with the snow outside. Every bit of light from cabin windows was reflected and enhanced by the sparkling white depths covering every available surface. It was still snowing, burying the last traces of furniture in the yard, the footpaths vanishing. While the hotel grounds crew had come through in the morning with the snowblowers to clear those walkways, the snow slowly reclaimed them, until all the defining lines were blurred.

Scarlett wrapped a blanket around herself and sat on a chair facing out the windows. That was her life right now, wasn't it? Defining lines were blurred. Here on this road trip, they were in a liminal space, a period of transition where they could make their own rules and live out of each other's pockets. But in another week or two, they'd be back to Florida—separate homes, separate lives, separate ambitions. Megan would find some new project and commit fully to it, and Scarlett would continue stringing together temp jobs, their lives orbiting similar stars but never crossing.

Sleeping with Megan was a bad idea, but she couldn't bring herself to regret it. This was some of the best sex she'd ever had, sure, but she'd also had the privilege of watching Megan Harris lose her composed exterior and fall apart beneath Scarlett's hands and lips. And it wasn't just sex, either. Megan had opened up in other ways—her dreams, her fears, the ways she'd held herself back. Megan wasn't going to be the same person after this trip.

Maybe Scarlett didn't have to be, either.

"You okay?"

Megan's voice behind Scarlett made her jump. She hadn't heard her come downstairs, and now she stood behind Scarlett's chair, visible in the reflection on the windows. Scarlett met her gaze in that reflection. "I keep thinking about after all this is done," Scarlett said.

"The snow?"

"The trip."

"Oh." Megan came around to the side of her chair. "I'm trying not to think about it."

That kind of denial would make it easier for Scarlett to sleep. She tried to smile. "Probably for the best."

"You think we shouldn't have slept together?" Megan asked, in her characteristic Megan bluntness.

Scarlett rubbed a hand over her face. It was way too middle-of-the-night for them to be having this discussion. "I don't know. Probably."

"Maybe we should stop. Take a few steps back." Megan shrugged, like it was a casual decision to make, on par with choosing a fast-food place for drive-thru lunch.

If she could offer it up that casually, then she wasn't nearly as affected by this as Scarlett was. "Yeah. You're probably right."

"You want me to sleep on the couch tonight?" Megan asked.

Scarlett shook her head. "Nah. It's fine. The couch sucks."

"Come on back to bed."

Megan held out her hand. If only she were making that offer under different circumstances. If only she wanted the same things as Scarlett, things she'd always wanted but could never have.

She took Megan's hand and let herself be led back upstairs.

Chapter Fifteen

Scarlett was acting weird. She'd been acting weird since the previous night, when Megan had found her sitting in front of the windows after sex looking forlornly into the snow. They'd had a leisurely morning together waiting for the storm to stop, but Scarlett had been more withdrawn than ever. Megan had thought it was about being stuck in the cabin and worried about the wedding, but it was probably something more. If she hadn't known better, she'd assume Scarlett was upset about not sleeping together anymore. But Megan had been upfront the whole time about this just being fun and not having to mean anything else. It wasn't *Megan's* fault if Scarlett... what? Misinterpreted? Wanted something more? No matter what it was, a weird undercurrent of guilt settled on Megan's shoulders. She hadn't promised Scarlett anything, though. She shouldn't feel guilty.

Scarlett's funk persisted, even after they'd had lunch, even after the snow stopped and they got the car dug out. Now, with the two of them back on the road at dusk and a timeline of a late evening arrival in Quebec, Megan had hoped Scarlett would snap out of whatever blues she seemed to be wallowing in. Instead, she stared out the window and didn't even sing along to the songs on one of Megan's CDs.

"You got your passport?" Megan asked at last, interrupting a long stretch of painful silence.

"What?" Scarlett jolted out of what must have been a daydream.

"Your passport. We're near the border." Megan gestured to a sign indicating that they were going to be crossing into Canada very soon.

"Oh. Right." Scarlett dug her bag out of the backseat and began rifling through it. "It's right here."

"Good. Hate to get stranded at the border." Megan forced a smile. "Unless it would shake you out of whatever's gotten into you today."

Scarlett thumbed through her passport. "It's weird to be almost there."

"I know." Megan was feeling a mixture of excitement and sadness. Whatever world they'd created together, it was coming to an end soon.

Not *that* soon, though. "But," Megan added, "we do have the whole drive home."

"That's true." Scarlett smiled. It didn't reach her eyes, but it was at least a smile. "And we're going to the wedding. I do love weddings."

"See, that's the spirit. Cheer up." Megan reached across the console and gave her a playful shove.

"I could always tell border patrol that you've kidnapped me."

Megan's smile vanished. "Don't you dare."

That, at least, made Scarlett laugh. "Don't worry. Somebody's gotta drive me the rest of the way to Quebec."

Their border crossing was uneventful, and as soon as they passed into Canada, Scarlett made them stop immediately on the other side. "You need a picture with the sign!" she announced, and Megan dutifully posed in front of the "Welcome to Canada" sign for Scarlett to fumble with the instant camera and get the shot for her scrapbook. They set the picture on the dashboard to finish developing and drove on.

Megan did the entire last stretch of the drive, since she probably owed it to Scarlett after Scarlett's terrible snowstorm drive. When Old Quebec came into view, lit against the dark sky, Megan's throat closed up with emotion. They were here. After all this driving, they were *here.*

The Château Frontenac was the most obvious landmark, but they still needed the GPS to guide them through a maze of narrow one-way streets and steep, winding hills to the parking garage. Then, it was a flurry of gathering their stuff, shoving loose snacks into bags, unloading, and then apologizing in broken French at the front desk while the immensely patient clerk found their room reservation information. Finally, at just past nine thirty, they unlocked the door to their hotel room.

"Wow." Scarlett tossed her stuff onto the bed and immediately went to the windows, which gave a breathtaking view of the St. Lawrence River. Megan joined her. The riverbanks heaved with icy mountains on both sides. In the center, a tiny ribbon of moving water cut through the vast swaths of ice to wend its way downstream.

"It's beautiful." Megan's voice sounded too loud in the stillness, even though she was whispering. The city was illuminated beneath them, spread out like a tapestry of tiny lights. A cathedral came to mind. This view felt holy.

And somehow, having Scarlett by her side felt like the most perfect way to witness it. Scarlett didn't crack a joke about her sentimentality, or say it was only a city. Scarlett's gaze was soft, her lips turned up in a tiny smile of wonder.

"I can't believe we're really here." Scarlett turned to her, and for a moment, her gaze flicked to Megan's lips at the same time Megan wanted to kiss her. Instead, Megan took a step back on shaky legs, and Scarlett turned away. "Maybe it's all the time in the car," Scarlett said, "but this is all making me really emotional." She laughed, and that laugh came out as unsteady as Megan felt.

"Yeah." Megan was relieved that her voice didn't tremble. "Me, too."

Scarlett started to unpack her bag onto the bed. "Remember to burn your candle."

Megan had nearly forgotten. "Thanks."

"What happens if you forget a day?"

Megan hadn't asked. It wasn't like her to forget anything she set her mind to. This was just another example of how distracted she'd been. "Maybe it doesn't work."

As Megan lit the candle, Scarlett's gaze followed her motions. She hadn't yet asked Megan what it was for, although Megan kept waiting for the question. It didn't come.

"I should probably put it somewhere where it won't set off any alarms, right?" Megan didn't want to burn down the hotel, or trigger a sprinkler system.

"You should be fine, as long as you don't leave it burning." Scarlett turned away and continued unpacking. Megan did the same, and when the candle's top layer had fully melted into a pool of wax, she blew it out for the night. She didn't feel any closer to direction or clarity since she first burned the candle a few nights ago. In fact, she felt *more* confused; her feelings toward Scarlett were a jumble, and she didn't like jumbles. She liked order.

Megan had only spent two nights sharing a bed with Scarlett, but her bed already felt empty as she slid beneath the sheets that night. Would it be wrong to ask if Scarlett wanted to share again? She put the thought aside before she'd even fully formed it. They'd agreed to stop fooling around together. Sharing a bed would probably lead to more, if the last few nights was any indication. Space was good.

Too bad what she really wanted was closeness.

Scarlett had not anticipated what a fancy wedding this would be. Everything was a whirlwind of top-tier extravagance, from the gorgeous flowers filling the room of the wedding itself to Juliet's spectacular gown. A few times throughout the evening, Megan audibly gasped near her—at the sight of Juliet coming down the aisle, later at the lavish decor of the reception hall, at the giant ice sculpture of a pair of doves. Privately, Scarlett thought it was a little over-the-top, but Megan seemed to be really into all of it.

"It's really something, huh?" Scarlett asked as they searched for their seats at the reception.

"It's unbelievable, that's what it is." Megan laughed. "I mean, it's gorgeous, don't get me wrong. It's the most beautiful thing I've ever see. But it must have cost a fortune."

Scarlett automatically pulled out Megan's chair for her, not realizing what she'd done until Megan already sat down. Oops. That was definitely a relationship thing, not a friend thing. She'd have to be more careful.

"If I ever get married," Scarlett said, taking her own seat, "I want something small. Maybe a backyard party, or an event at a park. No big extravaganza."

Megan sighed, resting her chin on her hand and looking wistfully at the room. "I used to think I wanted a big event like this, but now I don't know. Maybe if I married somebody rich like Juliet did with Gabriel. But I can't see that in the cards."

"Do you think you'll ever get married?"

Megan smiled, but it was a sad smile. "I don't know." Her gaze drifted toward the windows that overlooked the setting sun.

God, Megan was beautiful. Her lilac dress hugged all of her curves and flowed gracefully to the floor like a lace waterfall, and she'd put her hair up in an elegant twist that Scarlett had helped pin into place this afternoon. She looked like a movie star, like Audrey Hepburn or some other classic film actress. Scarlett had thought Megan was cute, but she really was more than cute. She was beautiful. How could someone be so beautiful, and so smart, and still be single? Scarlett didn't want Megan to be alone. She wanted to confess her love, to apologize anew for all the ways in which she'd been hurtful, to kiss those petal-soft lips and ask Megan to stay with her forever.

She was rescued from these dangerous thoughts by more people joining them at the table, finding their seats and introducing themselves. Fortunately, Juliet had seated them with people who spoke English, albeit with some gorgeous French accents. Apparently, they were some of Juliet and Gabriel's college friends, several singles and a couple, folks who knew each other but went out of their way to make Megan and Scarlett feel part of the conversation rather than just talking about their college days. They were all beautiful people, all in their mid-to-late twenties, and in another situation, Scarlett could see herself hitting on one of several of the single guys or definitely the woman, Victoria. Tonight, though, all she could think about was Megan.

Megan excused herself to go get a drink from the open bar, leaving Scarlett alone with the rest of the table. "So, how long have you two been together?" asked Henri, one of the single guys.

Scarlett stared at him blankly for a moment before realizing his meaning. "What, me and Megan?" She looked back over her shoulder out of reflex, catching sight of where Megan was talking to the bartender. "We're—" She paused, wanting badly to lie, to make up some story about their beautiful and non-existent romance. "We're just friends," she finally said, the words feeling strangled in her throat. "We've been friends most of our lives."

Henri's eyebrows went up, then drew together in a look of puzzlement. "I'm sorry. I misunderstood."

"That's all right." Scarlett tried to laugh. It sounded forced. "So. Uh. Tell me about what you do for work."

Megan came back midway through Victoria's story about something hilarious that had happened at work the previous week, and she slid a glass in front of Scarlett.

"What's this?" Scarlett asked quietly, not wanting to interrupt the story.

"I figured you'd want something, so I got you their specialty drink. It's a little bit sweet, a little bit sour, the kind of thing you like." Megan looked hesitant. "Is that okay?"

Scarlett smiled. "Thanks." Megan got her a drink, and she'd given thought to what Scarlett would like. *The way any friend would*, a little voice reminded her.

As the meals arrived, the rest of the table drifted into conversation about something related to college, giving Megan and Scarlett some time to talk quietly together. "You know," Scarlett said, because she couldn't *not* say it, "they thought we were together."

"Really?" Megan raised her eyebrows and glanced at the rest of the table. "I guess that's not so strange. We came together. And we do match."

Scarlett looked down at her gray velvet suit. She hadn't been thinking of Megan's dress when she bought the purple camisole to go under it, but it pretty obviously looked like they dressed to match. "I didn't even notice that."

"I thought you did it on purpose." Megan flushed and took a sip of her drink.

Scarlett's stomach clenched in longing. She was going to say something, she was going to say how beautiful Megan was and how she wanted everything to be real between them, but she was saved by the arrival of Juliet and Gabriel.

"Look at you both!" Juliet swept Scarlett and Megan into one crushing hug, and all their years of friendship came rushing back in an instant. They'd been inseparable, the three of them, making this friendship work during the years when most friendships fell apart. And then Juliet had moved away, and Megan and Scarlett had stayed close...until they weren't.

They'd wasted so many years.

"I'm so sorry I didn't get to see you before the wedding today," Juliet said, stepping back and looking between Scarlett and Megan. "I thought I'd have more time. It's been a blur."

"It's all right," Megan said. "We thought we'd be in days ago."

"That snowstorm, right?" Juliet shook her head, little curled tendrils bouncing around her face. "It passed just south of us. Lots of guests couldn't fly in until the last minute. I am so glad you're here."

She introduced Gabriel, who seemed nice enough, and he looked at Juliet like she was the most incredible woman in the world and he was lucky to be married to her. That was how *all* spouses should look at each other. They caught up briefly, the abbreviated conversations of any newly-married couple trying to visit everyone at the reception, and then she and Megan said goodbye with promises to talk more as they made their way to the rest of the table.

"They look wonderful." Megan smiled at Juliet and Gabe's retreating forms once they moved onto another group. "It's good to see her happy. I'm glad we came."

Scarlett went back to eating. "It's kind of weird, though right? We do this whole drive, just for today. For this brief time, to support them, and then they're off and we don't see them again."

"I know. The wedding is the culmination of this trip, but it's kind of anticlimactic." Megan gave Scarlett a long, searching look, and then went back to her meal.

By the time they finished dessert, and after two more trips to the open bar, Scarlett was feeling the alcohol more than a bit. The dance floor was starting to fill up as the music got louder. She leaned into Megan. "You want to dance?"

Megan made a face. "I'm not drunk enough for that."

"So have another drink." Scarlett smiled.

Megan rolled her eyes. "Okay, sure, I'll dance."

They moved out onto the floor together, joining the throng moving along to the music. Megan was a competent enough dancer, letting loose as the song went on, laughing at the way Scarlett deliberately exaggerated her movements. She wanted to make Megan laugh like that forever.

The next song was slow, some melodramatic ballad in French that definitely sounded like a boy band from when they were in elementary school. Scarlett pulled Megan in close with a dramatic flair, singing in her made-up-French. "Oui…madame…le baguette…bonjour…"

Megan started laughing so hard she started to snort, which made her laugh even harder, but she didn't pull out of Scarlett's arms. And then they were dancing, actually dancing, laughter dying away as they moved together to whatever ridiculous, saccharine song this was. This was silly, and at the same time, Scarlett didn't want it to end. When she turned, they were looking right into each other's eyes.

The song ended, fading right into something else that was far more peppy and upbeat, and Megan stepped back and swallowed. "I'm gonna go...use the bathroom." She gestured vaguely at the door.

Scarlett nodded and let her go.

Almost immediately, an older woman sidled up to her, smiling broadly and lazily with the look of someone who had had a few too many glasses of wine. She yelled something in French, but Scarlett had to stammer that she didn't understand. "You and your girlfriend are adorable!" the woman repeated, this time in heavily accented English.

"Thank you." Scarlett didn't bother to correct her, her attention still on Megan as she left.

Chapter Sixteen

Megan stared at herself in the bathroom mirror. This was one of those overly elaborate powder room–style bathrooms, with an entire sitting area and a wall of large ornate mirrors, but she was fortunately alone as she made direct eye contact with herself and tried to calm her racing heart. All these feelings were the result of lowered inhibitions brought on by too much proximity and too much alcohol. That's why Scarlett kept looking at her with those deep, longing looks, and why Megan hadn't turned her away. Scarlett had been pretty clear in their car rides: she falls in love with everybody. The problem was, she might think she was in love with Megan.

Megan could not be in love with Scarlett.

She left her reflection to rest in one of the sitting room chairs—seriously, who had a bathroom antechamber?—and fiddled with the armrests. She just needed to gather her thoughts. Scarlett was too close to her after they'd slept together (twice, Megan amended) and that's why they'd decided to keep their distance. Megan didn't want to be in love with Scarlett! Scarlett was fickle and capricious. She'd thrown Megan's friendship away over ego, and maybe she'd worked to make amends for it, but who's to say that wouldn't happen again? Scarlett had broken her heart, once.

Could Megan ever trust her again?

Megan was going to wear through the fabric of the armrests, so she made herself get up instead and went to fix her lipstick in the mirror. Her hands shook, and she had to lean down and rest her elbows on the counter in order not to screw it up. Scarlett had fixed her lipstick, once. Scarlett had helped her with her hair, too, pinning the strands into place with deft, deliberate fingers.

Those deft, deliberate fingers had been useful in other ways, and Megan's cheeks grew hot at the memory.

No. She was going back in there, but she was going to keep her emotional distance, and maintain this friendship, and ignore all the hormones and dangerous impulses that she'd spent her entire life trying to avoid.

Head held high, she returned to the wedding.

Scarlett's face lit up when Megan walked back in. She'd been staring off to one side, but at Megan's entrance, her gaze tracked onto her like a homing beacon as she smiled. A quiet voice in Megan's head reminded her that no one else had ever looked at her like that. Her boyfriends, her girlfriends, her one-night sexual partners, nobody looked at her like she was the sun and the moon and the stars.

"I thought you'd be dancing with somebody else by now," Megan said, sliding into her chair, the heat from Scarlett's arm somehow tangible across the inches of space between them.

Scarlett shook her head. "I got asked, but I'm not in the mood for that." She pushed a water glass over to Megan. "I thought you might want an ice water. I got one, too. Don't want a hangover tomorrow."

"Are you drunk?" If Scarlett was drunk, it would be easier to excuse these feelings.

But Scarlett shook her head. "Nah. I wouldn't drive, but I'm fine. Thinking clearly." She gave another of those beautiful, lazy smiles to Megan. Megan was very grateful for that water, and guzzled some of it down.

"You want to dance again?" Scarlett asked.

Megan shook her head. She kind of *did* want to, but being so close to Scarlett was making her want things that she shouldn't want. And instead of saying she didn't want to dance at all, she said, "Not right now," and cursed herself for that weakness. "You go, though. I'll sit here."

Scarlett looked between the dance floor and Megan, visibly deciding. An upbeat pop song came over the speakers, then, and Scarlett made up her mind and got to her feet. "Come join me if you change your mind," she said, and joined the crowd on the dance floor.

Megan was content to watch. Scarlett wasn't dancing with anyone in particular, gyrating and jumping around with an abandon that Megan couldn't ever match. She was vivacious and untamed and beautiful, and she looked smoking hot in that suit that Megan wanted to run her hands all over. *Damn*, she should do something about these hormones. Because that's what it was, right? Hormones.

It took Megan a moment to realize Juliet had slid into the empty seat next to her. "Hey," Juliet said.

"Hi!" Megan gave Juliet another hug, reaching awkwardly across the empty space. "How are you doing?"

"I'm good. Just taking a break from all the mingling and the dancing." She squeezed Megan's hand. "I wanted to say again how good it is to see you two."

"Thanks. I'm glad we could come."

Juliet looked fantastic, still, even after dancing for the last few songs. She was glowing. "How was the road trip? Looks like you and Scarlett got pretty close, right?" Her eyes sparkled, and she nudged Megan. "You could've told me."

"What do you mean?"

Juliet looked between Megan and Scarlett, who was out on the dance floor. "You're together now, right? I saw you dancing."

Megan's face must be crimson. "Oh. Um...no, not...not really." To be anywhere but here right now.

Juliet covered her mouth. "I'm sorry. I thought... I shouldn't have assumed. I got so excited, I got carried away."

"It's all right. We've been getting that a lot, lately." Megan swallowed and tried to look nonchalant about it. "Your wedding is beautiful. And the food was fantastic. I can't believe you put this together in such a short time frame. I was expecting something small."

"It blew me away, too, to be honest. Gabe's father has worked with so many organizations, he was able to call in a lot of favors all at once. And now, look at us." She sighed happily before looking over at Megan, something in Megan's expression making her shift from happiness to concern. "Are you doing all right, Megan? I know we never talk anymore, but I want that to change. I think of you and Scarlett all the time. I've been terrible about keeping in touch." Juliet took both of Megan's hands in hers.

"I've been the same. I'm good, Juliet. I really am. I'm doing fine." It was hard to shrink away or deflect with Juliet's open honesty looking her right in the eye. "I'm figuring out what's next for me."

Juliet nodded empathetically. "Transitions are hard. Sometimes, getting your routine shaken up is just what you need to see everything more clearly."

Megan squeezed Juliet's hand. "That's a comforting thought. I've had enough of a shakeup."

Juliet looked at something past Megan's shoulder, then gave her hand a return squeeze. "Gabe's calling me over, and I've gotta run. Don't be a stranger, all right? Keep in touch. We'd love to have you come out this summer and stay with us, if you'd like. You and Scarlett both."

"That would be nice. Thank you." Megan could picture them visiting the city again in the summer, walking through the streets, eating at outdoor cafes. In all those mental images, she walked alongside Scarlett. The image was hard to swallow down. She said her goodbyes to Juliet, wrapping her up in another hug, and then let her go.

Scarlett was still out there dancing. She caught Megan's eye and beckoned, but Megan shook her head and gestured to the door. Scarlett frowned and tipped her head to the side, but Megan turned away and left.

She'd only gotten a few steps into their shared hotel room when the door opened behind her, and Scarlett came in with her brow furrowed. "Are you okay?"

"I'm tired," Megan lied, lighting her orange candle on the windowsill. "I'm all wedding-ed out."

Scarlett was still frowning when Megan made eye contact again, her expression indicating she did not believe a word of what Megan was saying. "What?" Megan sounded more defensive than she intended, but she struggled to rein it in. "Not everybody wants to party the night away like you do."

"It's barely nine. Things are still going strong up there." Scarlett folded her arms. "Is it me? Do you just want a break from me?"

"It's not always about you, Scarlett." Megan tossed the matches down onto the table. She slipped off her shoes, the

Berber carpet rough against her bare feet, and stared out the window so she didn't have to look at Scarlett.

The silence stretched out behind her, and as Megan knew she would, Scarlett finally spoke. "I kinda feel like it's about me *this* time."

Megan spun, anger rising suddenly inside her like a hot wave. "Maybe it is a little bit about you, yeah. Everybody thinks I'm your girlfriend."

Scarlett smiled, just a hint of one that she tried to suppress, but the little up-tilt of her lips was enough to make Megan even angrier. "It's because we match," Scarlett said, but Megan shook her head.

"It's not just that. It's because of how you look at me, and the way you touch me, and dance with me...you treat me like you want to be with me, and other people can see that." Megan's heart was thundering in her head by this point.

"So what? Maybe I do. Maybe I do like you. Maybe I thought you liked me, too." Scarlett's smile was gone, hurt and anger warring on her expression instead. "Maybe if you weren't throwing me so many goddamned mixed signals, I'd know where you stood, too."

"Mixed signals?" Megan took a step forward. "What are you talking about?"

"You cuddle with me, you have sex with me, you say it's a bad idea, and then you have sex with me again? What am I supposed to do with that?" Scarlett started to pace.

Remembering those nights in the cabin made Megan's face heat, and then her body, the hormones flooding through her even alongside the irritation. "You weren't objecting."

"Because I thought you wanted me." Scarlett stopped pacing and folded her arms across her chest, like they might be armor to protect her. "I didn't realize you were just using me to get your rocks off."

Megan blinked, her stomach dropping. "I wasn't doing that."

"Are you sure? Because it feels a little bit like that from my end." Scarlett took a step forward. "Yeah, I told you I fall in love with everybody, and that was a little bit of an exaggeration. You know who I have fallen in love with? You. I had such a crush on you in high school, and I was so ashamed of not being good enough for you, good enough for your perfect vision of yourself, that I ended our friendship. I thought on this trip, I might be able to connect with you again. Get back that friendship. Instead, though, I figured out that I'm in love with you. I can't go to bed with you and have it mean nothing. Not with...not with you." Scarlett's voice trailed off, and she stood standing in front of Megan, her chest heaving, her face flush with emotion and eyes bright with anger and tears.

Megan's emotions caught in her throat. She'd been terrified of these exact words, terrified that Scarlett would want something different than friendship, would get too attached and ask for more than Megan wanted to give. But she also couldn't stand here and say it was meaningless. "It's not nothing," she said, her voice coming out strangled. "It didn't mean nothing."

"It was fun. That's what you said, right? Fun." Scarlett's smile turned bitter. "I like when people see us together and think we're *together.* I like being with you. But you don't want me. You don't know what you want, but you know it's not me. I don't know if it's because I'm too loud, or too clingy, too something, or maybe I'm not enough. I've been terrified of being not enough for you. And now, I'm pouring my heart out here, and you're just *standing* there. Like you don't know what to do."

"I don't know what to do!" The words burst out of Megan like a dam breaking. "I'm *scared*, Scarlett! I'm scared of what my future holds, and of what I haven't done with my life. And

I'm scared to let my guard down and get hurt. I'm scared of failing, and I'm scared of being alone, and I'm scared of making the wrong decisions." She was crying, damn it, tears welling up because she was an angry crier and a frustrated crier and her emotions were too much for her body to contain. "I asked that Salem witch woman for direction and clarity, and I've been burning this candle every single fucking night because I don't know what to do. I'm paralyzed. I've spent my entire adult life protecting myself, putting other people's needs first, never getting close to anyone, terrified of getting my heart broken. I've spent this entire trip trying to keep myself from getting in over my head. And you stand in front of me and tell me that I don't want you?"

Megan was shaking, with frustration but also fear, the fear that clawed its way up inside her even though she would not let that fear win. "Fuck you, Scarlett. Of *course* I want you. I'm terrified of how much I want you. I want to kiss you, and be with you, and I'm scared that you're going to leave again, and I'm scared of how much I...of how much I want to be with you anyway. I'm scared because I love you, too."

Scarlett sucked in a breath, her face lighting up with desperate hope, and then she closed the distance between them and crushed Megan's mouth to hers. Scarlett kissed her like she was drowning, and Megan was the only air, and Megan clung to her with the same intensity. She was crying, they were both crying, wrapped around each other and holding tight like each was the other's lifeline.

Their lips parted, scant inches apart, breathing each other's air, and Scarlett pressed her forehead against Megan's. "Wait. Wait."

Megan gulped air. "I can wait."

"I want to be with you. Just you." Scarlett held Megan close with an arm around her back. "Is that what you want?"

"Yes." Megan nodded, her head bumping Scarlett's, laughing despite the tears still wet on her cheeks.

"And you're willing to be honest with me, even when it's scary?"

Megan nodded again. "Yeah. I can do that." She swallowed. "And you meant what you said earlier, about not running away again, right? Even from this."

"Even from this." Scarlett nodded. "Will you trust me?"

Megan's heart was too full, the kind of full that didn't translate well into words. Scarlett had been worried about living up to Megan's expectations, like she wasn't already the most wonderful person Megan knew. "I trust you," Megan said. "And…you're enough. You're more than enough."

Scarlett's face lit up with a beaming smile of relief, and then she kissed Megan again, clumsy through their smiles. "We're a mess," Scarlett said. "We're such a mess."

"Yeah." Megan wiped her tears away. "I think I can stop burning my candle now."

"That's it? That's all the direction and clarity you need?" Scarlett laughed. "Come on. You still said you're trying to figure out the rest of your life. You should keep burning it."

"Maybe we can talk that through on the drive back." Megan imagined the road stretching back out ahead of them, the miles to sing along to more CDs and plan their relationship. "If you can still stand me by the end of it."

Scarlett pursed her lips. "It's gonna be hard, but I'll do my best."

"Do you want to go back to the wedding?"

Scarlett looked out the window at the night, at the snow falling outside the window. "I think I'd like to stay here with you, if you don't mind."

Megan couldn't help the happiness that bubbled up inside her. "I'd like nothing better."

★ ★ ★

Scarlett couldn't stop smiling as Megan kissed her, leading her back to the bed with every step. She was already pulling at Scarlett's suit jacket, and Scarlett had to slow her down before they ruined both sets of formal wear. Between kisses and touches, they undressed, careful to toss their clothes onto Scarlett's bed rather than the floor, and tumbled together onto Megan's bed, laughing.

"Finally." Megan pinned Scarlett's shoulders to the bed, arching up to look down at her. "I've been wanting to get you out of that suit all day."

"Fuck." Scarlett dropped her head back onto the pillow, her desire skyrocketing with just those words. "I thought you didn't want to sleep with me anymore."

"I didn't want you to fall in love with me." Megan dropped a kiss on her lips. "I think I've been lying to myself for a while now."

"I think I've been in love with you for a while now." Scarlett wrapped an arm around Megan and dragged her down for another, deeper kiss, their curves pressing against each other. Megan wedged a thigh between Scarlett's legs and Scarlett arched reflexively against it as Megan kissed her way down Scarlett's chest and sucked a nipple into her mouth. Before this trip, she'd never expected Megan to be this aggressive in bed, so confident and completely comfortable with her body. It was fantastic. "Fuck, Megan, you keep that up, I'm going to fall in love with you even more."

Megan gave her a nip that made her jump, and then moved to the other breast. "Wait until you see all the sex toys I have at home."

That was a terrifyingly good prospect. Scarlett was about to say so when a sharp jolt of pleasure stole her words. Megan's slender fingers flicked over her clit, then lower, sliding inside her. She swore loudly, making Megan chuckle again. "You like that?"

"Can't you tell?" Scarlett gasped, bucking against Megan's hand. "God, if I'd known you could do this, I'd have taken you to bed forever ago."

Megan lifted her head to smile down at Scarlett, her fingers still working magic over Scarlett's clit. Backlit by the lamps, her hair was illuminated in a halo, her perfect French twist coming loose in wild strands. She was beautiful. "Return the favor, and I'll call it even."

Scarlett nodded, already building toward that precipice, her orgasm bearing down on her like an unstoppable tidal wave. "Deal."

Hours later, they lay side by side on Megan's bed, sweaty and breathless. Megan threw an arm over her head. "I lost count of how many times you made me come."

"Same." Scarlett rolled up onto her side to look down at Megan. "You know we still have time to spend here, right? We've got the hotel for four days."

"Four days." Megan licked her lips. "I have to hydrate more if we're gonna fuck like that for four days."

Scarlett laughed. "I'm not talking about that. I'm saying, we don't have to rush back onto the road. We're in Quebec. We can sightsee. Don't you have a whole page in your scrapbook about this city?"

Megan nodded. "I have a lot of pictures still to take. But that involves leaving this bed."

Scarlett bent to kiss her. Megan was going to drive her crazy, but that was worth it. "I do love you, you know."

Megan nodded. "I know. I love you, too. Are you getting all sappy on me?"

"Probably."

Megan's smile was as bright as Scarlett had ever seen it. "Good."

★ ★ ★

If Megan were going to envision a perfect way to spend her last day in Quebec, it would be this moment exactly: sitting in a cafe in the middle of the old city, sipping chocolat chaud and eating macarons across from Scarlett, who was exclaiming over the desserts and making deals about their future.

"All right how about this." Scarlett held a single elderberry macaron aloft. "I'll apply to two colleges if you apply to two radio stations."

"Are there even two radio stations in Crystal River?" Megan snatched the macaron from Scarlett's hand and bit into the crisp shell, the flavor exploding sharp on her tongue. God, these were amazing. "One radio station, two colleges."

"You can look beyond Crystal River. We're driving distance from lots of other towns. Two and two; that's fair." Scarlett stole the macaron back out of Megan's hand and ate the entire rest of it in one bite. "Get your own," she said around a mouthful of macarons. "These are mine."

"I thought we were sharing."

Scarlett made a face. "That was before I tried one, and discovered how good they are. I hope you don't expect me to share all my desserts if we move in together."

Megan paused, hot chocolate halfway to her mouth. "Did you want to move in with me?" She hadn't considered it seriously, hadn't thought Scarlett would want to take that step so quickly.

Scarlett ducked her head, looking away as a faint blush colored her cheeks. "I don't know. My lease is up at the end of May, and I haven't talked to Jacen about renewing or not. Maybe we could see how it goes for a while and then talk about it?"

"I'd like that." Megan could see a future shaping itself with each new suggestion, each possibility they laid out for the two of them together. "You really think some radio station might hire me?"

"I think you've got a better shot of that than I do for finishing my degree." Scarlett shrugged. "But you promised to help me study if I get in, so what the hell? We're not getting any younger."

"You make it sound like we're ancient." Megan ate another macaron, pistachio this time, and that might be her new favorite.

"Speak for yourself."

Megan chewed thoughtfully. "And you have to stop insulting yourself. All this 'I'm not teacher smart' and 'no shot of finishing my degree.'"

"Now wait a minute," Scarlett protested. "That wasn't part of the deal."

"I'm making it part of the deal. No negative self-talk about your intelligence."

Scarlett rolled her eyes. "Okay, fine, fine. I guess it'll be good practice for working with students someday."

Megan smiled. Scarlett was going to make a great teacher, and maybe she really could run a radio show of some kind. "Okay, then you've got a deal."

"And I think you should get a mic and start a podcast."

Megan drank more hot chocolate. Scarlett had mentioned her starting a podcast before, but would anyone actually want to listen to her? "Aren't there enough podcasts in the world?"

"It's good practice for your radio show. Get yourself a following, talk about whatever you like. A project. Weren't you saying how you needed a new hobby?"

"I don't know… I think that was you." Megan could at least consider it, though. "You know we're going to have to tell our families we're together."

"My mom will be thrilled." Scarlett laughed. "She was

after me to ask you out way back in high school." Scarlett rolled her eyes. "I kept telling her you were straight, and she kept forgetting."

"Or maybe she was psychic." Megan considered taking another macaron, but decided against it. "My parents are going to be insufferable. They'll want to know all our plans, how serious we are, if we're gonna get married and have babies, all of it."

"Oh, god. Well, tell them to lay off. We've got careers to plan for. Right?" Scarlett raised her mug in a toast.

Megan gently clinked her mug to Scarlett's. "Right."

Outside, snow was lightly falling. This afternoon, she was going to a Quebecois salon and getting a pixie cut. Then tomorrow, they would get up early and start the drive back to Florida, with at least one scheduled stop in New York and a few more getting added to the list.

She smiled at Scarlett across the table. Next week, they'd be back home, back to the same place where they'd started, but nothing was going to be the same again.

Epilogue

May, a little over two years later

"Scarlett! Come out here and pose for a picture!"

Scarlett fixed the angle of her mortarboard in the mirror one last time, adjusting a bobby pin holding it secure. "I'm coming!"

Megan was waiting impatiently in the living room, tapping her foot, that instant camera held aloft in anticipation. She stopped tapping as soon as Scarlett appeared, gasping and holding her hands over her mouth. "Look at you!" She blinked rapidly.

"Are you crying? Don't cry." If Megan started to cry, Scarlett was going to start to cry.

"I'm not crying." Megan shook her head way too fast for that to be true, sniffed once, and held up the camera. "Okay. Strike a pose. This one's for the scrapbook."

Scarlett posed, and Megan snapped the photo, which whirred out of the little slot at the bottom. In what had become a tradition now, they both crowded around the photo while it developed, watching the blank slate resolve into first muted, then full colors. In a few minutes, they'd put this one into the new scrapbook, the one that had grown to catalog their first years together. Megan had already put together a page for Scarlett's college graduation, decorated with headings but with plenty of room for the photos and the program from the ceremony itself.

"Can we put it in the book now?" Megan looked at the clock. "I don't want you to be late for the ceremony."

"We've got time." Scarlett was used to Megan's fastidiousness around documentation, her desire to get photos into the book. Already, the scrapbook lay open on the kitchen table to the right page. After Megan affixed this photo, she went to grab something out of the other room, leaving Scarlett to leaf through the last few pages. There was one for Megan's radio job, decorated with photos of her in the studio and the temporary name badge she'd worn at her orientation, plus a cutout newspaper clipping advertising her as a new on-air personality. A page back was Scarlett's acceptance letter to the university. She'd talked Megan out of putting the full document of her transfer credits in here, too, but she'd posed for a photo beside the giant sign at the campus entrance. Although the Scarlett in the photo was rolling her eyes, she still looked happy, and the photo brought back that same sense of nervous exhilaration she'd felt upon going back to school. Megan's confidence had carried her through, though; Megan had believed in her even when she'd doubted herself, had even insisted on putting some of her ten thousand dollars toward Scarlett's first semester. The rest she'd invested, because—as she'd told Scarlett—they were going to want a house of their own someday.

Scarlett smiled until her face hurt whenever she thought about it.

Tonight, after graduation, they were headed up to Tybee Island for an extended getaway weekend, and Scarlett had agreed that Megan could get her up to watch the sunrise again. Hopefully, they'd be putting a new page in the scrapbook, a page Scarlett had been secretly crafting for weeks now. Tied to the page with ribbon was a simple gold ring.

"You ready?" Megan stood at the table, beaming with excitement, holding her bag and camera.

Scarlett took her hand. "I'm ready."

★ ★ ★ ★ ★

*Reviews are an invaluable tool when it comes to
spreading the word about great reads.*

*Please consider leaving an honest review for this
or any of Carina Press's other titles that you've read
on your favorite retailer or review site.*

*To purchase and read more books by Elia Winters,
please visit her website at eliawinters.com/books.*

Acknowledgments

Writing this book has been such a pleasure and privilege, and that's in no small part due to the people who supported its creation along the way. First, for my amazing agent, Saritza Hernandez, who has been in my corner since I first started publishing. Her words of wisdom and emotional support get me through each manuscript. Next, my incredible editor, Kerri Buckley, who has been excited about this book since I first pitched it. It's been a pleasure to work with her again. Also, a huge appreciation to all the folks at Carina Press past and present who have been instrumental in getting the Carina Adores line off the ground.

I wrote a lot of this book during coffee shop sessions with Felicia "Ray" Davin, who is simply a wondrous human being with a bottomless well of good sense (and great fashion). My social circle has been invaluable, especially as we all retreated to our homes for the long haul. I'm quite thankful for my people: Laura for commiseration, support, love, and laughs; Amanda for liveliness and steadfast determination; my work buddies who are also real buddies; and the Human Interaction Discord for cocktails and screaming into the void with me. Also, my quarantine pod: Chris and Crystal, who have been sharing this too-small condo with me since mid-March and who have put up with all the shenanigans that come from trying to create art during a global crisis. I love you all.

Finally, I want to thank everyone who's so excited about this book. My readership has been immensely supportive, and the response and anticipation have been greater than I ever expected. This is a book I would have loved to read when I was first coming to terms with my queerness, and I'm honored to write it and to share it with you. I'm hoping by the time you all read this, it's safe to take road trips again.

Available now from Carina Adores
and Cole McCade!

Summer Hemlock never meant to come back to
Omen, Massachusetts...
But with his mother in need of help,
Summer has no choice but to return to his hometown,
take up a teaching residency at the elite Albin Academy—
and work directly under the man who made
his teenage years miserable.

Read on for a sneak preview of what happens next in
Just Like That, *the first book in Cole McCade's*
new Albin Academy series.

Chapter One

Albin Academy was on fire.

Summer Hemlock saw the plume of smoke before he saw the school itself—just a thick coil of black puffing up into the cloud-locked sky, spiraling above the forest of thin, wispy paper birches that segregated Albin from the rest of the town. He ground his rental car to a halt at the foot of the hill and clambered out, staring up the winding lane...then over his shoulder, at the clustered handful of shingle-roofed houses and stores that barely qualified as a town.

No sign of alarm from the Omen police department. No fire trucks lighting up and screaming out into the streets.

With a groan, Summer *thunk*ed his forehead against the top of the Acura's door.

Business as usual at the boarding school, then.

He guessed seven years away hadn't changed a thing.

He climbed back into the Acura and sent it coasting forward once more, struggling with the gear shift on the steep hill and the narrow lane that crawled its way up the slope.

Thin fingers of branches kissed their tips across the road to create a tunneled archway, a throat that spilled him from the lane and into the academy's front courtyard.

He remembered, as a boy, walking up this lane every morning as the only local who attended the academy, the thick layer of mist that seemed a staple of Massachusetts mornings coming up to his shoulders, making his uniform cling to him damply. He'd always been a little scared, on those walks. Something about the fog, the thin black trees, the *silence* of it, where he could hear his own lonely footsteps on the pavement and imagine them echoed back by some strange ghost in the woods.

Maybe the ghost of Isabella of the Lake, the drowned girl who haunted the rowing pond behind the school.

Or maybe just his imagination, chasing him with all the fears he hadn't been able to face.

At the moment, though, he was driven less by fear and more by resigned curiosity as he forced the Acura to make the steep ascent. By the time he pulled into the courtyard, the plume of smoke had turned into a brooding cloud hovering over the school, wreathing its pointed spires in ominous black. Most if it seemed to be coming from one upstairs window in the front west tower, the pane pulled up to let the smoke escape.

The entire courtyard was crowded with teenage boys, all of them lounging about in loosely knotted groups. They wore ennui like cologne, draping it around them as casually as their expensively tailored uniforms—and utterly uninterested in both the burning school, and the harried-looking teachers trying to shepherd them away from it.

Maybe Summer was a little weird.

Because the chaos of it was a familiar, bittersweet ache of homecoming, and it made him smile.

He stole an empty parking slot, cut the engine, and slipped out to weave through the crowd, holding his breath against the stink of chemical fumes on the biting early spring air. As he pulled the front door open, a severe-looking man in a navy blue suit—someone new, Summer thought, no one he recognized—reached for his arm.

Without even thinking, Summer stepped back out of pure instinctive habit, pulling out of arm's reach and edging past the man.

Until he was forced to stop, as the man stepped in front of him, blocking the door.

"Excuse me, sir." The man looked at him coldly through half-rim glasses. "Visitors are not allowed at the moment. In case you can't see, we're in the middle of an emergency."

Summer smiled, not quite meeting the man's eyes. It made him uncomfortable, always, this feeling like people were crawling inside his skin with a single stare—but most never noticed that he was looking right over their shoulders, instead. "It's okay," he said. "I work here. And I'm used to Dr. Liu's explosions. I'm just gonna grab a fire extinguisher and help."

The man just blinked at him, cocking his head with a quizzical frown.

So Summer stole his opportunity and slipped inside, just barely managing to squeeze past the suit-clad man without touching.

He barely had a moment to register the disorienting feeling of familiarity—as if he'd traveled back in time, back to that rawboned thin pale boy he'd been, walking into the eerily quiet, high-ceilinged entry chamber of dark paneled wood and tall windows with his shoulders hunched and head bowed—before he vaulted up one side of the double stairway, taking the steps two at a time, and dashed for the northwest wing. The smell of bitterly acidic smoke led him on, beckoning him through vaulted corridors where the air grew thicker and thicker, until the murk fogged everything gray and stung his eyes.

Coughing, he pulled the collar of his button-down up over his mouth, breathing through the cloth and squinting. Just up ahead, he could barely make out a few shapes moving in the hallway—but a familiar voice rang down the hall, low and dry and authoritative, this thing of velvet and grit and cool autumn nights.

"Extinguisher first, then sand," the voice ordered. "Dr. Liu, if you insist on getting in the way, at least make yourself useful and remove anything *else* flammable from the vicinity of the blaze. Quickly, now. Keep your mouths covered."

Summer's entire body tingled, prickled, as if his skin had drawn too tight. That voice—that voice brought back too many memories. Afternoons in his psychology elective class, staring down at his textbook and doodling in his notebook and refusing to look up, to look *at* anyone, while that voice washed over him for an hour. Summer knew that voice almost better than the face attached to it, every inflection and cadence, the way it could command silence with a quiet word more effectively than any shout.

And how sometimes it seemed more expressive than the cold, withdrawn expression of the man he remembered, standing tall and stern in front of a class of boys who were all just a little bit afraid of him.

Summer had never been afraid, not really.

But he hadn't had the courage to whisper to himself what he'd really felt, when he'd been a hopeless boy who'd done everything he could to be invisible.

Heart beating harder, he followed the sound of that voice to the open doorway of a smoke-filled room, the entire chemistry lab a haze of gray and black and crackling orange; from what he could tell a table was...on fire? Or at least the substance inside a blackened beaker was on fire, belching out a seem-ingly never-ending, impossible billow of smoke and flame.

Several smaller fires burned throughout the room; it looked as though sparks had jumped to catch on notebooks, papers, books. Several indistinct shapes alternately sprayed the confla-gration with fire extinguishers and doused it with little hand buckets of sand from the emergency kit in the corner of the room, everyone working clumsily one-handed while they held wet paper towels over their noses and mouths with the other.

And standing tall over them all—several teachers and older students, it looked like—was the one man Summer had re-turned to Omen to see.

Professor Iseya.

He stood head and shoulders above the rest, his broad-shouldered, leanly angular frame as proud as a battle stan-dard, elegant in a trim white button-down tucked into dark gray slacks, suspenders striping in neat black lines down his chest. Behind slim glasses, his pale, sharply angled gray eyes flicked swiftly over the room, set in a narrow, graceful face that had only weathered with age into an ivory mask of quiet, aloof beauty.

The sleek slick of his ink-black hair was pulled back from his face as always—but as always, he could never quite keep the soft strands inside their tie, and several wisped free to frame his face, lay against his long, smooth neck, pour down his shoulders and back. He held a damp paper towel over his mouth, neatly folded into a square, and spoke through it to direct the frazzled-looking group with consummate calm, taking complete control of the situation.

And complete control of Summer, as Iseya's gaze abruptly snapped to him, locking on him from across the room. "Why have you not evacuated?" Iseya demanded coldly, his words precise, inflected with a softly cultured accent. "Please vacate the premises until we've contained the blaze."

Summer dropped his eyes immediately—habit, staring down at his feet. "Oh, um—I came to help," he mumbled through the collar of his shirt.

A pause, then, "You're not a student. Who are you?"

That shouldn't sting.

But then it had been seven years, he'd only been in two of Iseya's classes...and he'd changed, since he'd left Omen.

At least, he hoped he had.

That was why he'd run away, after all. To shake off the boy he'd been; to find himself in a big city like Baltimore, and maybe, just maybe...

Learn not to be so afraid.

But he almost couldn't bring himself to speak, while the silence demanded an answer. "I'm not a student *anymore*," he corrected, almost under his breath. "It's...it's me. Summer. Summer Hemlock. Your new TA." He made himself look up, even if he didn't raise his head, peeking at Iseya through the wreathing of smoke that made the man look like some strange and ghostly figure, this ethereal spirit swirled in mist and darkness. "Hi, Professor Iseya. Hi."

Fox Iseya narrowed his eyes at the young man in the doorway.

He had nearly forgotten his new TA would be arriving today—or, more truthfully, he had put it out of his mind, when he was not particularly looking forward to training and shepherding an inept and inexperienced fresh university graduate in handling the fractious, contentious group of spoiled degenerates that made up the majority of Albin's student body. He only needed a TA to ensure his replacement would be properly trained when he retired. Otherwise, having a second presence in the classroom was little more than an unwanted but unfortunately necessary nuisance.

The nuisance he had been expecting, however, was not the man standing awkwardly in the doorway, face half-obscured by the collar of his shirt.

The Summer Hemlock he remembered had been a gangly teenager, so pale he was nearly translucent, all angles and elbows everywhere. Fox recalled seeing more of the top of his head than anything else, a shaggy mop of black falling to hide blue eyes and a fresh, open face; he'd always huddled in his desk with his head bowed, and mumbled inaudible things when called on in class.

The young man in front of him almost mirrored that posture...but that was where the resemblance ended.

Summer was tall and athletic now, a lithe runner's build outlined against his dress shirt and low-slung jeans; pale skin had darkened to a glowing, sunny tan that stood out vibrant even in the smoke-filled murk of the room. The lank mess of his hair had been tamed into a stylishly bedheaded tousle, perhaps in need of a trim but framing his face and rather strong jaw attractively. Too-wide, nervous blue eyes had deepened, shaded by firmly decisive brows.

Considering that Fox guided his students through to senior graduation and rarely ever saw them again, it was rather bizarre to contrast the boy he had taught with the man who had apparently come to take Fox's place, when he retired next year.

But right now, he didn't have time to think about that.

Not when Dr. Liu was currently racking up exponential increases in charges for property damage.

Fox flicked two fingers, beckoning. "Sand. Join the chain. Let's do our best to keep this contained."

Summer's head came up sharply, and he looked at Fox for a single wide-eyed moment—and that drove home that sense of bizarrely unfamiliar familiarity, when Fox recalled quite clearly that direct eye contact could turn the boy into a stammering wreck, cringing and retreating. That moment of locked gazes lasted for only a second, before Summer nodded quickly and averted his eyes.

"Of course, sir—yes."

Summer strode forward swiftly on long legs, and skirted around Fox to pick up a bucket and scoop up sand from the massive black trash bin that had been repurposed specifically to deal with Dr. Liu's regrettably frequent "accidents." The man was a nightmare and a half, and Fox supposed they could consider themselves lucky it had been two months since the last time the good doctor had practically burned the school down.

But they were running out of empty classrooms to repurpose for chemistry lessons while previously damaged rooms were repaired, and Fox intended to have *words* at the next faculty meeting.

Honestly, he didn't understand how Dr. Liu still had a job.

And he quite firmly directed the chemistry teacher out of the way once more, as he returned to marshalling the emergency response group to put out the secondary fires that had erupted from jumping embers and ample fuel throughout the room. Fortunately this was rather a practiced habit, at this point—and within twenty minutes the blaze was contained, the last of it smothered beneath sand and fire extinguisher foam. They had, regrettably, learned years ago that Liu frequently worked with substances that only burned hotter when doused with water.

At Albin, the students weren't the only ones who often had to learn from experience.

Yet throughout the suppression efforts, Fox repeatedly found his gaze straying toward Summer. His apparent shyness had vanished the moment he dove into the fray, joining the others rather energetically and hauling bucket after bucket of sand to chase down one sparking blaze after the other before it could get out of control.

By the time the clouds of smoke began to thin, Summer was a mess—his once-white shirt smeared with soot and ash, streaks of it along his cheeks and jaw, underscoring one eye in a rakish dash like face paint. But he was laughing, as he helped an older student shovel sodden, charred remnants of notebooks into a trash bag.

But the moment Fox called, "Mr. Hemlock," Summer went stiff, every bit of ease bleeding out of his body to leave his back rigid and his shoulders tight.

Hm.

Interesting.

Summer glanced over his shoulder, looking toward Fox but not quite *at* him. "Yes, Professor Iseya?"

"Leave the cleanup to Dr. Liu. It's the least he can do to compensate for his crimes."

"Hey!" came from the corner Liu had sequestered himself in. Fox ignored him, crooking a finger at Summer.

"If you've brought your possessions, fetch them. You can use my suite to clean up and change. We have matters to discuss."

Summer ducked his head, scrubbing his hands against his jeans. Beneath the smears of soot streaking pronounced cheekbones, tanned skin turned a decided shade of pink. He nodded quietly, obediently.

"Yes, Professor Iseya."

Fox frowned. There was something...*off* about Summer's furtive behavior, something more than just a reticence he clearly hadn't shaken over seven years away from Omen and Albin Academy.

It didn't matter.

Summer's demons were Summer's demons, and Fox wasn't staying at the school long enough to figure them out.

Fox waited only long enough for Summer to retrieve his suitcase from his car, then retreated to his private suite in the southwest tower. While he let Summer have the run of the bathroom, Fox wiped off his face, washed his hands, and changed into a clean shirt, slacks, and waistcoat, then settled in the easy chair in the living room to wait; to keep himself busy he flipped to his last page marker in the absolutely abysmal Jordan Peterson book he was forcing himself to read for a class exercise.

Pop psychology, all of it, based in flawed and inhumane principles, but it provided an interesting exercise in logical fallacies and poor application of outdated psychological principles; examples he could use to demonstrate poor reasoning to students as a caution against falling into the same traps. He underlined another passage riddled with subjective bias in red, and jotted down a few notes on his legal pad, idly listening as the shower shut off with a faint squeak and an ending of the quiet, rain-like sounds of water striking tile.

A few moments later Summer emerged, steaming and still dripping, a pale gray T-shirt clinging damply to his chest and slim waist, a fresh pair of jeans slouching on narrow hips. He scrubbed a towel through his messy wet hair and peeked at Fox from under the tangle of it in that *way* he had, offering a sheepish smile.

"Sorry," he said. "Not really up to dress code, but technically I'm not checking in for work just yet."

"I hardly think you need to worry about work attire in my living room." Fox pointed his pen at the plush easy chair adjacent to the sofa. "Sit."

Like an obedient puppy, Summer dropped down into the

chair, resting his hands on his knees. "Thank you for accepting my application."

"Your qualifications met the requirements, and as a former student you're familiar with the school, the curriculum, and the standards of my classes." Fox crossed his legs, tapping his pen against his lower lip, studying Summer thoughtfully. "However, I don't think you're suited to teach."

"Wh-what?" Summer's gaze flew up quickly, then darted away. "Then why did you accept me as your assistant?"

"No one else applied." Fox arched a brow. "Look me in the eye."

Immediately, Summer bowed his head, staring fixedly at his knees. "Why?"

"You cannot, can you?"

"Does it matter?" Summer threw back, biting his lip and turning his face to the side.

"It matters." Fox set his pen, notepad, and atrocious tome aside to lean forward, resting his hands on his knees and lacing his fingers together. The longer he watched Summer, the more uncomfortable the young man seemed to grow, sinking down into his shoulders and curling his fingers slowly until they dug up the denim of his jeans in little divots. "Do you recall why most parents send their sons to Albin Academy, Mr. Hemlock?"

"Because..." Barely a murmur. "Because they're rich and horrible and don't want to deal with their problem children themselves, so they ship them off where no one can see them?"

"That is a more crass explanation of our function here, yes," Fox said dryly. "The point is that these boys have no respect for authority—and while we are not their parents or their disciplinarians, we do at least have to maintain the appropriate seniority and boundaries to keep them out of trouble. They will push those boundaries at every turn, and considering you haven't changed a bit from when *you* were a student... I don't think you're capable of dealing with that."

"That's not fair!" Summer protested. "I'm not a kid anymore. You don't know me. You've spent all of five minutes talking to me."

"One can generally make an accurate psychological assessment in less."

"Well, your assessment of me is wrong." Summer's jaw tightened. "I can do this job. And since you accepted me, you can at least give me a chance before telling me how much I suck."

So there was something of a backbone there, Fox thought—and wondered just what it was that had made Summer so shy, so withdrawn. Leaning back, he steepled his fingers. "You interviewed with Principal Chambers, did you not?"

"Y-yeah." Summer nodded.

"And what did he tell you?"

"That no one else wanted the job." Summer smiled faintly. He had a soft, sad mouth that seemed ill-used to smiling, yet was haunted by a perpetual ghost of warmth nonetheless. "And that my mother must be happy to have me back home."

"Are you?"

"Am I what?"

"Happy to be here."

"I..." There—an almost imperceptible flinch. "She needed me here. She's not young anymore, and it'll be better for her if I'm close by to help."

That, Fox thought, was not an answer. It was a reason, but not an answer to the actual question he had asked. He pressed his lips together, tapping his fingertips to his knuckles.

"I have a proposition for you," he said. "We can call it a training exercise, or a psychological experiment—whichever suits you."

"Am I a TA or a test subject?"

"Both, perhaps." Fox tucked a loose lock of hair behind his ear. Irritating mess; he always meant to cut it, and yet... He let his gaze drift to the mantle. The butsudan resting there, its deep-polished rosewood glinting in the afternoon light drifting through the windows, its doors currently closed and its contents private...as they should be. Tearing his gaze away, he made himself focus on Summer. "Once per day, I expect you to do something outside your comfort zone. Challenge yourself to take on a role as a leader, or mentor. Challenge yourself to approach this job with confidence, rather than asking permission to do what you must do. If you cannot learn to be bold, Mr. Hemlock, at the very least learn to fake it in the necessary environments so that your knees knocking together do not drown out the lesson you are trying to deliver."

Summer's lips twitched faintly. "Pavlovian conditioning is a little 101 level, sir. Are you trying to make me assert my own authority?"

"I'm not trying to *make* you do anything," Fox replied. "My only goal is to see if you can take the steps needed to face down a classroom of unruly, disrespectful children on your own. Do I need to hold your hand in that, or do you feel capable of attempting it under your own impetus?"

Summer plucked at his jeans. "The children don't scare me."

"Oh? Then what does?"

No answer. Simply a heavy silence, fraught with meaning, and yet—for all his understanding of psychology, of psychiatry, of the small markers that gave away intent and thought and emotion... Fox couldn't quite read what that meaning might be. Not when the Summer he had known as a boy was necessarily a stranger to him, with the appropriate distance between teacher and student; not when the Summer he saw now was a new person, shaped by years of experiences Fox as yet had no insight into, and technically stood on almost equal footing as his peer and assistant.

And if he were honest with himself...no matter how he tried, no matter what clinical understanding he possessed...

He somehow always felt at one remove from other people's feelings, observing them and yet never quite understanding them, the soul of his own emotions locked away.

Summer took a deep, slow breath, his shoulders rising and falling. "Every day? Does that include today?"

"You don't technically start work until Monday, so you may take the weekend to consider, if you'd like," Fox said. "Or you may start today. But that is still not an answer as to what frightens you."

"Okay," Summer said shakily, rising to his feet with wooden motions. "Okay then. I'll show you what scares me."

He stepped rigidly across the living room, navigating the low polished coffee table with an awkward bump of his shins against the wood. Fox watched, brow raised, as Summer drew closer to the couch—but startlement prickled down his arms in a rush like goosebumps and fine hairs raising as Summer bent over him, bracing one hand to the back of the sofa.

Before the young man captured Fox's chin, his jaw, in roughened fingertips.

Tipped his face up.

And kissed him.

Chapter Two

Summer had no idea what he was doing.

He hadn't meant to kiss Professor Iseya. He'd just—he—
after sitting there listening to Iseya list Summer's faults and
remind Summer that he hadn't changed at all, something had
risen up inside him. Something irritated, that whited out his
thoughts and smothered his common sense until he wasn't
really *choosing* to do anything; just reacting to provocation. If
he wanted to look at it from a psychology perspective, Iseya
had pricked at Summer's id.

Until it had bitten back.

But Freud had been a hack, and dissection of the psyche
couldn't explain why Summer was bent over Professor Iseya
with his mouth pressed hot against the man's and the taste of
him on his lips.

Iseya's mouth was a stern thing of cruel sensuality, made
for whispering cold-edged, cutting words of emotionless logic
with articulated precision, every curve and dip of his lips defined as if they'd been shaped by the razor of his tongue...but

for just a moment, those lips went soft. Slack. A moment that shot through Summer with a wilding heat; a moment that charged him with a vibrant rush and made his entire body go so hot he felt as though he burned with every harsh draught of smoke he'd inhaled just minutes before.

He'd thought about this more times than he cared to admit, as a boy. Back when he'd been fascinated by the older man's frosty demeanor; by the glint of eyes a silver as pale and in-scrutable as the forest's mist; by the controlled elegance in his minimalistic movements; by the quiet hint of command in his every gesture. When Summer had been a teenager, Professor Iseya had been a fantasy, out of reach, unreal.

Yet he was very much real, now.

Summer wasn't a boy anymore.

And the man whose mouth went fiery and firm against his own was very much not the icy caricature of his dreams.

That softening, that parting of Iseya's lips promised heat, promised more—and with a low sound Summer slanted his mouth against Iseya's, only for firm lips to lock and hold him, the lash of a rough tongue to whip him, his fingers curling and tingling with the sudden rush of warmth as Iseya's teeth grazed his mouth, teased him, left him shivering.

Until a hand pressed against his throat, seizing his breaths and stopping his heart.

He froze as long, firm fingers wrapped against his neck, a heated palm pressing down on his pulse just hard enough for him to feel it; just hard enough to make his next breath come shallow and tight. His knees trembled, an odd, weak-ening sensation seeming to cut the strength from his limbs and leave his gut liquid-hot and tight as slowly, Iseya pushed him back. That one hand held him in complete thrall, controlling his every movement and keeping him trapped in place in silent command as Iseya parted their lips from each other.

Frigid eyes as pale as cracked ice fixed on Summer, piercing him. For all the breathless heat that had lived in that stolen moment...those eyes were cold enough to smother it, frostbite in every slowly spoken word.

"I," Iseya said softly, "would thank you not to be inappropriate, Mr. Hemlock. And if I am what frightens you...you have every reason to fear."

For just a half-second longer, Summer's focus remained on those lips—their redness, their fullness. On the pressure of that hand against his throat. On the confusing and aching feeling it roused inside him, taut and shaking and thrilling with something not quite fear at all.

Before it hit him just what he was *doing*, when he had never been so reckless or so forward in his *life*.

He flinched back, breaking free from Iseya's grip. The man regarded him coolly, utterly calm and unreadable, yet for the few breaths that Summer held his eyes he couldn't help but imagine judgment there.

Judgment...

And rejection.

Because Summer hadn't been back in Omen for a day before he'd crossed a line, and proven he was still the same awkward, utterly hopeless boy he'd always been.

"S-sorry," he whispered, though it barely came out on a dry croak, his throat closing. "*Sorry.*"

Iseya said nothing—and Summer didn't know what else *to* say.

He just knew he couldn't stay here, not when he felt as though his every shortcoming and failure, his every maladjustment and cowardice, were laid bare for that cutting silver gaze to dissect before discarding him as worthless.

And so "*S-sorry,*" he stumbled over, one more time.

Before he bowed his head. Clenched his fists.

And ran.

★ ★ ★

He didn't stop until he was outside, and shut inside the safety of his rental car with at least the barrier of metal walls to hide him.

Clenching his hands against the steering wheel, Summer groaned and *thunk*ed his forehead against the leather of the upper curve—and then again and again, just for good measure.

What the hell, Summer.

What the hell, what the hell, what the hell.

His pulse was on fire, his entire body prickling as if a sunburn had crisped his skin to paper and left him feeling like he was going to split right out of it. He'd...he'd *kissed* Professor Iseya. Like he was still that same shy fumbling boy with a completely impossible crush, he'd kissed the man without so much as an if-you–please, and probably just fucked himself out of a job.

One more *thud* against the steering wheel, hard enough to make his temples throb.

Dammit.

He couldn't go back in there. Not today. He'd left his suitcase at Iseya's, but he'd wait until the man was in class Monday to get a janitor to let him in to retrieve it. Whether or not he'd be unpacking it in his faculty suite or looking for somewhere else to stay?

Would probably depend on if Iseya had him fired or not.

He'd deserve it if he did.

Welp.

At least if he was unemployed, he'd have more time to help his mother fix up a few things around the house.

And wouldn't have to worry about having an anxiety attack in front of two dozen staring, snickering boys.

Summer backed the Acura out of its parking slot and did a U-turn in the now-empty courtyard, the students already back inside and in class like nothing had ever happened, despite the fresh scorch marks on the upstairs wall and window frame. The drive down the high hill felt less ominous than the approach—every foot of space between himself and that mortifying moment of impulse letting him breathe a little easier, put it behind himself, tuck it away as something to be dealt with later.

The town at the bottom of the hill was still the same—cobbled roadways and colonial style homes, only the more modern shops, street lighting, and sidewalk bus stops reminding Omen of what century it was. Summer had always managed to find a way not to come back, even on holiday and summer breaks, instead flying his mother out to Baltimore when he wanted to see her; Omen had somehow always felt like its name, this ominous trap that would ensnare him in a life, a future, a *self* he'd never wanted to hold on to.

But he still remembered the way home—and he couldn't help but smile, as he pulled up outside his mother's house. The sunny little cottage hadn't changed, either, still overgrown with flowers everywhere. Daffodils nodded their sunny heads, while hollyhocks clustered around lavender and flowering azalea bushes; jasmine climbed the walls, dripping blooms whose fragrance nearly drowned him when he stepped out of the car, chasing away the last stinging scent of smoke in his nose. Little glass wind chimes and baubles hung in every tree and from every eave, catching the meager gray light and turning it into winking shards of color.

He'd barely made it past the wooden gate, stepping under the arch of the flowering bower overhead, before the front door opened and his mother came tumbling out. Small, round, Lily Hemlock was a compact bundle of energy swirled about by gauzy scarves, trailing her in a flutter of color as she nearly launched herself into him.

"*Summer.*"

He caught her with an *oof*, rocking back on his heels before righting himself and wrapping her up in a tight hug. "Hi, Mom."

"I was wondering when you'd get in. You didn't call, you just—"

"Sorry. I stopped by the school first." He grinned wryly. "It's burning again."

"Oh, it's always burning. The fire chief doesn't even bother unless they actually call anymore."

She pulled back, gripping his arms and looking up at him with a measuring gaze, blue eyes bright against the dark twist of her hair; when had those jet-black locks started to fade to iron gray?

When had she become so *frail*, the bones of her hands pressing into his skin?

But her presence was still larger than life, as she gave him a once-over and clucked her tongue primly. "Look at you. Have you been eating? You're too thin."

He laughed, taking her arm and nudging her toward the door. "I'm twice the size I was in high school."

"And you were too thin in high school, too. Too thin times two is still too thin." Suddenly *she* was the one tugging *him*, and he let himself be marshalled along without protest. "Come. Sit. I've just finished baking."

Summer only smiled, as his mother practically dragged him inside. The house was as warm and open inside as it was the outside, all weathered, unvarnished wood everywhere and sprigs of herbs strung up along the walls and ceiling, the aromas of her latest concoctions making the entire house smell earthy and clean. Familiar. Safe.

And as she ushered him to a place at the kitchen table, he was finally able to *breathe* again.

Even if he had no appetite for the orange crème muffins she piled on a plate in front of him; he still wasn't going to tell her that, not when she watched him like a hawk.

"Go on," she said. "I know they're your favorite."

"And you made them just because I was coming home?" He chuckled and picked off a bite of one steaming muffin, plucking it between his fingers. "Today's really not special, Mom. Within a week you'll be sick of having me underfoot."

"I could never." She dropped herself down into a chair opposite him, propping her chin in her hands and watching him fondly. "And knowing you, you'll probably still never be here what with living up at that school."

"It's mandatory. I've got to do my part as dorm monitor." He made himself swallow a bite; even if he'd loved his mother's orange crème muffins since he was old enough to talk, right now it tasted overly sweet, cloying, lodging in his still-tight throat. "Though I may just end up moving in with you and looking for a new job. I...uh... I kind of screwed up."

Her eyes sharpened. "Now how did you manage that when you've not even started yet?"

"...nothing. I didn't do anything."

"So you managed to screw up by not doing anything?" Her brows lifted mildly. "That's unlike you. Usually when you screw up, you're at least trying."

"Funny."

"Darling, what did you *do?*"

He winced. "...*IkissedProfessorIseya*," he mumbled under his breath.

"Try that one more time, dear. With air."

"Oh *God.*" Summer let the muffin plunk back to the plate and dropped his face into his hands. "I kissed him. Professor Iseya. I just...kissed him."

His mother gasped. "*Fox* Iseya? Oh dear."

"...I don't think 'oh dear' really covers it."

She made an odd sound, before pressing her fingers to her mouth—but that didn't stop her lips from twitching at the corners. "Oh—oh, darling, I still remember you doodling his initials in your notebooks. And learning how to read those—what were those letters?"

"...hiragana..."

"...yes, that. Just so you could write his name the proper way."

"Oh my God, Mom, *stop*." He pressed his burning cheeks into his palms, closed his eyes, and told his churning stomach to calm the hell down. "I was seventeen."

"And it was *adorable*." She chuckled fondly. "But whatever possessed you to kiss him today?"

"He pissed me off."

"One, language. Two, *that* is highly unexpected, coming from you. My mild-mannered boy." She patted his hand, and he cracked one eye open on her warm, indulgent smile. "Three, most people don't kiss people when they're angry."

"Yeah, well, I'm weird. We've always known that." He sighed, dropping his hands and folding his arms on the table. "He didn't even give me a chance. He just told me I haven't changed and I'm not fit to teach a class, which makes me wonder why he even agreed to work with me. Then he challenged me to like...assert my authority or something just once every day, if I want to prove myself. So... I kissed him."

She clucked her tongue. "Well, that *is* certainly quite assertive."

"I can tell you're trying not to laugh." Groaning, he dropped his head and thudded his brow against his forearm, burying his face in his arms. "Go on. Get it out."

"I wouldn't laugh at you, darling." Her small, warm hand rested to the top of his head, weaving into his hair...and it struck him with a quiet ache just how *weightless* her hands were, as if her bones had turned hollow as a bird's. "I take it, though, it didn't go over well."

"How did you guess?"

"Because it's Fox. Not because of you." His mother sighed gently and tucked his hair back with a lingering touch. "You were too young to know him before his wife died. We were actually fast friends, he and I, before he shut everyone out and isolated himself."

Professor Iseya's...wife? Summer lifted his head sharply, staring at his mother, his heart thumping in erratic sick-lurch rhythm. "He was married?"

"For some time when he was close to your age, yes." She smiled, blue eyes dark, soft. "He was really the kindest, sweetest man...but when he lost Michiko, well..." She shook her head. "Loss and grief can change people."

"When did this happen?"

"When you were...about four or five, I would say. Terrible tragedy, truly. She fell asleep behind the wheel one night on her way home from her job in Medford, and lost control of her car on the bridge over the Mystic. Her car sank right to the bottom of the river." His mother bowed her head, lines seaming her round, soft features. "Fox was never the same after that."

"I...oh." Guilt plunged through Summer in a hard strike, sinking deep as a spear into his flesh. He knit his brows. "Why haven't I ever heard about this?"

"You were quite young, dear, and it was grown-up business. And over time, the whole town learned to stop speaking about it out of respect for Fox. I don't think the man's ever stopped grieving."

Or he never allowed himself to grieve in the first place, Summer thought with dawning realization.

And just like that, far too many things fell into place.

When he'd been a student at Albin, all he'd seen was Professor Iseya—aloof, untouchable, mysterious, his icy armor all the more fascinating for the secrets it promised. As a boy it had been too easy to daydream about being the one to tease past that armor to discover everything hidden inside; to be the *special one* the cold, somewhat frightening professor defrosted for. There'd been a touch of the forbidden, too, when Iseya had been nearly forty by the time Summer graduated, and that stern, subtly domineering demeanor had inspired a few whispered thoughts of just what he might *do* to Summer in private when Summer was young, vulnerable, inexperienced.

But those had been childish fantasies, entirely inappropriate and impossible, and suddenly that frigid exterior took on a wholly different meaning when seen through older eyes.

When it was the defensive shield of a man in pain, struggling to find a way to function in his everyday life, fighting his pride to keep from putting his grief on display for all the world to see.

Yet if Summer had been four or five years old when Iseya's wife had died...then Iseya had been shut inside himself for twenty years, now.

And maybe Summer was reading too much into it, thinking a few psychology and education courses gave him any insight into the workings of a distant man's mind...

But he wondered if Iseya even knew how to find his way out, anymore.

Or if he was trapped inside himself.

And completely alone.

Summer sighed, rubbing his fingers to his temples. "I'm an asshole."

"*Language.*"

"I'm twenty-five."

"And I'm still your mother, and this is still my house." She reached across the table and curled her thin, papery fingers around his wrist; her skin was cooler than he remembered, and brought back that pang, that quiet unspoken fear, the entire reason he'd been willing to take a job in the town he'd once been so desperate to escape. "You didn't know, Summer. Now you do. It's up to you what you do with that information."

"Yeah...yeah. I know." He smiled and caught her hand, squeezing it in his own. "I've got to think for a bit, but... I think I know what I need to do, in the end."

"What's that, dear?"

"I," he said, holding her hand just a little tighter, as if he could give her his warmth to hold and keep, "am going to do something brave."

And he couldn't think of anything that would take more courage than walking up to Fox Iseya...

And apologizing to him flat out.

Fox sat on the shore of Whitemist Lake and watched the sun rise over the spires of the school.

The mist always made sunrise at Albin Academy a strange and silvered thing, when the thick blanketing layer of fog rose almost to the treetops and captured the sun to glow strange and ethereal about the edges. The mornings tasted cool as rain, and every blade of grass around him clung on to condensation like dewdrops, soaking it into his slacks. At times like this he often felt as if the threshold between one world and the next had somehow blurred. And if he looked hard enough, stared deep into the clouds weaving tendrils through and about the trees...

He might somehow see through to the other side.

But this morning there was nothing to see but his reflection, as he looked down into the water and watched the ripples spread while, one at a time, he plucked up clover flowers from the grassy shore and tossed them in. If he followed with the legend of Isabella of the Lake, he was supposed to weave the clovers into a crown for her to wear, down in the watery deeps.

Yet this morning, his mind wasn't on Isabella.

It was on Summer Hemlock, and yesterday afternoon's bizarre encounter.

Whatever had possessed such a shy, timid young man to actually kiss him—*him*, of all people?

And why, for just a moment, had something sparked inside him when he had neither needed nor wanted such things for nearly twenty years?

You are a case study in denial, Fox.

That was what the grief counselor had told him, a decade ago.

Then again, she'd also told him he was a pain in the ass, considering most psychotherapeutic methods didn't work on someone who knew them by heart.

He plucked up another clover flower, its stem cool and crisp against his fingers as he began tying a delicate knot—only to still at the faint sound of footsteps at his back, rustling in the grass. Probably one of the boys; they liked to make wishes in the lake, throwing flower crowns down to Isabella and asking her for better grades on their midterms or for one of the students at the public school one town over to go out with them. Fox prepared himself to shut away behind the mantle of authority and excuse himself, drawing silence around him like a cloak.

Until a soft "Hey" murmured at his back, and Summer Hemlock sank down to the grass at his side.

Fox stiffened, eyeing Summer sidelong—but as always, Summer wasn't looking at him. He never looked at anyone, and not for the first time Fox wondered just what had ingrained that particular behavior. That fear. For Fox direct eye contact had other implications, ones few around him understood…

But Summer seemed to be carrying some weight on his shoulders, that bowed his head and kept his eyes downcast.

Summer settled with one leg drawn up, draping his arm over it and leaning back on his other hand. He still wore the same close-fit T-shirt and jeans as yesterday, albeit as rumpled as his hair, and an odd, quiet little smile played about his lips even if it hardly reflected in pensive blue eyes that looked out across the lake as if he, too, could see something in the mist.

Fox looked away, letting the clover flower fall to the grass and leaning on his hands. "Mr. Hemlock," he greeted. "I presume, since you've not changed your clothing, that you returned to fetch your personal effects."

"No," Summer answered quietly. "I came to say I'm sorry."

Fox arched a brow. "For...?"

"You know what." That smile strengthened, strangely cynical and self-mocking. "But you're going to make me say it, aren't you?" Summer turned his head toward Fox, almost but not quite meeting his eyes. "I'm sorry for kissing you yesterday. I'm sorry for not asking first. I'm sorry for crossing your boundaries. And I'm sorry for running away."

"I hardly expected you to be so forthright."

"One brave thing per day, right?" Summer let out a breathless, shaky laugh. For all that he had grown into an athletic young man, there was a softness about him, a gentleness, that made every laugh, every gesture a thing of uncertain sweetness. "This was my brave thing. Apologizing to you. I'll figure out what tomorrow's is. And Monday's...if I still have a job."

Fox realized he'd been watching Summer—the way his lashes lowered to shade the oddly deep blue hue of his eyes, the nervous curl of square, strong fingers—and diverted his gaze to the lake, pressing his lips together. "Why would you not have a job?"

"Because what I did was an asshole move?"

"And I don't have the authority to fire you. I'm tenured, not all-powerful." With a sigh, Fox relented and added, "...but I hadn't intended to discipline you in the first place. It was an impulsive kiss. Not the end of the world. And I should likely apologize as well, for needling at your nervous tendencies and subjecting you to anxiety-inducing scrutiny. Not that I understand why *that*, of all things, was the choice you made to show your courage."

Summer let out a sudden low laugh; like his voice, it was a quiet thing that always seemed just a touch breathless, whispering deep in his throat. "I guess I wasn't as obvious back then as I thought."

"Obvious...?"

"I was in love with you when I was a student, Professor Iseya."

Fox blinked. His chest tightened. "You most certainly were *not*."

"I thought I was. At least, with who I thought you were. I know now that's not actually who you are...so I guess you're right that I wasn't." Another laugh, startled and hesitant. "God, this 'being brave' thing sucks. I can't believe I just blurted that out to you, and you're still sitting there with that same empty expression like I just told you it's going to rain."

"You're speaking of feelings you had as a child. They have no bearing on now, or on our professional relationship as adults. Am I supposed to react any other way?"

"No...no, I guess not." Summer's laughter faded into a sigh, and he glanced at Fox—for just a moment really looking at him, Summer's dark eyes half-lidded, messy hair framing his gaze in black tendrils. "But I do still find you attractive. And you made me angry. So I kissed you to make you stop saying those things about me. I still shouldn't have done it."

Fox opened his mouth.

Then closed it again.

Then scowled, a *most* disquieting feeling of uncertainty settling in the pit of his stomach, light and strange. "This has to be one of the most bizarre conversations I've ever had."

"Me too." Summer tilted his head back, looking up at the sky, lips curling. "But this is me, Professor Iseya. And I guess you need to know that if we're going to work together. I'm a walking bundle of anxiety waiting to trip into a panic attack, but every once in a while I hit a break point and just... do what I have to do, and say what I have to say." His shoulders shook with silent laughter. "Don't worry. Once I leave I'll probably hyperventilate."

"I'd rather you didn't. Challenging you to be brave was never meant to upset your anxiety."

"Sometimes I want my anxiety to be upset. Sometimes I... I..." He trailed off, lips remaining parted, before he shook his head. "Nevermind. It doesn't matter. Do you want to just put this behind us?"

Fox watched Summer from the corner of his eye; the way the rising light fell over his profile—his straight, somewhat awkward nose, the stubborn set to his jaw, the softness of his mouth. In this moment he looked older than his mid-twenties; not in his fresh, clean-shaven face, perhaps, but something about the way he carried himself, some tiredness that spoke of long hours of thought, of introspection, of weary self-awareness that he carried with him heavily.

And Fox didn't quite know what possessed him, what it was about that soft quiet air about Summer, that made him ask, "...first... I'd like you to answer a question."

Summer was silent for some time. And it was in that moment that Fox realized Summer might actually refuse him; he didn't know when it became a foregone conclusion that people would simply do as he said, but...

When his only human contact was with children or other teachers who were intimidated by him, it became too easy to stop seeing others as...

Others.

As entities who existed outside the thin shallow projections by which he defined their presences, ghosts he could banish at will.

He couldn't banish Summer at will, he thought. Couldn't summon him at will. Couldn't compel him to speak.

And that made him a strange new thing.

Something with thin bright edges that cut at the cloud of distance surrounding Fox at all times, slicing narrow gashes that forced him to look into the harsh, raw reality of the world outside.

How strange, he thought.

How strange indeed, that the world suddenly became more real, more crisp, the colors sharper about the edges in the slow span of breaths it took to wait for Summer to answer.

"Maybe," Summer said after those long, waiting breaths, choosing the words carefully. "It depends on the question."

Very well, then.

"Why are you attracted to me?" Fox asked.

And Summer laughed.

He laughed, quick and startled, a short light thing that made Fox think of mayflies startled into taking flight. Wide blue eyes darted to him, then away—very firmly away, Summer turning his head to stare across the grass, toward the stark cliff edge that led down the other side of the slope, into dense forest. His mouth pressed to his upraised shoulder, muffling his laughter into a muted sound, and the tips of his ears turned quite a shade of red against the dark backdrop of his tousled hair.

Fox blinked. "Did I say something funny?"

"*No*," Summer mumbled against his shirt. "I'm just embarrassed, I... Why would you ask me that?"

"Because I want to know," Fox said. "I would think that would be entirely self-explanatory."

"Oh *God*." With a groan, Summer closed his eyes, letting his head fall back limply on the toned arch of his neck, hanging between his shoulders, face tilted up to the sky. "I forgot how literal you are. You really haven't changed."

No, Fox thought, and wondered at the tight feeling like his ribs were pressing in too hard on his lungs. *I suppose I have not.*

"But that's one reason why I'm attracted to you." Summer opened his eyes, looking up at a morning sky that reflected in his eyes to give them a gray-blue sheen like glacial silt; a small smile touched his lips, warm and sweet. "Maybe I don't know the real you, but I know some real things *about* you. I like the way you talk. You're literal and while you hide a lot, you say what you mean when you do talk. If you don't want to say something you just won't, instead of deflecting or falling back on social niceties that are just a step away from lies. But even though you're so straightforward...there's all kinds of subtle nuance, too. Soft things between the lines. Sometimes even though you mean what you say...you mean something else, too."

Fox blinked again.

And again.

And had to look away from this strange young man with his equally strange smile, clearing his throat. "Perhaps you're only imagining what you're reading between my lines."

"It's possible. Projection is a thing." Even without looking at him...that smile was still in Summer's voice. "But it's not the only reason I'm attracted to you."

"I can't imagine more than one reason," Fox muttered.

"I can imagine a thousand. Only I don't have to imagine,

because they're as real as the color of your eyes and the way you wear your hair." Summer laughed. "I don't know how I'm not hyperventilating right now, but I guess I hit 'fuck it' mode and can freak out later. Why do you think I *wouldn't* be attracted to you?"

"I..."

It was almost instinct for Fox to *want* to deflect around that, and yet somehow Summer's quiet faith in his honesty, his straightforwardness, made him at least want to be somewhat truthful.

"I consider myself a non-entity on that front," he said. "If romance is a playing field, I benched myself long ago. Most do not pay attention to players who are not actively on the field."

"You're bad at sports analogies," Summer teased softly, and Fox scowled.

"I have little interest in the sports ball."

"...'the sports ball.'" That prompted a soft snicker, barely repressed. "And there's another reason. You're funny without meaning to be. But just because you've benched yourself doesn't mean you aren't still someone's favorite MVP."

"Now who is making terrible sports analogies?"

"I don't watch the sports ball either." Summer shrugged one shoulder ruefully. "Swimming turned out to be my thing."

Fox arched a brow, risking a glance back at Summer. The way he'd tanned and filled out, building into compact athletic musculature with a sort of flowing, liquid grace to it rather than thick-honed bulk...he could see it. Summer cutting through the water in smooth, fluid strokes.

He should not be picturing this.

"So is that how you finally hit puberty?" he shot back. "Swimming?"

"There it is. The defensive barbs because I managed to fluster you when you're supposed to be made of stone." Summer was still looking up at the sky, but his lips curled sweetly, almost slyly. "Keep insulting me, Professor Iseya. It just means I get under your skin a little. Although that's kind of regressing, don't you think? Child psychology. I thought we universally agreed as a field to stop telling children when a little boy pulls your pigtails and kicks dirt in your face, it means he likes you."

"*I don't like you!*" Narrowing his eyes, Fox growled, tearing his gaze away and glaring at the water.

What was even happening here?

How was this shy, anxious young man sitting here with that smile on his lips, needling at Fox and leaving Fox completely uncertain of how to handle this at all?

Yet that smile never wavered, even as Summer lowered his eyes from the sky, looking at Fox with a strange and quiet frankness, a soft ache in his voice when he said, "I know."

That…should not sting.

A sudden sharp pang, as if an arrow had been fired straight from Summer's bleeding heart to Fox's own.

With a soft hiss, he clenched his jaw and looked anywhere *but* at Summer. At the mist slowly beginning to burn away from the surface of the lake, hovering like the last remnants of ghosts that refused to let go with the dawn.

"This," he bit off, "is the most absolutely *ludicrous* conversation. What makes you think I'm even attracted to men?"

"Hope," Summer answered simply, softly, and yet *everything* was in that one word.

Hellfire.

Fox closed his eyes, breathing in and out slowly, if only so he could keep his tone even and calm. He wasn't accustomed to this—to feeling out of sorts, shaken out of place, his stone foundations cracked and no longer holding him so steady.

Being around Summer was like seeing the sun after decades buried in a subterranean cave.

And the light hurt his eyes, when all he wanted was the quiet and comforting dark.

"You don't want me, Summer," he said firmly. "I'm quite old, used-up, and I don't even know how to be with someone anymore."

"I don't think that's true," Summer murmured.

"Isn't it?"

Silence, before Summer said slowly, "Maybe I'm wrong... I'm probably wrong. Or maybe you were a good enough teacher that I can figure some things out. But either way, I think you shut yourself away while you needed to...but your protective walls turned into a cage when you didn't need them anymore, and now you can't find your way out."

Shut yourself away while you needed to.

The simple memory of just *why* he'd shut himself away cut deep, digging down to a tiny pain that lived at his heart. He'd made it tiny deliberately, so he could compact it down into a thing so small it could fit in the palm of his hand, all of that agony crushed down into nothing so that he could never touch too much of it at any one time, its surface area barely the size of a fingerprint.

And then he'd tucked it away, burying it down where he couldn't reach it.

But those simple words threatened to expose it, even if it meant cutting him open to do so.

No.

He stood, reminding himself to breathe—to breathe, and to wrap himself in his calm. He was nearly twice Summer's age, and quite accustomed to rebellious boys who thought they were intelligent enough to outsmart their teacher, put him on the spot, leave him floundering. Summer was just an older, larger version of that.

And Fox could not forget that he was the one in control here.

"Is that so?" he asked, looking down at Summer—the top of his head, the hard slopes his shoulders made as he leaned back on his hands. "If that's your analysis, you aren't fit to teach elementary school psychology."

"They don't teach psychology in elementary school." Summer chuckled, those firm shoulders shaking. "Insulting me already didn't work, Professor. Why do you think it's going to drive me back from the walls this time?"

Fox turned his nose up. "Is that your intent, then? To breach my walls?"

"Not breach them, no."

Summer tilted his head back again, then, but this time instead of looking at the sky...he looked up at Fox with his eyes full of that sky, the first morning clouds reflected against liquid blue.

"I'm not going to get inside unless you let me, Professor Iseya. But I can stand outside the walls and wait...and ask."

Fox stared.

He could not be serious.

One minute Summer had arrived to apologize for that egregious and utterly ridiculous *kiss*, and now he...seemed to be emboldened to some kind of *designs* on Fox?

All because Fox had not summarily dismissed him from his position?

Absurd.

He pressed his lips together and took a few steps away from Summer, drifting along the lake's shore, putting more distance between them. Giving himself space—to think, to sort himself out, when he wasn't accustomed to this.

Wasn't accustomed to someone who took one look at his walls and saw not someone cold, not someone cruel, distant, detached, inhuman...

But simply that those walls were made not of stone, but of pain.

He did not like it.

His walls had served him quite well for some time, and they did not need to be broken down.

"Do you think Rapunzel was comfortable in her castle?" he asked. "Perhaps, since it was all she knew…it never even felt like a cage."

Summer let out a sunny little laugh. "Are we talking Grimm's Rapunzel or Disney's Rapunzel?"

"Does it matter?"

"Considering in one I end up losing my eyesight trying to reach you, and the other I just get hit in the face with a frying pan?" A wickedly amused sound rose from the back of Summer's throat. "Yes."

Fox wrinkled his nose. "Please do not project us into the roles of fictional lovers."

A soft rustle rose, denim moving against grass, the sounds of fabric against skin. It was an oddly intimate sound, one that made Fox remember the sound of flesh on sheets, the pad of soft footsteps in the dark, a quiet room where he never wanted the light to find him and wake him from a dream of being in love.

He couldn't breathe.

He couldn't breathe, and he couldn't seem to move even though everything inside him wanted to *run* as Summer drew closer, *closer*, until he was a warmth at Fox's back, this bright thing that kept trying to chase away the cold touch of ghosts, of yurei whose icy spirit-fingers wrapped around Fox's neck, choking off his air, but Fox didn't want to let them go. Didn't want to let in the breath they were strangling from him.

When if he remembered how to breathe, that one tiny swelling of his chest might just shatter him.

"What about real lovers, then?" Summer asked, husky, low, his breaths and his voice like a lick of flame on a frozen night.

Fox stared blankly straight ahead, curling one hand against

his chest, against his shirt, clutching up a handful of the fabric. He couldn't turn around. Couldn't face that warmth.

Didn't Summer realize?

Didn't he realize if he burned away Fox's wall of frost...

There was nothing beneath, and he'd just melt and evaporate and wisp away?

"Why?" he whispered. "Why do you want something like that?"

"You told me to be bold." Soft, entreating, yet...so inadvertently seductive, too. Fox didn't think Summer realized just how seductive his sweetness was. "I can't think of anything bolder than asking the most terrifying man in Albin Academy to kiss me." Summer drew closer, the crackle of grass beneath his feet, his shoulder brushing Fox's in a sudden quiet shock-jump of sensation before it was gone as Summer stood at his side, looking out over the water as well with that strange, gently melancholy smile on his full red lips. "Once per day."

Fox watched him from the corner of his eye, brows knitting. "That's...a bizarre proposition."

"Is it?" Summer slipped his hands into the pockets of his jeans, his shirt drawing tight against leanly toned musculature, wrinkles seaming against the flex of his biceps. "It's motivation. If I'm bolder, if I prove to you I can do this job... I get rewarded with a kiss. With one caveat."

There. One caveat.

All Fox would need to end this ridiculous game.

"And what would that be?" he asked.

"Only if you really want to." Summer shook his head slightly, messy hair drifting across his eyes. "I couldn't stand it if you felt like you had to. Like you were obligated, or like..." He trailed off, eyes lidding, voice quieting. "...like I didn't really care what you want. I think... I kind of think 'no' is the most important word we know, and not enough people listen to it."

"You have to know that I would say no right in this instant, Mr. Hemlock," Fox said through his teeth. "Which makes your proposition quite pointless, as it is."

Summer lifted his head, then, once more looking at Fox directly. Considering how he avoided eye contact so pathologically, Fox...didn't understand why Summer seemed inclined to so often look at him so fully, so intently, when he claimed to be afraid of Fox, claimed to be so anxious he actually found Fox terrifying.

But perhaps that's what bravery was, Fox thought.

Summer was afraid of him...

And yet still looking at him.

Trying to *see* him.

And telling him, in his own way...

That for some bizarre reason, he found Fox to be worth facing down that fear.

He didn't understand.

And he didn't understand how intently Summer looked at him, those rich blue eyes subtly dilated, turning them smoky.

"Summer," he whispered. "Call me Summer."

Fox's eyes widened. His fingers clenched harder in his shirt.

Did Summer not...understand what using given names meant, to him?

Perhaps he was only half-Japanese, his mother a white American woman who gave him his gray eyes in a rare genetic fluke, but he still knew so much of so many things from his father, things passed down to him like traditions written in blood.

Given names could be used with fondness for children, for family, for close friends who might as well be family...

But in certain circumstances, someone's name could be a love word.

Intimate and shivering, rolling off the tongue.

He turned his back on Summer, on those eyes that pleaded

with him to be that intimate, to be that close, curling his shoulders in and digging his fingers against his shirt as if he could claw down to his heart and grasp it to stop its erratic and sharp beating.

"*Mn.*"

"You said it once before," Summer said softly, and Fox caught his breath.

He had.

Letting it roll off his tongue, easy and fluid, but he'd tried not to taste it, tried to simply use it to capture Summer's attention, to impress on him that he wasn't someone Summer should ever want.

But he wondered, now.

Wondered now what he'd let slip past his lips without feeling its texture, its flavor.

He glanced over his shoulder. All he could see was Summer's profile, the tanned slopes and lines of him catching the sun until he glowed. Amber-soft and gentle, and Fox swallowed thickly.

"...Summer," he said again.

It tasted like sighs. Like the taste not of summer, but the spice of autumn leaves turning and falling and crackling under every step. It tasted like the color of the sky just as the sun touches the horizon at sunset.

And it felt like silk on his lips and tongue, passing over his skin in liquid, smooth caresses.

He didn't like it.

He didn't like how *close* it felt, when he still remembered the taste of Summer's lips against his own, that same crackle-bright hint of warmth and sharpness, while Summer's pulse throbbed and trembled underneath his palm.

"Yeah," Summer said, a low thrum turning his voice husky. "Just like that."

Closer he stepped. Closer still, until he was a wall of heat at Fox's back, this vibrant living thing trying to make Fox re-member *he* was alive, too.

"Would it be so terrible?" Summer asked softly. "To kiss me just once per day. Operant conditioning works better with a reward."

"I..." Breathing was so hard, right now, and Fox didn't un-derstand this feeling. "I refuse to answer that."

"Shouldn't it be easy to say no, then?"

He scowled. "You are baiting me."

"Maybe a little." Summer smiled sweetly, just a faint curve of his lips visible in the corner of Fox's eye. "It's not every day I get to make the man I was in love with for my entire childhood *blush*."

Fox caught a strangled sound in his throat.

He was most certainly not *blushing*.

His face simply felt warm because of the rising sunlight, the heat chasing the last of the mist from the pond, the trees.

"If you are attempting to pique my pride, *Mr. Hemlock*, it won't work."

"I'm not."

Then Fox felt something he hadn't felt in decades:

Fingers in his hair.

Just the lightest touch, catching one of the damnable tendrils that would never stay in the clip, lifting it and making him shud-der and tense with the prickling feeling of the strands moving against his neck, kissing his skin, then pulling back to leave him strangely deprived of *touch*, as if the sensitized flesh was ach-ingly aware that it wasn't in contact with...skin, warmth, *texture*.

"I'm just riding my bravery until it runs out." Summer stroked his thumb down the strands captured in his fingers, handling them delicately. "Think about it, Professor Iseya. I'll be ready for class tomorrow. Tell me then."

Then: the feather-soft sensation of his hair free-floating,

falling, drifting down to lay against his neck and coil over his shoulder again.

The quiet fall of footsteps, whispering and sighing against the grass.

The wild pounding of Fox's heart, a drumbeat calling the day into existence.

He turned.

He turned, but Summer was already gone.

And already...

Already, the world was turning gray again.

Don't miss
Just Like That *by Cole McCade,*
available now wherever
Carina Press ebooks are sold.

www.CarinaPress.com